SHAUN HUTSON
EPITAPH

orbit

www.orbitbooks.net

ORBIT

First published in Great Britain in 2010 by Orbit
The paperback edition published in 2011 by Orbit

A CIP catalogue record for this book
is available from the British Library.

ISBN 978-1-84149-763-1

Typeset in Bembo by Palimpsest Book Production Limited,
Falkirk, Stirlingshire
Printed and bound in Great Britain by Clays Ltd, St Ives plc

Papers used by Orbit are natural, renewable and recyclable
products sourced from well-managed forests and certified
in accordance with the rules of the Forest Stewardship Council.

Orbit
An imprint of
Little, Brown Book Group
100 Victoria Embankment
London EC4Y 0DY

An Hachette UK Company
www.hachette.co.uk

www.orbitbooks.net

By Shaun Hutson

EPITAPH

He closed his eyes tightly and tried to obey the inner voice. It was impossible.

You've been buried alive.

'Oh, Jesus Christ,' he gasped. 'Jesus. Jesus.'

He screamed again. And again. And again. He banged on the lid and the sides of the coffin. He hammered away until his fists hurt, frustrated by the fact that he couldn't create much of an impact because he couldn't get the leverage in his cramped and confined position. Nevertheless he continued shouting and thumping, not really knowing why but unable to think of anything else that he could do. He even kicked out with his feet, feeling the bottom of the casket. For five minutes solid he thrashed and kicked and pounded.

And screamed.

'They have digged a pit before me, into the midst thereof they are fallen themselves.'

Psalms 57:6

'O, what a tangled web we weave,
When first we practise to deceive.'

Sir Walter Scott

1

When they reached the gates they ran as if they were being chased.

No running was allowed inside the school corridors and not even in the courtyard and playgrounds but, once they reached the gates that opened out on to the school field beyond, there was no stopping them.

Free from these strictures, they hurtled out on to the vast expanse of greenery like greyhounds released from their traps.

Laura Hacket led the charge, whooping as loudly as her eight-year-old lungs would allow, her long plaits whisking around her face like a duo of benevolent whips. She stumbled once but remained on her feet, giggling as the first of her friends caught up with her and they narrowly avoided colliding with a group of boys who had already sprinted on to the field and were busily pulling off their blazers, putting them down as goal posts as another of their number dribbled a football agitatedly back and forth.

The boys looked around briefly at Laura and her friends but were more interested in their game than in these irritating girls. Laura tugged at her school tie and loosened it slightly as she walked, her pace now slowing as the initial excitement of escaping school once more began to wane.

High above in a cloudless sky, the sun was beating down relentlessly. A promise of good weather to come throughout the school holidays, Laura hoped. She shivered with anticipation even at the thought of six whole weeks of freedom to come. She and her parents were going on holiday to their caravan on the east coast in less than ten days. Laura loved the caravan. She loved the seaside, too. Her grandparents lived there and she would probably stay on with them for another week after her mum and dad returned home. That was what she usually did. Then, when she returned, she had another three or four weeks to look forward to, playing with her friends and just generally whiling away the time until school began again in early September. This holiday was her favourite. No contest (apart from Christmas, of course, when she got so many presents) and she and her friends had been looking forward to it for so long it seemed.

Beside her, two more of her friends were talking about their own forthcoming holidays. One of them was going to Spain but Laura wasn't jealous. She didn't want to leave the country. Everything she loved was already here. Besides, at least she was going with both her parents. Her friend was going to Spain with her dad and younger sisters and then, two weeks later, she was spending a week at a holiday camp in this country with her mum and her stepdad. Laura was only too happy that her mum and dad were still together, unlike so many of her friends' parents who were separated, divorced, about to split up or just plain unhappy. She had no such problems and she was grateful for that.

Once across the school field, past the tennis courts and their high mesh fence, there was a concrete path that led between some trees and bushes and eventually to another smaller metal gate.

2

Beyond this was a picturesque lane leading towards the estate where Laura and most of her friends lived.

Some of the older boys and girls were sauntering down the path towards this last barrier now. Alone or in small groups, they made their way along it towards their homes, some of the boys shouting excitedly both at each other and at those who shared the path but most were content to amble along cocooned within the world of their own conversations, uninterested in those round about.

Laura saw two boys from her class prodding a spider's web with a stick, another holding a struggling crane fly near the sticky web. He finally released the unfortunate insect, he and his companions cheering as it flew helplessly into the spider's trap and wriggled there.

One of Laura's friends commented on how cruel the boys were but they merely laughed and watched mesmerised as the spider advanced hungrily on the stricken crane fly. Laura shook her head disapprovingly and muttered something derogatory about boys in general.

She and her group of friends reached the rusty gate and turned left into the lane. Blossom had fallen from the branches of many trees that lined the walkway, their fallen bounty looking like fragrant snow on the tarmac of the path beyond. Laura picked two vibrantly yellow flowers from the side of the path and placed them in her school bag. One for her mum and one for her dad, she decided.

At the bottom of the lane there was a set of concrete posts inserted into the tarmac to prevent the passage of cars, and it was here that Laura and her friends separated. Laura's house lay to the right, across an open green and then down beneath an underpass. Her friends would take different routes. Even so, they should all be home within ten or fifteen minutes. Laura bade effusive farewells then turned and hurried off across the green towards the underpass, promising first that she would ring each of her friends when she got home for a chat and to arrange what time they were meeting the following day.

Halfway across the wide, overgrown green, Laura slowed to a walk. She was hot and thirsty and running, she reasoned, would only make things worse.

As she headed towards the path that led down into the underpass she saw a man walking his dog and she paused to look at the dachshund that was waddling along in the heat looking as if it would rather be curled up in its basket. The man smiled warmly at Laura who stepped on to the cracked path leading down into the underpass.

As she reached the bottom she let out a deep breath. There were words and images spray-painted on the walls and Laura giggled to herself as she recognised some of the words. Rude words, her mum would say. She did not know who was responsible for putting them there. Yobs, her dad had said. Laura wasn't completely sure what that word meant but her dad used it in connection with quite a few of the boys on their estate. It was a bit smelly inside the underpass; it always was and Laura had no idea why. Nevertheless, she enjoyed the coolness in the subterranean walkway, sheltered as it was from the sun. She slowed her pace and looked at the large, painted letters that had been sprayed on to the underpass walls, mesmerised by their size. There were some empty beer cans scattered across the pathway that led through the underpass and Laura was careful to step over them. Perhaps, she reasoned, they had belonged to the people who'd spray-painted the rude words on the walls.

Laura walked on.

4

Paul Crane closed the door behind him and leaned against it for a moment, eyes closed, head thumping.

He remained in that position for a moment longer then reached out a hand and slapped on the light. A welcoming glow filled the hallway and Paul finally opened his eyes slowly. He sucked in another weary breath then dropped his briefcase. It landed with a thud on the expensive carpet.

The hall was pleasingly cool compared to the heat he'd struggled through outside. Paul hated the warm weather, especially in the summer. The often unrelenting heat that bathed the country for days or weeks at a time. He enjoyed the chill of autumn and winter far more. During the summer he had to retire all his favourite jackets for the duration of the heat. His office, naturally, was air-conditioned but, once he'd left that safe and temperature-regulated haven, he was out on to the streets surrounded, it seemed, by people with pink tinted skin and scarlet cheeks. People who seemed to be impervious to the sunshine or, at any rate, incapable of ensuring that it didn't cause them to look so comical.

This particular evening, the amount he'd drunk seemed to have exacerbated his dislike not only of the heat but of other people. He had studied those he'd ridden home with and experienced emotions ranging from contempt to hatred.

Everyone he'd looked at he'd imagined to be happier than he was. More financially secure than he was. Had more to look forward to in life than he had. Everything he was about to lose, they probably had.

Normally he would have taken a taxi home from work but, he reasoned, normally he wouldn't have been thinking about the cost of a cab. He wouldn't have been considering the cost of anything because financial concerns weren't high on his list of priorities. This particular evening, however, was different. Since receiving the news he'd got earlier that day, suddenly everything financial seemed of the utmost importance. Every penny was crucial from now on, he told himself.

It had been the first thought to hit him when he'd heard he'd lost his job.

There had been no sense of failure, no sudden onset of self-doubt and thoughts of rejection. He had been overcome by one all-consuming and unshakeable conviction. He was going to lose everything. His home, his lifestyle and everything he loved. In the middle of the worst world recession in living memory, Paul Crane had been made redundant and he didn't know how he was going to cope.

He ran a hand through his hair and wandered through from the hall into the kitchen to his left, dropping the mail he'd collected on to the kitchen table. He pulled a bottle of vodka from the freezer, retrieved a glass from the cupboard above his head and poured some of the clear liquor into it. He swallowed most of it in one motion, as if he were dying of thirst, then he put the glass on the kitchen table, pulled out one of the chairs there and sat down. His head was spinning. He'd already drunk half a dozen large measures and a couple of tequila shots before coming home and now he looked at the bottle, common sense telling him not to consume any more of the vodka but a louder voice inside his mind urging him to drink until he collapsed. To anaesthetise himself against the pain of the day. Blot out the reality of the situation until at least the following morning.

Fuck it. Why not? What reason have you got to stay sober?

He held the glass in one hand and the bottle in the other, the cold surface numbing his flesh.

To drink or not to drink. That is the question.

He shook his head.

A job, a job. My kingdom for a job.

He lifted the vodka bottle and poured more of the liquor into the glass.

Employment, employment. Wherefore art thou, employment?

Again he shook his head.

Funny fucker, aren't you?

Paul took a sip from the glass and then put it down, letting out a weary breath.

It was quiet inside the room; his neighbours in the flats above and below and to either side of him were out or going about their business in their usual subdued and undemonstrative ways. That had been one of the things that had attracted Paul to the flat in the first place, its solitude. He knew his neighbours to nod at if he passed them in the walkways or met them in the lifts but, apart from such cursory meetings, everyone including him seemed to keep themselves to themselves. There was very little community spirit within the block of thirty luxury apartments but that was something Paul was grateful for. He was comfortable in the company of others but had always truly enjoyed keeping his own counsel more. He had plenty of friends and always had done. From his various occupations he had amassed the requisite collection of acquaintances during his thirty-six years but, with a handful of notable exceptions, Paul Crane was more content alone.

And, at this precise moment in time, he felt more alone than he ever had in his life.

3

'I've got to go.'

Gina Hacket glanced at her watch as she sat up in bed.

'Just another few minutes,' said the figure lying next to her. He ran one hand up the inside of her right thigh as he spoke, his fingers gliding along the smooth, taut skin there.

'We've been here for three hours already,' Gina reminded him.

'Not moaning, are you? You weren't complaining when we first got here.'

She glanced around the room and shook her head almost imperceptibly.

The hotel room was basic, to say the least. Thirty-five pounds bought functional rather than luxurious. A rough, dark brown bedspread that resembled and indeed felt only two or three degrees softer than hessian lay untidily upon the bed. The sheets beneath were rumpled and sweat-soaked from earlier exertions. The carpet was worn and threadbare in places. There was a sofa beneath the window, its cushions badly in need of a steam clean. The same was true of the orange curtains. Blinds hung at the windows, the slats waving lazily in the breeze from the opening. There was no air conditioning and only the warm air from outside circulated inside the room. The air within smelled musky. A smell of sex and hastily snatched pleasure. From outside, she could hear the sound of passing traffic.

Gina looked at the no smoking sign above the small sideboard to her right, perched above a grubby white kettle and a bowl of coffee sachets, tea bags and single-serving milk cartons.

There were two empty soft drink bottles there, too. She and her companion had brought them into the room when they'd first entered. Gina felt like something stronger.

Her companion trailed two fingers gently between her legs and felt the heat and moisture there. When he removed the digits he offered them to her and she flicked her tongue over them, tasting both herself and his saltier emission, too.

'Just a quickie,' he grinned.

'There's no such thing with you,' she told him, trying to inject a note of disapproval into her voice but failing miserably. 'There never has been.'

'That's good, isn't it? Better than it all being over within a couple of minutes.'

'Time's like money; it's fine when you've got it to spare.'

'Smart-arse.'

'I was just saying.' She shifted position slightly on the bed, her attention caught by a long crack in the ceiling. She lay gazing at it.

He pulled her hand down towards his groin and she felt her fingers brush against his erection. Gina looked down at it, her fingers closing briefly around his shaft.

'It won't take long,' he assured her, moving closer to her, kissing her slender neck.

'I'm sure it won't,' she breathed as he pushed more insistently against her, his penis butting against her thigh.

'Come on.'

'You've got to be back at work, haven't you?' she continued.

'Eventually.'

'They'll notice you're not there.'

'No one checks up on me. As long as the work gets done they don't stand looking over my shoulder, you know.'

Gina felt his hand on her face and he stroked her cheek softly. She turned her face towards him and he kissed her. She responded almost in spite of herself. When she pulled away she was breathing more raggedly.

'I knew I'd persuade you,' he grinned, his hand now gliding to her breasts, his palms brushing over the erect nipples. 'Don't tell me you don't want it again. I know what you're like.'

'Not now,' she whispered.

'Why have you always got one eye on the clock?' he wanted to know.

'You know why. I want to be home when Laura gets there. I don't like her coming home to an empty house.' She swung herself off the bed, picked up her knickers from the floor and walked through to the tiny bathroom.

'Perhaps we should meet up earlier in the day, then you wouldn't have to worry about that,' he called.

'We'll both have to worry about it soon. It's the school holidays. She's off for six weeks.' Gina inspected her reflection in the mirror, fluffing up her shoulder-length auburn hair with her hands. She pulled on her knickers then returned to the bedroom.

'What are we going to do? When are we going to meet up?' There was something like irritation in his voice.

'She's staying with her grandparents for a week. We can see

11

each other then,' Gina told him, retrieving the remainder of her clothes from around the room. 'Don't worry about it.'

He watched her as she buttoned her blouse then slipped a hair band around her hair, pulling it into a ponytail.

'Are you getting dressed?' she enquired, looking at her naked companion who was now sitting on the edge of the bed.

'You can't leave me like this,' he said, raising his eyebrows and indicating his erection with one index finger.

Gina hesitated for a moment then dropped slowly to her knees between his legs.

'I told you,' he grinned. 'It won't take long. I promise.'

She dipped her head, closing her mouth around the tip of his erection, her tongue sliding across the sensitive glans. The carpet felt rough beneath her bare knees but she ignored it and concentrated on the stiffness in her mouth. She massaged his testicles gently as she slid her head up and down his shaft, hearing his breathing grow more laboured. After a moment or two, he bucked his hips upwards to match her movements. She felt one of his hands on the back of her head, keeping her in position as he neared his peak.

He groaned in appreciation.

'I told you it wouldn't take long,' he gasped.

He was true to his word. Gina felt his penis throb in her mouth and she kept her lips fastened around it as he climaxed, his thick fluid filling her mouth. She swallowed it quickly then straightened up, glancing back at him lying naked on the bed, his organ softening after his release.

'That's better,' he grinned, his eyes still closed.

She pulled on her jeans, stepped into her shoes and headed for the door.

'If you're still horny tonight your husband can take care of *you, can't he?' he called to her and she thought that she heard a note of sarcasm in his voice. She paused and looked evenly at him.*

'I'll ring you tomorrow,' he added, stepping through into the bathroom. She heard the shower sputter into life.

Gina dug in her pocket for her front-door keys and checked her watch once more. As long as the bus came on time, she should be home in twenty minutes.

Across the street, hidden by the shadows of the doorway in which it stood, the figure that had been watching her since she arrived at the hotel now watched her leave.

4

In all of his thirty-six years on the planet, Paul Crane had never felt the sense of helplessness he now experienced as he sat at his kitchen table.

Combined with a growing feeling of anger and desperation, it closed around him like an invisible vice, tightening with every passing moment. Perhaps, he told himself, he'd had it too easy in his life up until this point. Maybe that was why this current chain of events had hit him so much harder than he'd expected. But, as he considered his situation, he knew that wasn't true. He'd worked hard for everything he had. None of what he'd achieved had been down to luck; it had been down to sheer bloody hard work and, now, all that counted for nothing.

With no job he knew that he would lose everything that mattered to him. His home. His way of life and, even more cripplingly, his self-belief and confidence. He had no savings to fall back on. He'd never been one to plan ahead and make provision for such shattering eventualities.

He earned money and he spent it. It was as simple as that. He bought the best clothes, the finest wines and when he ate out he did so at the best restaurants. He always paid top price for theatre, concert or event tickets and, when he took holidays, he never considered travelling any other way but first class and enjoying his breaks in nothing less than five-star hotels. The money had always been there. That was why he worked, to ensure that he could afford the best that life offered. He'd never envisaged the day when all that would change so why, he wondered, should he have seen it coming? He was good at his job. Well liked by his colleagues and those he dealt with. There was never any reason why he should have suspected that when job cuts were made at his firm he should be one of those who was so simply and easily discarded.

And that was where the desolation turned to anger. There were others he knew of who were less competent than him. Others who deserved to lose their jobs.

He'd been at Meyer and Banks advertising agency for close to fifteen years. He'd done a bit of everything there in his time. Market research at the beginning, then design, direct marketing and finally copy writing. There'd never been any complaints about his input, commitment or dedication. Customers had always liked him. Some of the agency's most successful campaigns over the years had been because of him. The quality of his work had been consistently high. Unlike some he could think of even now as he sat helplessly at his kitchen table.

He wanted to smash something. To pick up the glass and hurl it at the nearest wall and bellow his rage and frustration.

He wanted to know why it had to be him. Why did he have to be the one who lost his job?

Of course the subject had been mentioned briefly during the course of the afternoon but, upon hearing the news of his release (dismissal made it sound as if he'd been removed because of some inadequacy) he had been too shocked to probe his bosses about the reasons for his removal from the position he enjoyed so much. They had spoken of things like redundancy payments and working until the end of the month but all of those subjects had floated past him. As if they'd been spoken while he was asleep. After the initial news that he was being released, very little had penetrated his consciousness. He wondered if this was what it was like hearing you had a terminal disease. Once the word terminal had been uttered, everything else was subordinate and unnecessary.

Had this happened a year or two earlier then he would not have received the news with such despair, but to be laid off in the middle of such a deep and seemingly endless recession offered little hope of salvation. A year or two earlier there would have been other firms willing to employ him. Other companies only too willing to take on his expertise. He would have looked upon his redundancy as a chance to take a holiday. A hiatus from the daily grind. He would have used that time between jobs to relax and enjoy some of the life that his handsome salary brought him.

But not now.

Paul poured himself another drink and slumped back in his chair, the anger he'd felt now replaced once again by that same creeping despair he had grown so accustomed to since leaving his office earlier in the day.

The sensible side of him said that he should get up early in the morning and scour every available outlet for a job to replace the one he'd lost. But sense didn't feature too strongly in his mindset at this precise moment. It was hard to think logically and begin formulating plans when you felt so much distress and helplessness. Anyone who thought otherwise had never been in this position.

The other side of him had already decided that there was nothing to do at present but wallow in self-pity and that no amount of enthusiasm, drive or desire was going to get him a comparable position in a firm of equal or better standing. It was a matter of logic. It was nothing to do with trying to work out some kind of strategy for moving on. His position was intolerable and, right now, there seemed nothing that could be done about it. More to the point, the mortgage would need paying. A reasonable redundancy payment might keep him solvent for a few more months but it wouldn't last for ever.

Words like repossession began to circulate inside his already overcrowded brain and he finally sucked in a deep breath and got to his feet, his hands shaking slightly.

He shrugged off his jacket, hung it on the back of the chair and walked through into the sitting room, switching on the lights as he did so. He looked around the immaculately decorated room for a second then glanced in the direction of the polished wood table close to the wall to his left.

The red indicator on his answering machine was flashing a five.

Five people had rung him. Paul wasn't sure if he wanted to speak to any of them, whoever they were. Nevertheless, he moved towards the machine and rested an index finger gently on the PLAY button.

'You have five messages,' the electronic voice confirmed.

When Paul heard whom the first one was from he jabbed the STOP button.

He couldn't listen to it. Not now.

5

Laura Hacket heard her own footsteps echoing in the underpass as she walked. Light, unhurried steps.

She was moving towards the upward ramp when she heard heavier footsteps behind her.

Laura thought about turning to look and see who the footsteps belonged to. She knew lots of people on the estate, especially those who lived near her. There was the old lady who lived across the street with her daughter. Laura spoke to both of them on a regular basis. The old lady had something wrong with her left foot and walked with a stick. She was a big woman so Laura discounted the possibility that it was her purely and simply because her footsteps would have made more noise, and it wasn't the daughter because she always wore high heels and Laura told herself she would have heard them clicking. She always knew when the daughter was leaving or arriving home because she heard that familiar click, click, click on the pavement.

She wondered if it might be one of her neighbours. On one side there was a family of four complete with their large dog,

19

Bruno. A mum, a dad and two teenage boys. Laura didn't speak to the boys much but she sometimes heard their voices when they were playing on their PlayStation. Sometimes she heard shouting coming from their kitchen, too, when she was in her back garden. She didn't like the shouting.

On the other side there was another family. They reminded Laura of overstuffed cushions. Each one of them was a little on the overweight side. There was the mother with her short black hair, the son with his bright blond hair and his grandmother who had vivid red hair. Laura had never seen the man of the house and sometimes she felt sorry for the boy because he obviously had no dad. No one to play with him in the garden. No one to kick a football about with him. Not that he played much; he was too big for that. All three of them sometimes ambled out into their back garden to cut their grass, trim their hedges and do some weeding but that was about as active as they got. When they emerged, their dog came with them. A little terrier that ran around a lot and barked at the birds that landed on the lawn.

Laura had asked her dad if they, too, could have a dog. She felt left out, what with Bruno on one side and the terrier on the other but her dad had said no. He'd said that it wasn't fair because they were all out of the house all day. He'd said that Laura would have to make do with her hamster until they moved to a bigger house. Then perhaps – and that was the word he always emphasised – perhaps they could get a dog.

So, Laura walked on, convinced now that the footsteps in the underpass behind her didn't belong to any of the people she'd thought of.

She stopped for a moment to fasten her shoe.

The footsteps stopped, too.

Laura straightened up and continued walking, a little more slowly this time.

Behind her, the footsteps she could hear also moved more slowly.

There were about ten yards left before Laura reached the end of the underpass and, for reasons she couldn't explain, she suddenly felt as if she wanted to be out of this subterranean walkway. It was dank and musty down there and she didn't like it any more. Perhaps if the footsteps hadn't been behind her she wouldn't have cared so much but she felt the need to hurry towards the light that signalled the end of the underpass.

She began to increase the pace of her steps.

The footsteps behind her also speeded up.

6

'Hello, Paul, it's Mum.'

Paul listened to the first faltering words then stabbed the STOP button and cut off the voice in mid-sentence.

He sat down next to the answering machine, his head bowed.

It was a full five minutes before he could bring himself to reach for the PLAY button again. The familiar and slightly frail voice continued:

'I just wanted to thank you for that beautiful birthday card,' it went on. 'I don't know how you find them. The words were lovely. I had a little tear when I read them.' There was a pause. Then a light chuckle. 'You shouldn't have put that cheque in, though. I really appreciate it but it was too much.' Another pause, longer this time. 'I just wanted to say thanks. I'll ring again later. I know you're busy at work.' The longest pause of all. 'It'd be lovely to see you again soon. I know you're busy but, well, hopefully we'll get to see you and thank you for the card and the cheque.' The voice ended but the phone hadn't been put down. It was as if the caller was waiting for him to pick up at his end.

The message ended.

Paul swallowed hard and looked at the machine, as if he was somehow going to magically see his mother standing there at the other end of the phone. He exhaled deeply, almost painfully. How long had it been since he'd seen her? Six months? Longer?

'We'll get to see you,' she'd said. *We.*

She still used the plural, despite the fact that his father had been dead for almost a year now.

The Royal We.

Paul smiled humourlessly.

They said that when men were shot in wartime they didn't call for their wives, girlfriends or lovers as they lay dying. They called for their mothers. Paul knew that feeling now. He wished his mother was here with him. He needed to see a friendly face. He wanted someone who would just listen to him without judging him but he also feared that time to come when he must confess his failure to her. When he would have to sit down with her and let her know that her son wasn't the success she had always imagined but that he had failed. But he didn't want to burden her with that now. Not over the phone either. The news he had received earlier that day was the kind to be delivered face to face.

She would tell him not to worry. That everything would turn out all right. She had always said that to him throughout the years when he'd confided in her and, up until now, she'd been right. Her faith in him had been well-founded. His father had been similarly supportive when he was alive. The two of them basking in their son's success at his chosen profession.

Not any more.

Paul thought how much this would have hurt his father. Despite himself, Paul had admired him and was haunted by the fact that he'd never let him know that when he was alive. They were polar opposites in attitude and behaviour but Paul had learned many lessons from his father, albeit grudgingly at times. The main thing that he had respected about the man was his ability to provide for his family. To keep a roof over their heads, no matter what. He may not have been the most communicative person ever to walk the earth, and not the easiest to get along with, but he had his own set of ethics that he lived by and they worked for him. Others might not always have liked him but they respected him and they recognised the code that he lived by and that he had tried to pass on to Paul as his only son.

If his father had been alive now he would have told Paul to go out and look for another job. To prove the other bastards wrong for getting rid of him.

'They'll be sorry before you are, son,' he would have said.

Paul afforded himself a thin smile at the thought.

He listened to the message once again and checked the time it had arrived. Lunchtime. He hoped his mother didn't ring back now. He was in no frame of mind to chat to her about anything at the moment. Feeling a little guilty he told himself that, if she rang, he'd simply leave it to the machine again.

He listened to the second message.

24

It was from his optician. His latest appointment had been confirmed for two days from now.

Paul stopped the machine again.

The third message had been timed at just after five that afternoon. About an hour after he'd learned of his redundancy.

'Paul, it's Martin. I just heard about them getting rid of you.'

Paul pressed the PAUSE button on the machine, hitting it so hard that he almost knocked it off the table it was perched on.

'Fuck you,' he growled in the general direction of the answering machine, his remark directed at the owner of the voice.

Martin Anderson was a year older than Paul. They'd known each other since primary school. Always been close friends, shared the same interests and, unlike so many childhood friends, they'd kept in touch throughout their lives, seeing each other regularly for lunch, drinks or for any other reason that appealed to them. Anderson had started his own photographic business upon leaving college and Paul, during the course of his work, had done advertising for him. But the two men were completely opposite in character and attitudes. Anderson was a cautious, sensible man who had managed to build up a very successful business, father two boys and remain married to the same woman for the last fourteen years. He'd always been scrupulously careful with the money he earned, saving where he could, paying chunks off his mortgage when possible and now he was reaping the rewards. Successful, solvent and comfortable.

At this precise moment, Paul hated him for it.

He listened to the remainder of the message, the sound of Anderson's voice washing over him.

'Give me a ring. Perhaps I can help,' Anderson said at the end of the message.

'Doubt it,' Paul breathed.

The next message made him even angrier.

7

Frank Hacket cupped his hand around the lighter flame and took a deep draw on his cigarette.

He blew out the smoke and leaned back against the wall, the sun beating down on his face. He was sweating, not just from the heat here in the car park of the hospital but because of his recent exertions. It had taken him almost twenty minutes to get an appallingly overweight woman from the back of an ambulance into a wheelchair even with the help of a paramedic.

The woman had complained about her aching joints and her swollen legs and just about everything else. It wasn't her fault she was overweight, she had told Hacket and the paramedic repeatedly. It was in her genes. She ate for comfort. She'd trotted out all the usual clichés and Hacket had nodded in all the right places as he'd struggled to help settle this human behemoth in the wheelchair that, for one awful moment, he'd feared wasn't going to take her weight. Once into the chair he had pushed her through the main entrance of the building to her designated destination within, listening the entire way to her incessant complaints.

'I'm big-boned,' she'd told him.

Dinosaurs were big-boned, Hacket had felt like telling her as he'd strained every sinew to transport her through the hospital.

He smiled a little to himself. He had to find the humour where he could in his job. For almost thirteen years he'd been a porter here at the same hospital. The incident with the woman was the kind he dealt with every day of his working life. If it wasn't that, it was mopping up the sick or the blood in A&E, removing or delivering bed linen to the wards and any one of another hundred different tasks that came under his job description.

Hacket wandered over to one of the wooden benches just outside the entrance to MATERNITY and sat down, nodding good naturedly to a nurse as she left at the end of her shift. He watched her walk across the car park and onwards towards the large and poorly maintained hedge that offered a barrier between the hospital and the road beyond. He'd thought about having a word with one of the hospital supervisors concerning the hedge. For a fee, Hacket would trim the hedge for them. Anything to bring in a little extra money but he knew that there were contractors employed to take care of that and the rest of the hospital grounds. It just appeared that they didn't care too much for their responsibilities. The grass, he noted, also needed cutting.

He took another drag on his cigarette, glancing at his watch. He still had another ten minutes of his break left then it was back to the daily grind until his shift ended. He dug a hand into his overall pocket and pulled out the scratch card, selecting a coin from the same pocket to rub off the circles covering the prizes.

He'd bought the card that morning, just as he did every single day, saving it until this time every afternoon, hoping against hope that when the symbols were revealed he would have won the jackpot but knowing in his heart that his dream would never come true. People like him didn't win lottery jackpots. It wasn't part of the grand scheme of things as far as he was concerned. Even so, it didn't stop him praying for such a win every now and then, especially when it was a particularly large jackpot. When he thought of what that kind of money would do for him and his family it almost made him weep. He had a mental list of things he would spend it on. The people he would help. What must it be like not to have any money worries, he mused. Those people who said that money wasn't everything were those who had plenty of it. He sighed and turned his attention once again to his scratch card.

Hacket revealed the first of the symbols, took a drag on his cigarette then proceeded. He raised his eyebrows when he saw that the two he'd uncovered were the same.

One more and he'd have won a hundred thousand pounds.

He rubbed it off.

Nothing. Just as he'd expected.

He sighed and folded the useless card, pushing it back into his pocket until he could dispose of it. He finished his cigarette and was about to get to his feet when his mobile phone rang.

When he saw who was calling his heart sank.

8

'Hello, Paul, it's Ian.'

Paul glared at the answering machine for a moment as if holding the contraption personally responsible for the call.

'Just thought I'd give you a call,' the voice went on. 'I'm back in hospital.'

Paul raised his eyebrows unconcernedly.

'They did the operation again but they fucked it up again,' Ian Garrett's voice went on. 'I'm in here for another ten days at least. It's the same hospital as before. Give me a ring.'

Paul pressed the STOP button.

'Fuck you, too,' he muttered.

He'd known Ian Garrett for the last eight years. They'd met while Paul was working on an advertising campaign for the company where Garrett was employed. The two men were the same age and they'd had the same interests. Their friendship had grown quickly and unexpectedly, blossoming from formal business lunches to nights out at pubs and clubs and, most regularly, cinemas. Like Paul, Ian Garrett was a film fanatic and the two men would often spend many pleasurable hours in the cinema watching films and then even longer afterwards talking about them.

However, three years earlier, Garrett had been badly injured in a motorcycle accident. The damage to his left knee and ankle had left him with a pronounced limp, something not corrected by the surgery recommended to him. In fact, the surgery had been so badly botched that there had been a danger for a while that he might even lose the leg. On Paul's insistence, he had sued the consultant and the surgeon responsible and a compensation payment approaching two million pounds had been mentioned.

Even now Paul sat staring at the answering machine preparing to erase Garrett's message.

'Two million,' Paul murmured through gritted teeth. 'You're getting two million fucking quid and you're still moaning. So you might have a limp for the rest of your life. Big deal. I'd limp for two million fucking quid. Perhaps the newest cock-up will add a few hundred thousand to your settlement.' He shook his head. 'Cunt.'

He ran a hand through his hair and listened to the other two messages.

The first was from a call centre. Something about his mobile phone and getting extra minutes. He deleted it. The last was from another work mate (or, rather, ex-work mate) offering commiserations about his redundancy. Paul deleted that, too.

He remained perched on the edge of the leather sofa for what seemed like an eternity, wondering what the hell to do next.

And what are the thrilling choices? Ring your mum and tell her how you've lost your job and how deep in the shit you are? Or call one of the others?

Neither of those two possibilities interested him in his current mood.

His most immediate choice came down to whether or not to stand up again or simply flop back on the sofa. He hadn't eaten since lunchtime, he reminded himself; he really should eat. However, he didn't feel like cooking himself anything and he couldn't be bothered to go out and get a takeaway. Perhaps he'd have a sandwich.

So, what's the decision?

He decided to get changed. Take off his work clothes and put on something more comfortable.

Have a shower. Try and wash away the dirt of the day.

He wished he could wash away the events of the day as well. Wash them away and start again as if nothing had happened. As if this day had never happened. Continue as if life was still good and had meaning. Carry on as if he still had some hope.

Paul shook his head again and got to his feet. He wandered across to the television set and switched it on, standing there switching channels aimlessly. There was news on a couple of them. A reality show of some description or another. The obligatory celebrity-orientated programmes on two others. Paul tutted and switched to a cable channel. There was something on about the Second World War (there always was on that channel). He left that on. Just so there was some sound inside the flat. Purely and simply because he wanted more inside his head than just the sound of his own thoughts.

He was about to move towards the bedroom and the bathroom beyond it when the phone rang.

'Fuck it,' Paul said, waving a hand in the direction of the ringing contraption. The answering machine could get it.

He heard his own-recorded voice intone:

'Leave a message after the beep.'

Whoever was calling could wait.

However, when he heard who it was, he realised that they couldn't.

9

Laura Hacket felt as if she was the only person left in the world.

As she started up the exit ramp of the underpass she glanced around towards the trees and bushes on either side and towards the open area beyond.

There was no one there. No other children playing among the trees and none on the open area of greenery she could see. There were usually some boys kicking a ball about or running after each other, shouting and yelling. But not today. The nearest houses were fully one hundred yards from the underpass, reachable by the pathway that she now walked along.

Laura didn't know why she felt nervous, she didn't know what made her feel uncomfortable about the footsteps behind her. It was a beautiful day, the sun was still shining and she was almost clear of the underpass, out of the gloom below ground and back out into the brilliance above it once more. And yet still she could not find the courage to turn and look over her shoulder. She could still hear the footsteps, moving at the same pace as hers. When she speeded up so did they. When she slowed down, they did likewise.

That was what had made Laura nervous.

If someone had been wandering through the underpass behind her and wanted to get to wherever it was they were going then surely they wouldn't have stopped walking when she did. Would they? Why would they do that? If they were going home or visiting someone or walking to the shops or whatever they were doing, they would do it at their own pace, wouldn't they? Not copy her movements, her pace.

Laura swallowed nervously and wondered what her best option was.

Should she run? Try to escape whoever had followed her into the subterranean walkway?

Or should she merely stand still and put her theory to the test? If someone was following her then, if she stopped, they would stop, she told herself.

Laura seemed pleased with her own logic and decided to try the second of her strategies. However, she reasoned, if someone was following her then if she stopped that would make her an easier target. The person following would simply be able to reach her more easily. She sighed, confused now. If there was someone following her then surely if they wanted to catch up with her then they could simply speed up. If they wanted to catch her that badly then that's what they'd do, wasn't it?

Laura was beginning to wonder if there was even anyone there any longer but she knew there had to be because there was no way out of the underpass other than the path on which she now walked. Unless that person had doubled back but, she told herself, why would they want to do that?

All this thinking and wondering was really becoming quite tiring. Laura decided that her best bet would be to run a little way, so that she reached home more quickly. After all, home was where she wanted to be. Home was where her mum would be waiting. Home meant safety.

Laura moved a little quicker for about twenty yards then decided that it was too hot to run.

She slowed down and listened, still determined not to look behind her. It was like when she was lying in bed at night and she heard strange noises. Her mum had told her that if she heard anything at night to just ignore it, that there was nothing to worry about. Just close her eyes and go back to sleep. The same when there was a thunderstorm. Her dad had told her that the thunder was just the clouds bumping together and that there was nothing to be frightened of. Imagination could cause all sorts of problems, she decided. A bit like imagining that there was some-body following you when there most probably wasn't. Laura was ready to blame her overactive imagination.

She wondered for a moment if it could be one of her friends trying to scare her but rapidly decided that wasn't the case. They all lived on the other side of the estate, they wouldn't have followed her all this way and, besides, none of her friends would be that rotten. Why would they want to frighten her?

Why would anyone want to frighten her? Unless it was that man that she'd heard her dad talk about sometimes. What was his name? Peter something. She remembered hearing it on the television news, too. He was a horrible man who did nasty things to little girls like her. Now, what was his name?

Peter what? Her dad had said that he should be strung up for the things he did to kids.

Laura frowned as she tried to remember this awful man's name.

Peter. She smiled to herself. Peter File. That was it. Her dad had been angry about a man called Peter File because he hurt children.

Laura hoped that it wasn't that man who was following her. She didn't even know that he lived in her town. All she knew was she didn't want to meet him.

She now decided that perhaps running was the best option after all.

10

'Hey, sweetie, it's me,' trilled the voice of the caller as soon as Paul's recorded message stopped.

Recognising it, Paul lunged for the phone and lifted it, simultaneously jabbing the STOP button on the answering machine.

'Amy,' he said quickly. 'It's me. I've got it.'

'Hey, you,' the voice on the other end of the phone said. 'I didn't expect to get your machine at this time of night. Where were you?'

'I was here, I've not long got in.'

'I'm not checking up on you, sweetie,' she chuckled. 'I was joking. I guessed you were working late or something.'

Paul held the phone limply for a moment.

'Paul?' Amy Thomas continued. 'Are you still there?'

'Yeah, I'm still here.'

'Can you hear me all right?'

'Fine. How're things with you?'

'I've been busy. Things were a mess here. I don't know how the hell they managed. I spent most of yesterday trying to get their office in some kind of order.'

'And how's New York?'

'I haven't really seen much of it apart from what I've seen from the cab going from the hotel to the office. But it's so, I don't know, so alive. There's a fantastic vibe here. I thought I was going to be jet-lagged when I got off the plane but as soon as I got to JFK I just felt so . . . energised.'

Paul nodded as she continued. Normally her enthusiasm would have made him smile. But not tonight.

'A couple of the people in their marketing office have promised to take me out for a meal, show me some of the sights, that kind of thing, but I don't know when,' Amy went on. 'I mean, I'm only here for another two days and there's so much to see. And I wanted to do some shopping, too. I mean, you can't visit New York and not buy something from Bloomingdale's or Macy's, can you?' she chuckled.

'You enjoy it while you can.'

'I just wish you were here with me.'

'Yeah, me too.'

'Maybe we could come here for a long weekend or something. The flights aren't too expensive and the hotels are really reasonable considering how good they are.'

There was a long pause.

'Paul?' she persisted.

'Yeah, I heard you,' he said flatly.

'What's wrong?' Amy asked.

'Nothing,' he lied. 'I'm all right. I went for a drink earlier and I think I had too much. I've got a lousy headache.'

'Who did you go with? Someone from work?'

'No. I went on my own. I didn't feel like company.'

There was a moment's silence at the other end of the line then Amy spoke again, her voice lower.

'Paul, something's wrong,' she insisted. 'You sound really down and you never drink alone. Not unless you're really, really pissed off and then you only do it in the flat. What's the matter?'

'I've lost my job.'

There you go. How hard was that? Better than bottling it up, eh?

Silence at the other end.

'I found out today,' he continued. 'They made me redundant. That's it. End of story.'

'Oh, Christ, Paul, I'm sorry. Did you have any idea?'

'If I'd seen it coming I'd have been prepared for it,' he said, cutting her short. 'I'd have made plans.' He smiled bitterly. 'They said they were very sorry to lose me. That they wished me all the best but that they had no choice. That the company had to make cutbacks. The usual bullshit.'

'Who told you?'

'Oh, Mr Banks himself,' he exclaimed sarcastically. 'Wasn't that an honour for me? Getting the bullet personally from one of the directors of the firm. Fucking shithouse. I never liked that bastard from the first time I met him. You know you get gut feelings about people? I had one about him when I first took the job. He's a cunt.'

'So what happens now?' Amy asked.

'You tell me. All I've got to do is find a job that pays comparable wages in a market that's more depressed and recession-hit than anything in living memory, find some way of paying my mortgage and bills or try to sell my flat. Piece of piss.'

He sucked in an almost painful breath.

'Listen, Amy,' he began. 'I don't really feel like talking about this, babe. I'm sorry but it's hit me much harder than I realised. I'm going to lose everything.'

'No you won't. You won't lose me and you'll find another job, Paul, I know you will. Just because Meyer and Banks don't want you doesn't mean someone else won't. There are plenty of other advertising agencies out there.'

'And none of them are hiring,' Paul interjected.

'You don't know that until you start looking,' Amy countered.

He exhaled wearily.

'You can't take this lying down, Paul,' Amy insisted. 'You've got to fight. If only to show those bastards that they were wrong to get rid of you.'

'You don't know what I feel like at the moment,' Paul intoned. 'I haven't felt this bad since my dad died.'

'You're one of the best copywriters around. You're too good at what you do for someone not to want you.'

'Thanks for that but I've already had enough bullshit for the day.'

'It wasn't bullshit. It's true. But I can understand how you feel.'

'No you can't, Amy,' he corrected her, butting in. 'You have absolutely no idea at all how I feel.'

He sighed.

'Who else knows?' she enquired.

'Who was I going to tell? It's not exactly the kind of thing you want to shout from the rooftops, is it? But

I'm sure that a few people will be smiling when they find out.'

'Like who? Who's going to be pleased that you've lost your job?'

'Oh, come on, Amy. I've always been so fucking sure of myself. Like I was invincible. Don't tell me there aren't some people who'll be having a quiet giggle when they see what's happened to me.'

'You only feel like this because you've just found out. When you've had a night's sleep and had time to consider your options, you'll feel better.'

'What fucking options? Trail around other ad agencies begging for a job, hoping that I've got something to offer that the thousands of other guys in the same position as me haven't got or go and sign on? Great.'

There was another long silence finally broken by Paul.

'I'm sorry, Amy, but I'm not really in the mood for a chat at the moment. Perhaps you'd better call me tomorrow,' he sighed.

'How does this affect our plans?' she wanted to know.

'Plans?'

'You know what I mean.'

'Not now, Amy.'

'But we were going to talk about it when I got home.'

'Then that's what we'll do, talk when you get home. Not now.'

'But we'd decided, Paul.'

'That was before I lost my fucking job, wasn't it? Just drop it, will you?'

'I think I'd better go,' she told him sternly.

'That might be best.'

'I'll ring you tomorrow.'

'I'll be here. I've got nowhere else to go.'

There was a loud hiss of static on the line.

'Amy?' he said, fearing he'd lost the connection.

She said something that he didn't hear. He only heard his voice drift through the crackling.

'Amy. Say that again,' he urged.

He was sure the line was dead.

11

Frank Hacket thought about ignoring the ringing mobile. He looked at the name displayed on the screen, waited a moment longer then answered.

'Hello, Gina,' he said, trying to inject a note of enthusiasm into his voice. 'I can't talk for long, I'm just finishing my break.'

'I know that,' his wife told him from the other end of the line. 'I assumed you'd be outside having a fag and playing with one of your scratch cards.'

'Am I that predictable?'

'Yes,' she told him humourlessly.

'Well, we haven't won anything so don't get your hopes up,' he told her.

'I stopped hoping years ago, Frank,' she announced.

Hacket rolled his eyes and was about to say something when Gina continued.

'I was just ringing to ask you to bring some milk home with you when you come,' she instructed him. 'Four pints should be enough. And some cigarettes for me.'

'How many?'

'Forty.'

'I got you twenty only yesterday. Are you smoking them two at a time? I've got plenty. Why can't you smoke mine until tomorrow?'

'I don't like the ones you smoke. You know that.'

'Couldn't you have picked some up yourself while you were out? You did go out this morning didn't you?'

'I didn't want to be late getting back. Laura will be home soon. I don't like her coming back to an empty house.'

'She'll have to when you get a job.'

'Well, that's not just yet, is it? For the time being I want to be here when she gets home.'

'Where did you go this morning?'

'Just to the town. I had to get a card for my sister's wedding anniversary. It's at the weekend.'

'See anyone you knew?'

'Like who?'

'I was only asking. I wasn't interrogating you.'

'Good. I don't want to go over all that again, Frank.'

'You were the one who had the affair, Gina, not me.'

'Why did you have to bring that up now?'

'I'm not bringing it up.'

'Yes you are. You mentioned it. That's bringing it up.'

'Do you blame me?'

'Look, we talked about it at the time. We sorted things out.'

'I know but that doesn't stop me thinking about what happened.'

'We said we wouldn't mention it again. You said you'd forget about it.'

'I've been trying.'

'Well, try harder,' she snapped.

There was a long pause, finally broken by Gina.

'I want to go home at the weekend and see my sister,' she said. 'Take her some flowers or something. They've been married for fifteen years this year.'

'I'll probably be working.'

'I know that. I'll take Laura. She hasn't seen her cousins for ages. She'll enjoy it.'

'Is your sister having a party for their anniversary?'

'No, just a few friends to the house, that sort of thing.'

Hacket nodded, held the phone a little away from his face and exhaled wearily.

'Did you get your prescription while you were in town?' he wanted to know.

'I've got to make an appointment,' Gina told him. 'They won't give out anti-depressants on a repeat prescription.'

There was a moment's silence.

'You could get some from the hospital pharmacy,' Gina insisted.

'No,' he told her. 'I'm not doing that again, Gina. I nearly got caught last time. They check these things, you know. They know who's got access to the pharmacy. I can't risk it.'

'I only need enough until the end of the week.'

'I daren't. If I get caught that'll be it. I'll get sacked and I'll probably get prosecuted, too.'

Another silence.

'Don't forget the milk and my cigarettes when you come home,' Gina reminded him coldly. 'What time will you be home?'

'They're a bit short of staff. I might have to do some overtime.'

'Good, we need the money.'

'I'll ring you if I get the chance, let you know what time I'll be home.'

'Don't worry about it. I'll expect you when I see you.'

'Give Laura a kiss from me,' he asked. 'See you later.'

'See you.'

He ended the call and stuffed his mobile back into his pocket.

12

'Can you hear me?'

Paul Crane raised his voice, trying to shout over the hissing static.

'Amy?'

Her voice finally broke through the barrage of interference.

'Paul, I can hear you,' she said. 'I'm still here.'

'I thought we'd been cut off,' he told her.

There was another silence then Amy spoke once again.

'I can fly home tomorrow if you want me to,' she informed him.

'No, there's no point. There's nothing you can do anyway. Besides, if you do that you might get in trouble. You might lose your job, too.'

'I'll come if you want me to.'

'No. Stay there. Enjoy yourself. Have a look around the city. Go out and have a meal. Do your shopping.'

'I'll bring you something nice back.'

'Unless you can bring back a job then forget it.'

He wanted her to go now. Wanted her to hang up. Although he liked hearing her voice, at this precise moment in time he just wanted to put the phone down.

And do what? Wallow in self-pity?

He didn't want to talk about how he was feeling because no matter how much he talked it wouldn't help. Nothing would help unless she was going to offer him a job and that wasn't going to happen, was it? All this aimless chat and pointless offers of solace were lost on him. If she was here with him now then he might hold her in his arms, he might kiss her and it might make him feel better for a fleeting second. Just a little human contact might relieve the pain he was so immersed in, no matter for how short a time. If she was here with him, he thought, he might even have sex with her. He didn't want to make love to her. He wanted to have sex and there was a huge difference. In better times he had made love to her, with passion and tenderness but, if she'd been with him now, he would have wanted to fuck her. To lose himself in the pure animal release of the moment.

But she's not here, is she? You're alone. Completely and utterly alone. Talking's not going to help so you might as well hang up.

'Listen, Amy,' he said slowly. 'You'd better go. Like you say, we'll talk tomorrow. I might be a bit more chatty then.'

'What I said about our plans, Paul. I meant it. They don't have to change, you know. We can still move in together like we said we would.'

'Not now, Amy,' he insisted.

Now he *did* want her to hang up. Those plans were for the future and, as it stood, he could see no point in discussing a future that he felt he didn't have.

'You should talk to Martin Anderson,' she offered.

'He left a message on my voicemail,' Paul told her. 'Why the fuck would I want to speak to him?'

'Because he might know if there're some jobs going.'

'He's a photographer not a fucking temp agency and I don't need his help.'

'You've got to take help from wherever you can get it at a time like this, Paul.'

'Thanks for the advice. I'll speak to you tomorrow.'

'What about freelance work?' Amy insisted. 'Get in touch with some of the people you've worked with over the years. There must be some favours you can call in.'

'It doesn't work like that, Amy.'

'You can ask, can't you?' she snapped.

'This isn't just about losing my job. This is about pride. Do you know how I'm going to feel going cap in hand to people, begging them for some work just to get me by? I can't do that, Amy. Besides, people only want to know you when you're successful. No one gives a shit when you're down on your luck.'

'You're so bloody stubborn. You never ask for help.'

'I've never needed help before. I've always been able to help myself.'

'Well, times change.'

'Yeah, for the worst.'

He thought about simply hanging up. Stop the call now. Tomorrow when he spoke to her he'd simply say that they were cut off. She wouldn't think anything more of it. Wouldn't be angry.

'I'd better go then,' Amy said wearily, apparently catching the sledgehammer hints in his tone. 'What are you going to do now?'

'Have a shower, go to bed. Try and sleep but I'm not holding my breath. Perhaps I should drink what's left of this bottle of vodka. Perhaps it'll knock me out.'

He expected her to protest but she didn't.

'If that's what it takes,' she said softly.

He nodded, wishing now that she was with him. He glanced to one side and could picture her seated on the sofa next to him. Shoulder-length brown hair, wide green eyes and soft lips. He closed his eyes tightly for a second and the image was gone when he looked again.

Alone again.

'I love you,' she told him.

More static.

'I love you, too,' he echoed.

And she was gone.

He replaced the receiver then pressed both hands to his cheeks for a second. Her voice was still ringing in his ears like some kind of auditory afterthought.

He finally turned and headed, once more, towards the bathroom.

Once inside he turned on the shower, listening to the jets of water as he undressed and prepared to step beneath them.

He looked at his reflection in the mirror and a haunted, expressionless man stared back at him, his image gradually obscured as steam from the shower began to cover the glass until at last he was hidden by the film of condensation. It was as if he'd disappeared off the face of the earth. It seemed a pleasing option.

Paul stepped beneath the shower and closed the glass door behind him.

13

Laura Hacket sprinted for about thirty yards, leaving the darkness of the underpass as far behind her as she could. Where the path had levelled out it was easier for her to pick up some speed now and she revelled in that opportunity, her legs pumping as she ran, her hair trailing out behind her.

She finally slowed down as she came to where the path became narrower. Not because it wasn't as wide but because bushes on either side of the walkway were so seriously overgrown that they seemed in danger of meeting across. Laura could see where some of the vine-like branches had been tugged free, she guessed by other people who didn't want to be ensnared by the out-of-control bushes.

And now, at last, Laura turned and looked behind her.

She was alone on the path in both directions. No one ahead and certainly, she was relieved and delighted to see, no one following.

For a moment she considered going back towards the mouth of the underpass, just to check if anyone was still down there but she swiftly thought better of that. On a list of plans it wasn't very close to the top of the list. Certainly not the favoured choice of options.

Laura stood still just beyond the overgrown bushes and waited to get her breath back. She could feel her heart pounding and not all of that was with the exertion of her sprint. She stared raptly at the path behind her, waiting for someone to emerge from below. Expecting her fears to be realised but no one came. Somewhere in the distance she heard a car drive past but other than that and the singing of birds high up in the trees on either side of the path, there was no sound detectable to her keen young ears.

She couldn't see over the bushes and the smell of leaves and vegetation suddenly seemed overpowering to her. It was a heavy, thick smell that clogged her nostrils. She didn't like it. It reminded her of the garden in the summer after a shower when everything was drying off again in the sunshine. That smell was thick and heavy, too, and she didn't like it. But, Laura told herself, she was more content having to inhale the smell of the bushes than she was to be running away from someone. From her imagined pursuer. From Mr File. Mr Peter File.

As she finally turned and walked on, she wondered if she should tell her dad about what had happened (not that anything really had happened, other than in her own imagination) and tell him that she'd thought that dreadful Mr Peter File had been chasing her. He'd laugh when she told him. She'd laugh, too. Her dad always made her smile. No matter what kind of mood she was in, if he wanted to her dad could make her smile. She'd even bought him a little plastic figure to put in the living room at home attesting to that fact. It was about three inches high. A tiny figure with a big head, smiling face and red cheeks that was holding a trophy with the number one on it. On the stand at the bottom it read:

My Daddy makes me smile.

She'd bought it for him last Father's Day and presented it to him along with his card. He'd cried. He always did when she gave him birthday or Christmas cards and she always felt sad despite the fact that he told her it was because he was happy. He always told her that she was the most precious thing in his life and that he loved her more than she'd ever know. He always said the same thing every time she gave him a present. Then he'd lift her up and swing her around until she was dizzy and they'd both laugh again.

Yes, she decided, she would tell her dad that she thought she'd been followed by Peter File. Just to see what he said. She hoped he wouldn't be angry like he was when that name was mentioned on the television or radio sometimes. She'd heard him say something to her mum about that same man once, when they'd been talking in the kitchen and she'd been in the living room listening at the door. Her dad had said something about a little boy being brought into hospital who'd been attacked by Peter File.

Laura could still remember her dad getting angry when he spoke of the marks he'd seen on the little boy's legs and the blood on his bottom.

It had been at that point that she'd run upstairs to her bedroom to play. She didn't want to hear any more talk like that. She'd had nightmares for the next two nights because of that. Her mum would have told her that it was her own fault for listening at doors.

So, now, Laura strode on towards the end of the pathway and the streets of the estate beyond.

The sun was still high in the sky and there were bees buzzing around the flowers in the hedgerows on either side of her. Laura glanced at them and smiled. She liked bees; they were like little *flying teddy bears, even if they did sting sometimes. But her mum had told her that they only stung people who bothered them so Laura was determined not to bother them as they went about their pollen-gathering duties, buzzing loudly and then flying off.*

Laura mimicked the noise they made as she skipped along the remainder of the path.

She was still skipping when the hands grabbed her.

14

Dressed in just a bathrobe, Paul Crane was seated on the sofa gazing blankly at his television screen.

After stepping out of the shower he'd pulled the robe over his body and dried himself to avoid dripping on the carpet. After that he'd briefly considered having the sandwich he'd promised himself earlier but then decided against it and plumped for more vodka instead. He didn't really feel hungry anyway. Why eat just for the sake of it?

He'd checked his mail and found that none of it was either interesting or important. The usual round of bills, circulars and other junk. Fortunately, none of the bills were for inordinately large amounts of money. It was one less thing to worry about and in this present climate anything he didn't have to worry about was welcome.

There was an advertisement break on the television. Paul reached for the remote control. He didn't want to sit and stare at a list of products that he could no longer afford, didn't care to be told of holiday destinations he wouldn't be able to visit or know of the latest technological advances that were shortly to be beyond the reach of his suddenly limited finances. He flicked on to another channel.

More adverts. A never-ending conveyor belt of aspiration for all those who would never be able to afford the treasures shown to them. People like him now, he thought bitterly. Those who didn't want to have products shoved down their throats. Paul suddenly felt as if he was the centre of some world-wide conspiracy designed to increase his misery and the realisation of how serious his plight actually was.

Looking at the adverts made him think about his own lost position, too, so that was another very good reason for switching them off, he told himself. He kept pressing the channel up key on his remote, becoming increasingly frustrated as each successive channel revealed yet more adverts. Paul pressed the button with more force each time, barely suppressing the urge to hurl the remote at the television.

'For fuck's sake,' he muttered under his breath.

Salvation came in the shape of a music channel. No adverts were on display this time but it was showing viewers around the ridiculously ostentatious home of the latest rap star. The presenter was squealing appreciatively at each brainless utterance from the gold chain-bedecked subject of the piece, flicking her blonde hair and spewing words like 'awesome' and 'amazing' with a regularity that made him sick. Paul decided that if it was a choice between the adverts or a glimpse into the privileged lifestyle of some talentless rich bastard with more money than she knew what to do with then the adverts were preferable.

He changed channels again and caught the tailend of a music video.

More tuneless posturing, this time from some boy band that had won a recent television talent show that he'd been fortunate enough to miss. Paul glared at them as they finished performing their latest single, wishing all kinds of ill upon them and hating them for not having to worry about money.

Then the adverts began again. Food. Cars. Insurance. A never-ending progression of images and sounds designed purely and simply to make people think they needed what they were being shown. Paul let out a weary breath and thought how good he himself had been at that.

Well, if you'd been that good you'd still have a job, wouldn't you?

The voice in his head was irritatingly persuasive.

'I didn't lose my job because I wasn't any good,' he said aloud and instantly felt slightly ridiculous for answering his own rhetorical question.

First sign of madness, talking to yourself.

'Fuck off,' he said to the empty air inside the flat although the words were directed at the voice inside his head.

The voice of reason?

The voice of truth, perhaps.

Paul shook his head, irritated by his own internal dialogue.

He hadn't lost his job because of his own ineptitude. That was a fact, and no amount of internal dialogue or any number of voices inside his head could persuade him otherwise. He'd been unlucky. That was it. Pure and simple. It hadn't been his fault. There was no way he'd have been able to avoid what happened to him. The choice had been taken away from him. If someone had offered him an ultimatum and told him that unless he did such and such a thing by this and that date then he would have done it. But no one did. Nobody offered him the opportunity to decide his own destiny. It was decided for him by others *(more powerful?)* who cared nothing for him or the way he lived no matter how they tried to persuade him that they did. They didn't give a shit. Bosses didn't care about their employees. They pretended to take an interest in them because that was how things worked. That was the accepted *modus operandi* in the workplace. No one really gave a fuck about anyone else. They merely went through the motions of seeming to be concerned because that was what was expected. If a worker felt more appreciated then he'd perform more capably. Fuck that. Paul Crane had never needed anyone to care about him or praise his work. All he'd ever needed was money. That was all the praise he wanted. All the recognition he sought. All the laudability he strove for.

A compliment and a caring word or a pay rise?

No fucking contest. Never had been. Never would be. Stick your compliments and your fake sincerity up your arse. Just pay me.

But no one was going to do that now, were they? No one was going to pay him because no one wanted to employ him.

The realisation seemed to hit him once again and he felt a cold shiver run the length of his spine.

You're finished. It's over. Everything you ever dreamed of, everything you ever worked for. All gone. Like it was never there.

He poured the remainder of the vodka into his glass,

cradled the expensive crystal between his palms for a moment and then drank, surprised that he wasn't paralytic by now. He was normally a bit of a lightweight when it came to drinking. Five or six shorts and he was well on his way to being merry.

But situations change circumstances, don't they? Or whatever that phrase is.

Paul sucked in a deep breath and allowed his head to loll back against the sofa.

His head felt as if someone had stuffed it with cotton wool but he hadn't yet acquired that feeling of total numbness and insensibility that he wanted so badly. How much more would he have to drink before that merciful oblivion enveloped him?

He thought about going to bed. Perhaps lying down in his bedroom would bring the nothingness he so badly wanted. Paul glanced at his watch.

Forget it. There's no way you'll be able to sleep just yet.

Might as well stay here and stare at the TV. Watch adverts all night. You might as well watch them, you won't be making any more. Ha, ha.

'Yeah, very fucking funny,' he murmured, changing channels again.

15

Gina Hacket groaned loudly as the mug hit the kitchen floor, slipping from her hand as she dried it.

It shattered immediately, pieces of the decorated ceramic spraying around like shrapnel.

Gina crouched down and hurriedly began to gather the pieces. Maybe there was some way she could salvage the mug, glue it back together, perhaps. However, as she collected the shards she saw that was a vain hope. It had broken into five distinct pieces but there were also dozens of much smaller fragments scattered across the tiles around her.

She held up the largest piece of the mug, gripping it by its still intact handle.

It should have read To Mum and Dad. The piece she was holding bore the legend

TO MUM AN

Laura had decorated it herself during an art class at school earlier in the year and Gina felt an inordinately deep sense of loss at breaking the mug. She tried to tell herself that it was, after all, only a mug but the fact that her daughter had painted those words on the ceramic seemed to make the loss infinitely more keen. For one ridiculous second, Gina thought she was going to burst into tears. She remained crouching on the floor for a moment longer then slowly straightened up, set the five pieces of broken mug on the nearest worktop and retrieved the dustpan and brush from a cupboard nearby. Wearily she set about collecting the smaller fragments.

Why, she asked herself, did it have to be that particular mug? Why not the one with the football crest on it (although her husband would have complained if that had fallen victim to her carelessness) or the chipped one with the picture of a bulldog on it? Any one but the one that had been broken.

No good crying over spilt milk, she told herself. Or broken mugs for that matter. The joke didn't seem so amusing as she dumped the tiny fragments into the pedal bin and returned the dustpan and brush to their cupboard.

She checked the oven, ensuring that the casserole she'd prepared earlier wasn't cooking too quickly. She and Laura would have their dinner at five-thirty, as they always did. She'd keep some of the food warm for Frank for when he got home. Whenever that might be. As she inspected the casserole, Gina caught a glimpse of her reflection in the glass of the oven door.

She ran a hand through her hair and noticed that her mascara was smudged. She wondered why she hadn't noticed that particular fact in the hotel.

The hotel.

Her thoughts drifted back to earlier in the day. She experienced that same peculiar and disconcerting mixture of feelings. Guilt mingled with exhilaration. Shame combined with pleasure. It was always the same. After every snatched meeting she ran the same gamut of emotions. Before the event she was like a child the day before her birthday. Almost breathless with excitement and longing and then, when it was all over again, the darkness descended upon her in the form of self-loathing and doubt.

Her affair had been going on for ten months, although Gina wasn't sure if affair was the appropriate word to describe her liaisons. She met with a man periodically and fucked him. That was a more apt description of her current status. The word affair tended to imply candlelit dinners in expensive and intimate restaurants followed by passionate lovemaking in fine hotels on crisply laundered sheets, not hurried fondling in a car followed by sweaty shagging in a Travelodge.

It was the second time they'd embarked on such a clandestine relationship (although the word relationship elevated it to something that it really wasn't). She'd known him, worked for him, nine years earlier, when she'd been in her early twenties. Their first encounter had lasted for six torrid months before she'd become pregnant with Laura although, Gina reminded herself, there was never any question of the child being anyone's other than her husband's. By mutual consent they'd finished the first affair and Gina had left work to concentrate on her daughter.

During the interim they'd spoken occasionally on the phone or seen each other around the town but, only a year or so ago, they'd met up for lunch and Gina had reached for that excitement she'd experienced before with him and agreed to begin seeing him again.

She didn't do it because she wanted to hurt her husband. She knew how much he'd been hurt by her first affair. She knew he loved her and would do absolutely anything for her.

Sometimes she was grateful that she was still married to him, that he hadn't demanded she leave after discovering her infidelity. But he hadn't because he cared too much for their daughter. He had said at the time that he would rather they stayed together for the sake of Laura and Gina had agreed. She was relieved that her daughter had never discovered what she'd done because it would have been impossible to explain that she'd done it because the crushing normality of everyday life was sometimes just too much to bear. The daily routine just too soul-destroying and without hope. She wasn't excusing herself. She wasn't looking for salvation. She was just trying to explain her actions to herself.

And what would happen if Frank ever found out about this latest indiscretion? Would he walk out and take Laura with him? Where, she reasoned, was he going to go? No, if he ever found out he would be hurt, as he had been before. Deeply and probably irrevocably hurt, but he would insist they worked their way through the problem once more and he would never stop loving her. And he would blame her lover and not her. He would be angry with her but he would lay the blame for the affair squarely at the door of the man she was sleeping with. She wasn't taking this for granted; she just knew him. That was his way. If confrontation could be avoided then Frank would find a way. And he would never jeopardise Laura's happiness. He would do everything in his power to ensure that their daughter was oblivious. What she didn't know wouldn't hurt her. That was Frank's way. Gina didn't hate him for it. She didn't think him any less of a man for it. That was just the way it was. However, in the meantime she would do all she could to prevent discovery. The feelings of guilt and shame might have been strong after the deed was done but before and during made those negative feelings almost worthwhile.

Gina returned to the washing-up, being more careful with the successive items of crockery as she cleaned and dried them. She glanced across at the electronic clock on the cooker and noted the time.

Laura should be home soon.

16

Paul Crane laughed.

It must be the drink, he told himself. If not for the unfeasible amounts of alcohol he'd consumed he would not have managed such a loud and unfettered explosion to escape him on this particular night. He gazed at the television and he laughed until his sides ached. However, there was no humour in the sound. No release of tension and no joyous exaltation. It was a resigned and weary sound. Almost painful.

And the cause of this alien sound?

'Isn't it time you started a new life?' the voice-over on the advert proclaimed.

Paul had heard that and begun to laugh. That was it.

'What are you offering?' he asked, his comment directed towards the TV but there wasn't anyone to answer if they could.

Except there's no one else in the flat with you, is there? No one else to answer the question.

That internal voice was becoming a bit of a pain in the arse, Paul decided. It was so logical. Too logical. He dealt with it the same way he had previously.

'Fuck off,' he grunted.

He changed channels for the hundredth time that night.

What exactly are you looking for? Something to watch? Something to stimulate you? Something to occupy your mind?

The internal voice refused to leave him alone. It persisted with its grindingly logical and irritating intrusions.

You haven't thought this through properly. I've already told you that. There are options. It's understandable you feeling aggrieved. That's fair enough. Even the self-pity is merited, perhaps even the anger. But you should be formulating plans now.

'Why don't you just fuck off,' Paul snapped, even more irritated by the fact that his internal voice seemed to have momentarily taken on the tone of a self-righteous, superior prick. Paul smiled to himself.

Call me what you like. I'm still here.

'Cunt,' Paul added to the empty air around him.

Very witty, very charming, I don't think. You were in advertising. You should be wondering which clients you're going to take with you, which ones might offer you freelance work and what favours you could call in. Why not return some calls? Snarling at the answering machine the way you did isn't going to help, is it?

Paul shook his head, so sick of the internal voice by now that he couldn't even be bothered to answer it. Even so, he forced out a handful of words in reply.

'You know fuck all,' he rasped, his words a little slurred.

Why not try to sleep?

Paul knew that he was merely postponing the simple act of having to go to bed because, once he left the sitting room and was lying in the darkness of his bedroom, the thoughts would come flooding in with even greater force. The thought of failure and fear for the future, such as it was.

What future? You haven't got a future.

Paul kept pressing the channel up button, finding mostly blank screens as he progressed. He didn't subscribe to the film channels, the lifestyle channels held little interest for him at the moment and the music channels even less. Then something filled the screen that did catch his eye and hold his attention, however briefly.

The two girls were in their early twenties. One blonde, one brunette. Both were naked on the large bed they occupied, supple bodies intertwined. They were kissing deeply, hands on each other's breasts, grinding enthusiastically against each other. Paul sat up slightly. Just as he did the screen went blank except for a caption at the bottom that read:

FREEVIEW OVER.

'Shit,' he grunted and jabbed the remote control once again.

The channels rose through TEENAGE NYMPHOS, past ASIAN SLUTS and on to C**K-HUNGRY HOUSE-WIVES. On each occasion, however, the screens were blank but for the captions at the bottom announcing the delights that could be had for a subscription fee. Paul smiled thinly and worked his way up through more of the adult channels that he had chosen not to subscribe to when his satellite dish had first been installed. He couldn't even remember seeing these before but, then again, he hadn't been sitting up pointlessly staring at the television trying to get drunk because he'd lost his job before.

This was a new, albeit not particularly exciting, discovery. He continued on through the array of blank channels, finally coming to one that announced itself as BANGBIRDS.

Now what genius did their advertising?

However, there was a girl on display. There was no sound, despite the fact that she was holding a phone against her badly made-up face, her thick and almost grotesquely red lips close to the mouthpiece. Callers could speak to her, the caption on the screen proclaimed, by subscribing and then calling the offered number.

She was dressed in just a thong and a pair of precipitously high heels and she was licking her lips in such an exaggerated way that it would have been comical at any other time. However, on this occasion, Paul found it quite mesmerising. He watched her face intently, trying on occasion to lip-read what she was saying.

Now you really have lost it.

He managed to make out a couple of words. One of which was fuck.

Not a great stretch to lip-read that one, was it?

He managed to make out pussy as well. This was followed by some more tongue flicking and then, he noticed, the word balls.

How about lip-reading as a new career? You seem to have a flair for it.

He saw her purse those huge lips again and blow a kiss towards the screen. To his surprise he felt the beginnings of an erection.

Must be the booze. She looks bloody awful. I'm sure she's a lovely girl, just trying to earn a decent living, but she looks horrible. Not your type at all.

The girl on the screen was now on her knees, running her hand up and down her stomach and over her breasts. She slipped her fingers into the top of her thong and leered at the camera once more in a parody of a lustful look that was almost comical. Paul felt his erection grow. If only he could hear her. And yet, there was something about the silence and just the image. With no sound he could imagine her voice. To him it could be soft and husky. He feared that, in life, it might be strident and harsh. Exaggerated and fake, like her make-up. He looked at her full lips once again, now completely enraptured by the image before him.

The girl was tugging off one of her shoes and Paul watched as she put the long, spike heel close to her mouth and flicked her tongue at it.

She mouthed DO YOU WANT TO FUCK ME? into the camera.

'Yes,' Paul murmured, opening his robe to expose his hard penis.

What the fuck are you playing at?

He fixed his eyes on her as she lay down on the hideous pink satin sheet, her legs now spread wide and one hand pushed down inside her thong. Even when she almost dropped the phone he didn't care. Not that it would have mattered to him because he couldn't hear what she was saying anyway. The room was silent. The girl leered out at him from the television and mouthed OH, YEAH.

Paul Crane began to masturbate.

17

Laura Hacket was more frightened than she'd ever been in her life.

She had been since the hands had grabbed her and yanked her from the path into the bushes.

She'd screamed for a moment but a hand had been clamped over her mouth as a bag of some sort had been forced over her head so that she couldn't see what was happening or where she was. Or who had grabbed her.

Laura could remember being lifted into the air and carried by a person who had run for a few yards, then she had vague memories of a car and the sound of an engine being revved.

And then nothing but the smell of the bag over her head. A damp, dirty smell that she hated.

She had wanted to scream out inside the car. She had wanted to tell whoever had grabbed her that she wanted her mum but she couldn't find the words. It was as if her throat and chest had tightened up, stopping her from inhaling enough breath with which to form the words. Also, she didn't like taking deep breaths with her head inside the bag because of the smell.

When the car had finally stopped, Laura had heard footsteps then the sound of the car boot opening and she'd told herself that then would be the time to scream but, before she could, she'd felt a sharp pain in her right arm. Close to the shoulder. A cold sensation that felt as if someone had stuck a needle in her.

Then there had been nothing but darkness.

How long ago that had been Laura had no idea but, now, the smells were different.

She still couldn't see anything and she still couldn't speak but the reasons for this incapacity were now different. Whoever had brought her to this place had covered her eyes and mouth with sticky tape, effectively sealing both. Laura knew that she was sitting on a hard chair; she could feel it when she flexed her hands. Her wrists were also secured with thick tape, as were her ankles. She was helpless. Unable to move, see or speak.

She just wanted her mum. Wanted her to come and fetch her. To release her. Take her away from this place. She wanted to be at home playing with her toys with the television in the background while her mum cooked dinner. Laura wanted to be able to smell cooking food. Not the cold, dusty odours she smelled now.

And her arm hurt where she'd been pricked. Her head ached, too, and she was upset because she couldn't remember anything that had happened since she'd been lifted from the car. Laura began to cry softly but the tears merely welled up behind the tape covering her eyes and made them sting even more. Some of the clear liquid trickled from behind the sticky blindfold and ran down her cheeks. She tasted the salty tears on her lips.

Laura swayed slowly backwards and forwards on her chair.

How she wanted her mum.

She heard a door open and close somewhere behind her and

she stiffened on her chair. Then she heard footsteps moving towards her and she felt even more frightened than she first had.

Please God, don't let it be someone who's going to hurt me, she thought. Please God, don't let it be the terrible Mr File. Don't let it be Peter File that's got me.

She tried to scream in pain as the tape was torn from her eyes, suddenly allowing her to see both her surroundings and her captor but the tape around her mouth stopped her.

In that split second, as the tape was ripped free and she saw what was in front of her, Laura wished that she had been taken by Peter File. At least he was only a man. He would have had a mouth and eyes and a nose. Unlike the face that confronted her. There were eyes but they were small and dark, hidden beneath huge overhanging eyebrows and sagging flesh. Where the nose should have been there was just an empty hole and there was only a zip across the part of the face where the mouth would ordinarily have been. Laura was sure that this was no man. It was something from her worst and most terrifying nightmare. And she was certain of one thing and one thing only.

Whatever was standing in front of her definitely wasn't human.

18

Paul Crane felt ashamed.

He didn't know any other word to describe the feelings that filled him as he sat staring at the silent television screen.

What the fuck are you playing at?

The internal voice was jabbing at him again but now it was throwing film dialogue at him, too. He remembered a film called *The Offence.* An old film, early seventies, with Sean Connery and Ian Bannen. Bloody good film, too. But, from that film, a line kept filtering through his mind and it seemed made for him. A description so apt it was almost painful.

'You sad, sorry little man.'

That was the line. Spoken by Ian Bannen with great derision and sneering contempt to Sean Connery. And now that irritatingly insistent internal voice of his was saying the same line to him over and over again.

You sad, sorry little man.

And that was what Paul Crane felt like. He looked at the girl on the television screen. She was laughing silently.

Laughing at you. Laughing at you and all the other sad wankers watching her. You pathetic bastard. You excuse for a fucking man.

Paul hurriedly changed the channel as if he couldn't bear to look at the girl any more. Like one of those mornings when you've drunk too much the night before and ended up in bed with a friend because she's been equally pissed and you've both ended up doing something you swore you'd never do. And then, in the morning, when you both wake up naked in bed or on the sofa or on the fucking floor you don't know where to look or what to say, do you? You both know that something happened the night before that shouldn't have and, at the time, you probably both enjoyed it but it still shouldn't have happened, should it?

A bit like the girl on the television and masturbating on your own living-room sofa. It really shouldn't have happened, should it?

He looked to one side of him, at the balled-up tissues he'd retrieved from his bathrobe. The tissues he'd cleaned himself up with when he'd finished masturbating.

The evidence of your sin. The concrete truth of your failure. The failure even to maintain any kind of self-control. It was some girl on the television. A girl you couldn't even hear. You were lip-reading her dirty talk. That's how fucking pathetic it was. If you really wanted phone sex that badly you could have called Amy back. She'd have obliged, wouldn't she? She's done it before when one or both of you has been away on business. Christ, if you wanted to look at porn you might as well have switched your fucking laptop on and looked at some porn. Some decent porn, not strained to lip-read that silly bitch on TV. Dickhead.

Paul shook his head, wishing that the voice inside it would shut up and bother someone else instead. But it couldn't bother anyone else, could it, because it was *his* internal voice.

Phone sex. Ha, ha. She was holding a phone, nothing else. You weren't having phone sex with her, were you, you fucking dickhead?

The voice was becoming more vehement. And he wanted it out of his head.

You're out of your head. You're out of your fucking mind.

It belonged inside his head, nobody else's. And it was doing what Paul himself always did. It was speaking as it found.

Speak as you find, son. You can't rely on other people's opinions. Trust your own judgement.

His father's words.

Yes, your dad's inside your head, too. All his homespun philosophy from years gone by. All his sayings and his views.

Paul bowed his head now. Almost like a penitent seeking absolution. He closed his eyes tightly and white stars danced behind the lids.

'Anybody else want to say anything?' he murmured aloud, eyes still closed.

But no one did because there was no one else in the flat except him.

And yet, despite the shame and the humiliation and the feelings of worthlessness *(something you'll get used to in the days and weeks to come, they'll be with you all the time)*, his brief foray into self-abuse had provided two very welcome and unexpected bonuses. Primarily, for the first time since he'd been told he'd lost his job, he'd felt something pleasurable. He hadn't, for the duration of his masturbation, thought about his situation or his lack of hope or anything else that had dogged him so determinedly for the evening and much of the night.

The second good thing was that he suddenly felt very, very tired. Not the kind of tired that he felt after a bout of particularly good sex but a tiredness that so much alcohol had been unable to induce. He slumped a little further back on the sofa and gazed blankly at the television screen, having flicked channels to a programme about Hitler and the SS. He turned the sound up slightly, trying to concentrate on the images before him, attempting to listen to what the narrator was saying.

Paul yawned. Was he, at last, going to be allowed the oblivion he had sought since he got home? He continued staring at the screen. His eyes closed a little more.

Another five minutes and he was asleep.

19

Gina Hacket adjusted the oven temperature once again, easing it down by a few degrees.

She didn't want the food to spoil. She wanted it to be perfect when she dished it up for herself and Laura. She wished that her daughter was home now. The silence inside the house was beginning to become oppressive. Even with the radio on and the vacuous ramblings of the presenters in the background she still felt as if there was no sound filling the void that surrounded her. As she listened she heard a woman giggling as she chatted to a man with a distinctly effeminate voice. They were talking about films and music and premieres and the kinds of thing that were beyond Gina's comprehension. The woman started talking about a showbiz party she'd attended and all the celebrities she'd seen drinking champagne. Gina felt her depression growing even deeper with each passing word.

She looked around her small kitchen wishing that she could taste some of that kind of life. Just once. That was all she wanted. Just a chance to live well for a short time. It might only be for a week but to live a life of excitement for even so short a time would be enough for her. If only so that she could say she'd experienced it, no matter on how small a scale. When she was out sometimes she saw groups of women shopping or sitting having coffee and she envied them so much that it hurt. She envied their friend-ships and their situations. She guessed that their husbands had such good jobs that they didn't need to work. How else, she reasoned, could they be sitting in a café in the middle of the day laughing, chatting and eating lunch?

She had friends but they were all in a similar position to her if she was honest. None of them had too much money to spend. Two were divorced, one was bringing up two children alone (the fact that she didn't see or even know the father of one of them didn't help). The others struggled by day-to-day in the same way that Gina did. They had nothing to look forward to. No excite-ment in their lives. At least she had her meetings with her lover, she consoled herself. The meetings might be snatched and hurried but they were better than nothing.

Weren't they?

What would ever come of the relationship? She would never leave her husband. She'd certainly never leave Laura. And yet, she'd told herself, if her lover should offer to whisk her away to a better life would she be able to refuse? It was a dilemma she'd thought about many times but one she feared she'd never become embroiled in. He'd never ask her to move in with him, would he? Instead she would have to make do with their illicit encoun-ters and the temporary rush of excitement and pleasure that they gave her. Crumbs of comfort in a world devoid of anything approaching fulfilment.

Gina wandered over to the radio and changed stations, twisting the frequency knob until she heard other voices. There was some static, some foreign words that she didn't understand and then more voices.

She listened for a moment. It was a discussion about politics. Gina shook her head and turned the dial once more. There was more music. Classical this time. She moved to another station and found a tune that she recognised and liked. She eased the volume up slightly, hoping that the infectious lightness of the song would somehow transmit itself to her.

It didn't.

Gina looked at the wall clock and checked its time against the electronic digits on the cooker. She sighed.

Laura should have been home by now.

20

Paul Crane bumped his head as he tried to turn over.

The impact startled him awake.

He muttered something under his breath, wondering what he had banged his head on and also why it was so dark in the room.

He tried to move a hand to touch the part of his forehead that he'd struck but he couldn't. His arm wouldn't move more than an inch.

Again Paul wondered why it was so dark. He couldn't see an inch in front of him and what the hell was that smell? Try as he might, he was unable to identify it.

He tried to sit up.

A couple of inches and his head collided with something once again.

'What the hell?' he grunted.

If this was a dream it was certainly more vivid than any he'd ever had before. What was going on? Why was it so dark and why couldn't he move more than an inch or two in any direction?

Beneath his hands he felt slippery material. It wasn't the leather of his sofa and it wasn't the cotton of his sheets so he obviously hadn't managed to make it into bed in his drunken state.

If you're not in bed, why are you lying down?

The internal voice was back again.

And why is it so completely and utterly pitch-black?

He didn't remember putting out the lamps in the sitting room. He certainly hadn't turned the television off. That much he was sure of.

So where's the light then, dummy?

He lay perfectly still for a second, breathing in that peculiar smell then he pushed outwards to both sides of himself, half expecting to fall off the sofa or discover that he was actually lying on the floor, wedged against the sofa and the coffee table.

That was it. That was what had happened. He'd rolled over in the night and fallen off the sofa, so anaesthetised by the amount he'd drunk that he hadn't even realised. He was still wearing his bathrobe. That had to be the answer.

So why is it pitch-black? Have you gone blind? That's what they say about too much masturbating, isn't it? Makes you go blind. See, they were right.

He tried to rub his eyes, to clear his vision but, once more, when he lifted his arms his elbows banged against something solid. Solid but covered in that same slippery material that was beneath him. He reached up and discovered that the fabric, whatever the hell it was, coated the

82

area above him, too. Just above him. Barely four inches above him.

'What the fuck is going on?' he said aloud but his voice sounded muffled. Constricted. Compressed. As if someone had taken his words and stuffed them into a matchbox.

Ha, ha. Hilarious analogy.

A thought struck him but he dismissed it immediately. It was too ridiculous to entertain for more than a split second. Too imaginatively crazy to be worth dwelling on.

Then why can't you sit up? Or turn over?

He felt the material beneath him, using his fingertips as a blind man would to read Braille. Only it wasn't words that were registering in his mind now; it was that thought that had come to him seconds earlier but been sent packing because it was so stupid.

Paul tried to swallow but his throat was dry. He always felt that way after a heavy drinking session. But this wasn't the dry-mouthed morning-after feeling he had now. His mouth was dry because he was suddenly frightened. He lifted his hands and ran them over the area above his face and chest, then he did the same on either side of him, still desperately trying to identify the material that surrounded him. There was something beneath it, too. Something harder and more solid. He balled both hands into fists and struck out to both sides simultaneously.

There were two dull thuds as his hands connected with the areas to his right and left.

The thought he'd dismissed so quickly because it was so ridiculous came thundering back into his brain and this time he found he couldn't dismiss it so easily.

Why are there no lights? Why can you feel satin beneath you, to both sides and above you? Go on, smart arse, what's the answer?

This was the most vivid dream he'd ever had, he told himself. It must all be part of it. Some kind of Freudian nightmare brought on by what had happened to him today. That was the answer. He was still asleep and this dream was so realistic because he'd drunk too much and his mind was more fevered than it had ever been before and. And.

And what?

This was no dream. He sucked in a deep breath. A breath full of that strange smell he couldn't identify. He trailed his hands across the satin beneath him and to both sides of him and, when he raised his hands, above him, too. He knew why it was so dark. He understood why he could see nothing. He realised why he was lying down.

The thought refused to be dismissed this time because it appeared to be, ridiculous or not, the only thought that was correct. The only assumption, irrespective of how inherently ludicrous it was, that ticked every box on his mental checklist. He had to accept the explanation because there was no other. He felt the breath catch in his throat as he tried to think of any explanation other than the one he now knew must be correct.

Paul Crane was lying inside a coffin.

21

Frank Hacket waved good-naturedly as he passed the door of the pharmacy, one hand guiding the trolley full of linen.

There was a faintly putrid smell coming from the piles of dirty cloth he was transporting. The linen had been removed from the bed of a burn victim barely five minutes earlier. Frank could smell the pungent odour rising from his cargo but he barely acknowledged it. He'd smelled worse.

He knew the woman who worked in the pharmacy. She was a little younger than him and she assisted the three pharmacists, one of whom was on duty more or less twenty-four hours a day themselves.

Frank knew those more exalted beings merely to nod at. He was beneath them otherwise and they never failed to let him know it. But the woman who worked there was different. More on his level. She didn't sneer at his lowly position. In fact, she chatted to him most days when she had some spare time. There was a large staff canteen housed within one wing of the hospital and Frank usually had his lunch there, sometimes with the woman from the pharmacy.

He sat patiently and listened to her problems and her complaints, nodding and smiling in all the right places, offering sage words where he thought it appropriate. She talked about her teenage daughter and how she had become increasingly hard to control and how, on one stupefying occasion, she'd returned home to find the sixteen-year-old naked on the living-room floor with her nineteen-year-old boyfriend. The woman from the pharmacy had been outraged but still laughed about it when telling Frank the story. He couldn't see what was so amusing but he'd smiled when he thought it appropriate. Just as he'd smiled when she told him of her drunken nights out with her friends and how much alcohol they each consumed in what, to Frank, seemed a pointless waste of time and money.

The exchange of information wasn't always reciprocated, though. She knew that he was married and that he had a young daughter but that was about it. Frank didn't mind hearing what other people had to say about their own lives but he'd always been reluctant to share too many details of his own, even with people he felt comfortable with. No one at the hospital knew any more about him than they needed to know and Frank was happy with that. What went on away from work he felt was his business, not something to be shared. Besides, he'd never been comfortable talking about himself. It had always been easier to listen to others.

Frank had been at the hospital long enough to have made plenty of friends among the other workers and one of his closest companions was a male nurse in paediatrics. The man hated being alone and when lunchtimes came around he invariably sought out company when eating his midday meal. That was how the two of them had first met. Frank had been sitting eating his sandwiches, reading his paper when the man had approached him and asked if he could share the table. Frank had assented and they'd hit it off immediately. There were, Frank had found over the years, some people who that just happened with. He could count them on the fingers of one hand and that included his own wife. Their relationship had been like that at the beginning. Not so much now, though, he lamented. Now was different. She was more demanding and yet, at the same time, more distant. He wished he knew why. He wished he could bring himself to ask her but, he told himself, perhaps he didn't want to hear the reasons.

He slowed his pace slightly as he passed the pharmacy door, peering back to look at it.

The door was left unlocked but that was partly due to the fact that at least one person was meant to be on duty in there twenty-four hours a day. However, that was not always the case. Sometimes, especially late at night, the solitary occupant of the pharmacy might have to leave for a couple of minutes even if it was only to answer a call of nature. When that happened, if someone entering knew what he or she were looking for and where to find it, they could acquire almost any drug they desired.

Frank stopped and looked up and down the corridor once more.

It was empty in both directions.

Later on that evening it would be even quieter.

He turned and began pushing the trolley once again.

22

Paul Crane screamed.

He couldn't think what else to do.

He opened his mouth and bellowed as loudly as he could. It wasn't a recognisable word that he roared in the confines of that satin-lined box. It was just an animal exhortation of dismay, horror and fear all mingled together in one wrenching cry.

This couldn't be happening. It was impossible. Things like this only happened in horror stories. He remembered a film he'd seen when he was a kid. An old black and white one with Vincent Price or Boris Karloff or Bela Lugosi. One of the old stars. One of the greats.

Does it really matter who was in the fucking thing?

The film was called *The Premature Burial*. It had been about some guy who had a morbid fear of being buried alive and, needless to say, he'd ended up being subjected to his worst fear.

Ray Milland. That was the actor who'd been in it. Not Vincent Price.

Does it really matter who the star was? You're in a fucking coffin.

Paul felt his body beginning to shake. It was like a spasm. The kind of muscular contractions that grip someone when they've got flu. Where you feel cold but you're running a temperature of over a hundred, that kind of feeling. Only this was ten, twenty, a million times worse, wasn't it? If only this spasm had been caused by flu and not by the realisation that he was in a wooden coffin.

He clamped his teeth together and closed his eyes tightly, hoping that the spasm would subside. He could feel sweat beading on his forehead. For a moment he wondered if he was going into shock. Perhaps the realisation of his situation had pushed him over the edge into a state of shock.

He tried to rise once again, as if that simple act would break this spell and return him to reality because, surely, this couldn't be reality. How could he be inside a coffin? Even considering his situation caused him to shake uncontrollably once again. Thoughts whirled around madly inside his mind, a mixture of the bizarre and the logical as he struggled to come to terms with what had happened here. Paul tried to take several deep breaths, tried to slow his racing heartbeat and attempted to stop his body from shaking so violently.

Think. Think. How can this have happened?

But did it really matter how it happened? All that matters is that it has happened. Somehow, you have ended up inside a coffin. Someone thought you were dead and they put you in this box and buried you.

'Oh, God,' he said aloud, his voice quivering just like his body. The contemplation of his situation was making him worse. He was breathing too rapidly. His head felt as if it was filling with air. Paul realised that he was hyperventilating but there was little he could do to stop himself. Fear washed over him in unstoppable waves. Terror poured through his veins like ice. His heart felt as if it would burst right through his chest.

Stop. For God's sake calm down. Try to think.

But he couldn't. He was unable to summon rational thoughts in his current state. Who the hell would have been able to calmly appraise what had happened to them and why they were here? Would anyone who had woken up inside a coffin be able to quietly consider how they might have got there? Anyone's first reaction would be the same.

You've got to get a grip. You've got to calm down and think.

He raised his head and thumped it against the lid of the coffin so hard that it hurt.

Slow your breathing down.

He closed his eyes tightly and tried to obey the inner voice. It was impossible.

You've been buried alive.

'Oh, Jesus Christ,' he gasped. 'Jesus. Jesus.'

He screamed again. And again. And again. He banged on the lid and the sides of the coffin. He hammered away until his fists hurt, frustrated by the fact that he couldn't create much of an impact because he couldn't get the leverage in his cramped and confined position. Nevertheless he continued shouting and thumping, not really knowing why but unable to think of anything else that he could do. He even kicked out with his feet, feeling the bottom of the casket. For five minutes solid he thrashed and kicked and pounded.

And screamed.

23

Laura Hacket watched the figure as it moved slowly around the room and she felt the tears running down her cheeks.

She couldn't scream because of the tape that was wound so tightly around her mouth but her body jerked almost rhythmically as she cried, lurching up and down in her seat with each inhalation. Her nose was running, too, and bubbles of mucus kept forming at each nostril the more she cried, bursting instantly as she sniffed.

Laura couldn't take her eyes off the figure even though she wanted to. She didn't want to look at this thing that had taken her. This thing with hooded black eyes, no nose and a zip where its mouth should have been. But no matter how much she tried to look away she couldn't.

She was beginning to wish that it had left the tape on her eyes, too. At least that way she wouldn't have been forced to look at it as it moved back and forth in the room.

Laura would ask it if she could go home if it should take the tape from her mouth. She would tell it that she had to be home or she would be in trouble with her mum. She would plead with it if she had to. Anything just to get out of this place and get away from this thing. Whatever it was. She wanted to ask it why it had grabbed her and stuffed her into the boot of its car. Why it had put grey sticky tape around her eyes and mouth and why it had secured her to this old wooden chair.

She would ask it if it knew Mr Peter File, that dangerous man who her dad hated so much and who did bad things to children like her. Above all, she wanted to ask it if she could see her mum.

She wanted that so much. She wanted to be held and cuddled by her mum. She wanted to be home. She wanted to be anywhere other than where she was now. Alone here in this empty room with this thing.

Laura was shuddering as she sat on the chair, her whole body trembling. It was deathly silent inside the room apart from her own sobs. She couldn't even hear the creature breathing unless it came close to her and then the sound was like someone breathing into their hand.

It had come close to her twice. Once to remove the tape around her eyes and another time when it had moved to within just three feet of her and stood silently looking at her, its head sometimes inclined to the right or left, as if it was studying her, taking in every single detail of her face.

Then, Laura had wanted it to remove the tape around her mouth. That was when she would have asked it the questions that plagued her. But all it had done was just stand there like some kind of horrible statue, just looking. Just waiting. Then, after a moment or two, she had watched as it had turned its back on her once again and wandered off behind her towards something that she couldn't see but, through her tears and her sobs and

sniffs, she had heard something that she couldn't identify. A sound
that was vaguely familiar and it made her cry even more.

It sounded like pieces of metal clanking together.

Like knives.

24

Paul Crane collapsed exhausted, his arms by his sides, his head to one side, perspiration covering his face and chest.

He was murmuring something unintelligible under his ragged breath.

Prayers, perhaps?

He had been hammering away at the coffin for more than fifteen minutes but to no avail.

Was it fifteen minutes?

He suddenly remembered that he was still wearing his watch and he tried to look at it. Pointless, really, because it was so impenetrably black inside the coffin that he couldn't even see the lid that was mere inches above his face, let alone the face of his watch. Perhaps if he could get the glass over the face off then he could feel the hands and work out the time that way.

And how are you going to get the glass off? Did you slip a chisel into your bathrobe pocket before you passed out?

Paul exhaled deeply, exhausted and drained of energy.

However, he noticed that his breathing had slowed somewhat. His exertions had taken his mind off his predicament for precious minutes and, in that time, his heart had slowed and his breathing returned to something like normal.

He sucked in a deep breath, held it, and then released it as slowly as he could. If he could get his breathing and his heartbeat under control, he reasoned, then he could calm himself and begin to think logically. Think of a way out.

He took several deep breaths and concentrated on releasing them slowly, forced himself to exhale a little at a time. The longer he did this the more the fuzziness inside his head seemed to clear. He had a headache.

It could be a hangover from all that booze the night before.

The night before. He had no idea of the time. He didn't know if it was the following day. An hour after he'd passed out or minutes after he'd achieved the oblivion he'd needed so badly. That was the first concrete fact that he was aware of. He had absolutely no idea what time of the day it was or, indeed, which day it was.

It's actually the second concrete fact, isn't it? The first is that you're in a fucking coffin. The first is that you've been buried alive.

'No, no,' he said to himself, as if denying the facts might change them.

Deny them all you like. You are buried alive. Face it and deal with it.

Paul felt sick. A wave of nausea that made him sweat again and, for one terrifying second, he thought he was actually going to be sick.

That'll be nice inside this box. The stink of your own vomit mingling with your own sweat and Christ knows what else. Don't throw up.

The feeling passed and he was grateful for that. What he wasn't grateful for was the terrible thirst that he was suddenly aware of. His throat felt raw. Some of it doubtless caused by his frantic shouting. His mouth was unbearably dry, too. Paul tried to generate some saliva by rubbing his tongue against the roof of his mouth and then against the inside of his cheeks. It helped a little but not much. What little saliva he generated he forced back and forth across his clenched teeth. The unbearable dryness inside his mouth began to recede somewhat.

Well done. Try and deal with one thing at a time. One problem at a time.

A line from a hymn suddenly popped into his mind.

'One day at a time, sweet Jesus,' he muttered.

One day at a time. Sweet Lord.

He didn't know why his brain was processing these random thoughts the way it was. They seemed to be flying about inside his head like tennis balls.

Sweet Jesus. That's who you need help from right now.

'Help.' He spoke the word quietly. How was he going to get help? Who was going to help him?

Paul tried to force those thoughts away, aware that his breathing was speeding up again. He knew he had to try and remain calm, irrespective of how difficult that might seem. He had to keep his mind clear and think his way through this.

He dug in his robe pockets, wondering if there was something in there he could use.

Use for what?

He found some balled-up tissues in one of them and that was it.

No chisels to dig your way out. No sweets magically placed there earlier to stop your mouth feeling dry? Tough shit.

'Think,' he told himself. 'Concentrate.'

On what? You're in a coffin, six feet underground. There's no way out. No one can hear you. No one knows you're here, and even those who do aren't going to think you're alive, are they?

Paul took a deep breath and held it.

What's the last thing you remember?

He exhaled slowly.

He remembered being in his flat, in front of the television. He'd drunk nearly three-quarters of a bottle of vodka upon arriving home. That was excluding whatever he'd drunk at the bars he'd visited before that. So, somehow, he'd gone from the sofa in his flat to the inside of a coffin. How? If he could figure that out then perhaps he could work out how to get out. Consider the whole problem. Think of it as an equation. Someone had to have put you in here so someone knows you're here. Think about how it could have happened.

Think.

'I *am* thinking,' he told the voice inside his head.

Better not talk to yourself. I told you before, it's the first sign of madness. Still, I suppose you're entitled to go a bit mad when you realise you've been buried alive. Carry on.

No one had been expected at the flat. It wasn't as if Amy had turned up and found him collapsed and called an ambulance or doctor or something. If that had happened then he would have remembered being taken to hospital. Wouldn't he?

What if you were in a coma?

The amount of booze he'd consumed wouldn't have put him in a coma. That was a fact. Even if it had, he would then have undergone all sorts of examinations and been certified dead. He didn't have a medical condition like a weak heart or one of those other mysterious medical anomalies that characters in horror stories always had that caused them to be buried alive. There were all kinds of tests that had to be done to determine brain death and shit like that.

Also, he reasoned, if he'd been examined, certified dead and then put in the ground by an undertaker he'd be wearing a suit or something smarter. They didn't bury people in bathrobes, did they?

So what's the answer? You were buried by mistake?

Paul was beginning to wonder if he'd already lost his mind. There was no sane reason why he should be inside this coffin.

Think.

He took another deep breath.

25

Gina Hacket checked the wall clock in the kitchen once more then she wandered through into the small sitting room and turned on the television.

As soon as the picture burst into life she reached for the remote and pressed the button that indicated the time. It duly appeared in one corner of the screen, confirming Gina's concern.

All the timepieces in the house, including her own watch, now testified to the fact that her daughter was ridiculously late getting home from school. Gina sat down on the edge of the nearest chair and tried to think rationally for a second.

Perhaps she'd gone to play with one of her friends after school.

Gina hastily dismissed that option, knowing that Laura would never go off to a friend's house without first asking permission. Also, in the unlikely event that that had happened, the mother of the friend would have rung by now to explain.

She got to her feet and crossed to the bay window, pulling back the net curtains and peering down the street in the direction from which she knew Laura would approach.

There were two or three kids dressed in the same school uniforms as Laura's making their way slowly along the pathways but of her daughter there was no sign. Gina looked at her watch again as if hoping that she'd somehow got the time wrong.

She hadn't. Just as her watch was right so was the wall clock in the kitchen, the electronic timer on the cooker and the digital readout that had displayed on the television.

Could a group of them have ventured down to the local shops, Gina wondered, but dismissed that theory as rapidly, realising her daughter had no money on her and also because she'd never done that before. Why would she start now? Besides, it was the final day of the summer term; all Laura would want to do would be to get home to begin what was to be seven weeks of play for her.

Gina stood beside the window a little longer, her breathing now increasing a little, her heart beating quicker. She wondered if perhaps the school had finished early; they sometimes did that at the end of term. Perhaps Laura had come home, found the house empty and then gone off around to a friend's house.

That particular theory was also discarded with uncomfortable haste. Gina now began to feel distinctly nervous. She remained at the window, aware of the sunshine high in the sky and of the blue sky. It was a beautiful day. Bad things didn't happen on days like this, did they?

And yet, despite the warmth in the air and the brilliance of the sunshine, Gina Hacket could feel what seemed to be light, cold fingers at the back of her neck causing the hairs there to rise.

Another five minutes she stood at the window, the curtains pulled back further with each passing moment.

Eventually, she let go of the curtain, walked outside and up the short path where she stood staring anxiously down the street.

The vantage point wasn't much better than the one inside the living room and now she had several greenfly to contend with as well. They flitted around her, causing her to swat at them with the flat of one hand.

Gina kept her gaze fixed firmly on the end of the street but, no matter how intently she looked, she still couldn't see her daughter.

She stood at the window for another ten minutes until she could stand it no longer. She had to do something.

Gina scooped up her keys and headed out of the house.

26

Paul Crane realised that even if he remembered how he'd got into his present situation it would still do him no good. Even so, he forced himself to think about how this could have happened but there was a cold, hard knot in his stomach that he knew would only be removed by him being released from his wooden prison and, if he was honest with himself, he could see no way that was possible. But he still racked his brains for answers, no matter how futile and pointless.

That knot in his stomach seemed to be growing. He rested his hands on his belly for a moment, wondering if he might actually be able to feel the knot. Could you physically feel fear? Obviously you could experience it but could it manifest itself as a tangible, somatic entity? Was that what he was feeling in his gut? Not a tangle of constricted muscles but a lump of manifested fear? People spoke of the taste of fear and the smell of fear; could it grow like a cancer, too?

Interesting but not really very helpful.

The inner voice was being irritatingly logical again.

Get back to the matter in hand. The reason why you're in this coffin can wait. The most pressing thing is getting out of it.

Paul nodded gently, acknowledging the inner voice and at least accepting that it was perhaps correct in its prioritisation. Getting out was the most important consideration. Everything else could be worked out later.

There was the time factor to consider as well. How long he'd been down here. Down here in the grave.

The thought made him breathe more rapidly and he attempted to think of the predicament in different terms.

It doesn't matter how you phrase it. You're still fucked. There isn't a nice way of putting it really, is there?

He couldn't, he told himself, have been in the coffin for that long.

And your brilliant logic for this is?

Paul doubted that he'd been in there for more than a couple of hours. Surely he couldn't have been in there for more than a day, could he? Wouldn't the air have run out by now if that were the case?

He let out a small murmur of despair. The thought of the air around him running out hadn't struck him before but it did now with sledgehammer strength.

You're going to suffocate.

His breathing began to increase in pace and he fought desperately to control it. If he were already running out of air then hyperventilating would use up the precious oxygen even quicker. He had to get a grip. Slow his breathing right down to a crawl. How long did it take to suffocate? Had there been studies done on this subject? Did he really want to know the results even if there had?

He felt a tightness in his chest.

You won't have to worry about suffocating. You'll probably have a heart attack first.

Again he sucked in a deep breath and shook his head as if the action would force the thoughts away. The tightness across his chest, he assured himself, was caused by tension. Muscles tightened when people were stressed. It was the old fight or flight routine, wasn't it? If the body couldn't run then the adrenaline that it pumped would cause muscles to tighten in readiness for a fight, be it real or imagined. Yes, that was it; the tightness across his chest was due to fear. That all-embracing emotion that he was coming to know so well. In fact, he was now on intimate terms with it. He and fear were more than acquaintances by this time. They were practically related.

Paul let out his breath slowly, his fingertips sliding unconsciously over the satin beneath him.

Why did they line coffins with satin? It was almost like an attempt to make them comfortable and welcoming. Wasted on the occupants, he thought. Well, in normal cases it was.

Not in this one, though. You can feel everything, can't you? So, do you feel at home? Comfortable? Suitably welcomed?

Paul tried to stop the inner voice as surely as he tried to stop the thoughts bouncing around inside his head. He just wanted to put them in some kind of order so that he could deal with them adequately. When thoughts ricocheted about inside his mind the way they were doing at the moment it was impossible to produce any order or discipline.

What the fuck are you talking about? What does it matter if the thoughts are random? You'll be dead in a couple of hours. There can't be that much oxygen in a coffin.

That one thought stuck in his mind like a splinter in soft flesh and it would not move.

Exactly how much oxygen did the average coffin contain? How much longer did he have?

27

Frank Hacket felt the mobile phone vibrating in his trouser pocket and he reached in to see who was calling.

Whoever it was he'd have to call them back. Mobiles were banned within the confines of the hospital. Frank wondered who would be calling him at this time. They knew what time his breaks and his lunch hour were. Whoever it was should know better than to ring during work hours.

A nurse hurried past him carrying a urine sample. Frank watched as she disappeared down the stairs leading to pathology, then he pulled the phone from his pocket and inspected it.

He frowned when he saw what was displayed on the screen. GINA-HOME.

Frank waited a moment longer, double-checking that he'd read it right, then he pushed the phone back into his pocket and continued on his way. However, as he walked, he could feel the phone vibrating constantly. Perhaps, he thought, he'd just nip outside and check what she wanted. Better that than have her moaning at him when he got home. It was probably just to tell him to get some extra shopping on the way home. Something trivial. It usually was.

The vibrating stopped and Frank breathed an almost audible sigh of relief. He carried on down the corridor, taking a right towards the lift that would carry him up to the first floor where he was supposed to clean up some vomit from outside the maternity ward. The store cupboard was on the same floor and he made a mental note to pick up some extra disinfectant from there before attending to the spillage.

Frank stood before the lift and jabbed the call button.

His phone rang again.

This time he pulled it from his pocket without thinking and once more saw the same letters and numbers displayed on the screen.

GINA-HOME.

Frank felt his irritation growing. What could possibly be so important that she needed to bother him now? She really should know better.

The lift arrived and the doors slid open to reveal an empty compartment. Frank prepared to step inside. He looked at the phone again. It was still throbbing as he gazed at it.

What was so important that it couldn't wait?

He hesitated, then, almost against his better judgement, he turned away from the lift and headed towards the main entrance of the hospital. This would, he told himself, take only a couple of minutes. Find out what she wants, remind her not to call again other than during lunch and breaks and then get that vomit cleaned up before someone gives you an ear-bashing over it.

Frank Hacket moved swiftly through the reception area of the hospital and out of the main entrance into the sunshine. He shielded his eyes from the blazing orb as he wandered towards *some bushes nearby and stood next to the wooden bench there. There were some cigarette ends strewn around the seat and he looked down almost yearningly at them, remembering how long it had been since he'd smoked one himself. He'd promised to give up but it certainly wasn't proving to be easy. Laura was always coming home from school with leaflets about good health for parents and she'd made him promise that he'd give up. He'd agreed half-jokingly but, as she'd reminded him, he'd never broken a promise to her in his life and this was important. He had to give up smoking.*

Frank thought about his daughter for a moment, looking forward to the moment when he could see her again. She'd probably be in bed by the time he got home but he'd still go into the bedroom and give her a kiss, like he did every night. Even the thought of her brought a smile to his face.

The insistent buzzing of the phone removed it again. Frank sighed wearily and inspected the screen once more, as if by looking at it with such resignation would somehow make it stop.

It didn't.

He checked to see that no one was watching then flipped the phone open and pressed it to his ear.

What he heard almost made him drop it.

28

For the first time since waking up, he thought about death.

Strange, since he'd been encased in a box designed specifically for the storing and disposal of the deceased, but the thought of his own demise hadn't hit him so powerfully up until now. To see it slipping away second by second, breath by breath, was almost unbearable. If the coffin contained enough air for a thousand breaths then the clock was running. Each inhalation was bringing him closer to the end. Five hundred breaths and he was halfway to death. How many times did an average person breathe in one minute? How many breaths did they take? Was his end to be measured in minutes?

'Stop it,' he snapped. 'Stop it.'

He didn't know to whom the words were directed. At his internal voice or his own mind. Either way he wasn't too hopeful of blotting out the less than savoury thoughts zipping around inside his head or of silencing that irritatingly logical and insistent voice that seemed impervious to all admonishments.

Everyone thought about death in his or her darkest moments, he was sure of that. Anyone who'd been on a plane when it had hit a patch of bad turbulence, or anybody who'd been in a car that had inexplicably swerved on a wet road must have entertained brief and terrifying thoughts of their own mortality. Any person admitted to hospital for an operation must consider the possibility that something would go wrong and they'd never leave the place. It was human nature. Unavoidable. One of the perils of being the most intelligent species on the planet. With that intelligence came the ability to contemplate your own death. Then again, dolphins were supposedly intelligent. Did they give thoughts to being attacked by sharks? To getting caught in the nets left for tuna? Cows were supposed to be stupid but he'd read or heard that they sometimes became more agitated upon entering a slaughterhouse. Were they really more astute than people gave them credit for, or was it just that they smelled the blood of others of their kind at that time and sensed their own fate? No one knew and no one ever would.

He himself had even given it a passing thought before now. But only ever in passing. Never in this way. Never in a situation where what life he had remaining was literally being sucked away moment by moment.

Then again, he'd never been in a coffin before with nothing else to think about other than his own demise. It focused the mind, the thought of slipping helplessly into eternity. And then, after the coughing and choking and the pain and the suffering were over, what then? Where to?

Heaven or Hell?

Don't start. Not now.

A sea of clouds or a lake of fire?

What do you think you deserve?

He clamped his jaws together as tightly as he could, until they ached, until he wondered if he might crack his back teeth. The thoughts drifted away slightly. They didn't leave completely, they just retreated a short distance. He knew they'd be back.

Where are they going to go?

He shook his head.

Go on, where do you think you deserve to go? Heaven or Hell? Have you been a good man or a bad man? Does it really matter? Who makes that decision anyway?

At the moment, he wished he knew there was something beyond where he now lay. He wanted more than anything to know that lying in this box wasn't the end. There had to be something more, didn't there? Please God, let there be something else.

You're calling on God. Do you believe? Or is it just that there's no one else to call on in situations like this? Everyone calls on God when they're in the shit. There are no atheists in foxholes, as they say. Then again, if there were a God He probably wouldn't have let you get into this situation in the first place. Looks like you're fucked all ends up.

Paul sucked in a deep breath and tried to calm himself down. Thoughts of death weren't helping, even if there was a certain inevitability about those thoughts considering the place and situation he found himself in.

He swallowed hard and tried to prevent the extraneous thoughts he had become so aware of from flooding into his mind with such reckless abandon.

'Would a God that was good invent something like death?'

It was a line from a film but he couldn't remember which one. For much of his life he'd been cursed – if that was the word – with the ability to dredge up lines of film dialogue completely unbidden, dependent on the situation. It was, he had joked, a sign of his inferior education. Others quoted Shakespeare, Shelley, Voltaire and people like that, but he quoted lines from screenplays. Not much of an achievement really but better than nothing. He always maintained that he'd inherited his love of films from his parents. They had been staunch cinema-goers and had done a good part of their courting in and around the local fleapits.

When he was as young as five or six, his special treat on a Friday night had been to sit up with his mum (his dad always went to bed because of getting up for work the next morning) and watch the old black and white horror films they showed on TV. A combination of that and collecting the plethora of film magazines that was available at that time had given him an appetite for cinema that had grown stronger as he'd grown up. His mother had taken him along to the local cinema more times than he could remember while he was growing up and then, once he reached his teens, he continued the odyssey alone or with friends, visiting one of the two local cinemas every Monday or Tuesday night to sample whatever was showing. It didn't matter what kind of film it was. Crime, comedy, drama or horror, Paul was there in his usual seat.

'All you can hope is that it won't be long-drawn-out and painful.'

Another line popped into his mind. Unwanted and unwelcome.

He didn't know if his own death was going to be long-drawn-out and painful. It might already be long and drawn out. If he had any idea of how long he'd been in the coffin, then he'd know exactly how long. As for painful, he tried not to think about it. Would it hurt as the air inside the box disappeared? Would the physical act of suffocating take long?

Paul tried to calm himself. He tried to think about anything other than his impending fate but it was impossible. It wasn't as if he could imagine what it would be like to be free again. There seemed no hope at all of ever escaping this casket. He felt himself beginning to shake again. The same kind of uncontrollable muscular spasms that he'd felt upon first realising his predicament.

How long ago had that been? An hour or more? Or was it only a matter of minutes? Time seemed to have been condensed the same way as his environment had been condensed. Telescoped down into this one one-foot by a half-foot box. Nothing beyond it and nothing inside except despair and the inevitability of death.

'Oh, God, help me,' he breathed once more but he knew that his entreaties were useless. He was praying for a miracle that wasn't going to come. Perhaps the sooner he accepted the end the better, he thought. Maybe that was how it worked. When people on a plane heard that they were going to crash perhaps that was how they reacted in the moments before impact, he mused. Rather than screaming uselessly as their deaths came unerringly closer, maybe they relaxed into an acceptance of that inevitability. A bit like people with terminal diseases. Didn't they say that there were several stages to be encountered and endured once they'd been told of their fate?

There was the anger, the sorrow and then the resignation.

What else was there to do but face up to the inevitable? And yet, even now, Paul couldn't bring himself to confront it. He could not will himself to stare head-on at the impending end of his life. So great was his desire to live, to breathe fresh air and walk on the earth again that he clung to that tiny fragment of false hope as if it were driftwood in a turbulent sea.

'Then do it,' he snarled to himself. 'Get out of this box.'

That was it; that was the answer. Get angry. Don't lie here waiting for death. Fight back.

There has to be a way. You can't just go down without a fight. You can't just surrender like this. Fight back. Get out of this fucking coffin.

Paul felt a surge of energy unlike anything he'd felt since waking inside the box.

'Don't give up,' he said through gritted teeth.

There had to be a way out. There had to be, and he was determined to find it.

29

'I don't know what you're talking about, Gina. Just calm down.'

Frank Hacket held the mobile away from his ear as he heard another loud shout from the other end of the line. It sounded like his name being bellowed loudly by his wife and it was the same sound that had greeted him when he'd first answered.

'Are you still there?' Gina shouted from the other end of the line. Her voice was cracking and full of emotion. 'Frank?'

'I'm here,' he told her. 'Just take it easy. I've told you not to ring me when I'm not on my break or at lunch. They don't like it.'

'Do you want to hear what I've got to say or not?' she snapped, the volume of her voice dropping a little even if the ferocity didn't.

'Just calm down.'

'I can't.'

'You've got to try. What's wrong?'

'It's Laura. She's not home yet. She should have been home two hours ago and she's still not here. I'm going out to look for her again. I've already walked the route from our house to her school and back. I'm going to do that and then, if she's still not home, I'm going to call the police.'

'Gina, wait a minute. Slowly. Just tell me what's going on.'

'I just told you. Laura's not home from school. She finished two hours ago and she's not back yet. There's something wrong. I know there is.'

'Have you rung her friends? She could be there.'

'I've done that. She isn't with any of them. And, anyway, she wouldn't go round friends without permission, Frank. You know that.'

'Perhaps she's playing out with some of them.'

'No, she isn't. Not until this time. Not for two hours.'

'She could be. It's a beautiful day.'

'Don't try and humour me, you bastard,' Gina yelled angrily. 'Why aren't you worried? You're normally worse than me if she's late coming in.'

Frank suddenly felt very cold, as if someone had draped an icy blanket around him.

'You can't just call the police because she's a bit late,' he said, trying to keep his voice as even as possible.

'How late does she have to be, Frank?' Gina countered. 'How much longer do I have to wait until you think it's serious enough? Where the hell is she, Frank? What's happened?'

'There's probably a really good explanation for this, Gina.'

'And what if there isn't?' she cut in.

'What do you think's happened then?' he wanted to know, still trying to retain the air of calm he hoped was permeating his voice.

'She could have been hit by a car crossing the road. Anything.'

'Ring the friends' houses then ring me back.'

'I've rung once. How many times do I have to tell you?'

'All of them?'

'She only ever plays around Daisy's house, you know that.'

'Ring the others. As many as you know.'

'There's no point. She isn't there. I know she isn't.'

'Just ring them.'

It was silent at the other end of the line for a moment.

'And then what?' Gina asked.

'Just ring, Gina, and ring me back straight away,' he insisted.

'You said you weren't supposed to take calls outside your lunch hour or your breaks.'

'I'm not, but this is different.'

'I broke that mug she painted for us.'

'What?' Hacket was suddenly puzzled.

'The mug she painted with Mum and Dad on it. I was drying it up this afternoon and I dropped it.'

'What's that got to do with her being late?'

'What if it was bad luck or something? An omen.'

'Oh, Gina, for Christ's sake. The mug's got nothing to do with it. Just ring her friends' houses and see if she's there. She probably didn't realise what the time was and she's worried now in case you're mad with her.'

'Are you blaming me now?'

'I'm not blaming anyone, I'm just trying to think logically about this.'

'I'll call now.'

'And ring me as soon as you've spoken to anyone. And, Gina, just stay calm.'

'I am fucking calm,' she rasped and ended the call.

Frank Hacket looked at the phone for a second longer then closed it once again. He sat back on the wooden bench and waited, the phone gripped tightly in one hand.

30

Paul Crane raised his hands very slowly above him until they connected with the satin that lined the lid of the coffin.

He'd guessed that there was about four inches of space above his face. To each side of him perhaps another five or six.

That's it. Use your brain for something other than this stream of pointless and harmful thoughts. Control yourself. Focus.

The first thing to do to escape the coffin was to raise the lid.

But if you're buried then there's six feet of earth on top of the lid, dummy. Even if you could lift the lid how the hell are you going to get through all that dirt?

'Shut up,' he snapped, banishing the voice as effectively as he could.

If he'd been buried recently (and every logical thought pointed to the fact that he had) then the earth would still be relatively loose. It wouldn't be as hard-packed as if he'd been in there for days. It wouldn't have settled. There was a chance that, once free of the box, he could push his way upwards through the dirt. A chance. Just a slim chance but that was all he needed. One single ray of hope in this blackness. One tiny fragment of belief to cling to that he hadn't had before.

That's it. Think positive.

He closed his eyes tightly for a moment and forced the voice away momentarily.

Paul wished that he could see something. He hated the darkness and this time it was so total that he felt it was almost a living thing surrounding him. He'd always been frightened of the dark as a child and, even now, he slept with a small night light switched on outside his bedroom. He liked to see something when he woke up in the night. Waking in total darkness made him think he was blind.

Idiot.

He laughed to himself. It was a loud laugh, completely out of keeping with his situation and his state of mind.

Another sign of madness?

He bit down on his bottom lip to curtail the laughter. If it continued it would use up his air more quickly. The air inside the coffin already felt humid to him and he wondered if it was actually becoming more tainted with exhaled carbon dioxide now. The thought sent a stab of fear through him again and he shook his head, trying to concentrate his mind once again on the task of escaping his wooden prison.

Right, so you get out of the box then you crawl up through six feet of earth and burst out into the fresh air. Piece of cake. Go on then.

The first task, he reminded himself, was to remove the lid.

And how do you do that then, smart-arse?

He raised his hands again so that the palms were flush with the satin. Beneath the slippery material he could feel the hard and unyielding wood of the coffin lid.

Haven't we already been here before? Haven't we tried this?

'Not like this,' he told himself.

There had been the frantic pounding against the lid and sides but not a concentrated and concerted effort to dislodge the top of the box that held him captive. Paul braced his heels against the floor of the coffin and his arms against his sides, preparing to use all his strength to shift the partition above him. He sucked in a deep breath of his precious oxygen, gritted his teeth and pushed.

'Come on, come on,' he grunted as he felt his muscles tighten with the effort. The veins on his face and arms bulged as he focused all his strength against the lid, pushing as hard as he could.

'Yes,' he gasped.

He continued forcing his hands against the coffin lid, letting out a loud cry of angry frustration when it wouldn't move.

'Fucking open,' he roared impotently.

The lid wouldn't budge. Not one solitary inch.

Paul slumped back, gasping for breath, momentarily drained by his exertions. He relaxed back on to the satin, feeling a stabbing pain in his left calf.

Not cramp. Not now. Not here.

He laughed again and didn't know why. A high-pitched, rattling laugh that rebounded off the coffin walls at him like a taunt.

Why are you laughing? The first part of your master plan just failed, in case you didn't notice. You can't move the coffin lid. If you can't get the lid off then you can't crawl through the dirt, can you, dickhead? Why are you laughing?

Because the thought of cramp in his leg had momentarily overshadowed everything else. The fear of choking, having a heart attack, smothering, starving to death or dying of thirst had just been superseded by the possibility of a muscular pain.

Oh, ha, fucking ha.

It was ridiculously amusing, he had to admit that, but he had to stop these bouts of almost hysterical laughter, if only for the sake of his oxygen supply. He nodded as if to affirm his thoughts and, once more, bit down on his bottom lip to stop himself. Paul forced himself to concentrate again.

The lids of coffins, he told himself, were fastened shut with screws or nails, weren't they? No amount of pushing and shoving was going to lift a lid held in place by screws or nails.

And six feet of earth. However many hundreds of pounds of earth must there be holding this box lid down? Even if the coffin isn't sealed by screws or nails it's still effectively closed by the sheer weight of the earth above it. You haven't got a chance of getting it open.

No, that wasn't the reason it wouldn't budge, he told himself. It was because he couldn't get sufficient leverage lying on his back the way he was. If he could just wriggle on to his side and use his shoulder against the coffin lid then he'd be able to employ the whole of his upper body strength against it. That would do it. That would be enough to shift it. Or, even if he couldn't lift it, perhaps he could crack it.

Yes, that was it. Crack the lid. Split the wood somehow then pull it open.

Another jolt of enthusiasm ran through him as if he'd been injected with a shot of pure adrenaline.

Break the lid if it won't lift. That was the answer. If the wood could be breached in some way from the pressure of him pressing against it then he could pull at the timber and open it.

But if you split it then the earth above will come pouring in like sand in an egg timer. The coffin will fill up with dirt. You'll suffocate quicker than if you ran out of air.

But Paul wouldn't believe that. He was determined now that he had a way out. He had a way to escape and he was unshakeable in his desire to achieve his goal. He pulled his shoulders in more tightly to his body and wriggled gently to the left, finding that he could turn his body almost halfway around so that the point of his right shoulder was wedged against the coffin lid.

That's it. Now use the strength in your upper body. Come on. You spend enough time at the fucking gym. Put that time to good use. Save yourself.

He gritted his teeth and began to push.

31

'No one's seen her.'

Gina Hacket spewed out the words as if they tasted bad. She gripped the phone in one hand, her other holding back the net curtains as she continued to gaze down the street, the sky now a worryingly dark shade of blue.

A cool breeze had sprung up about an hour ago, bringing with it thick banks of cloud that had obscured the sun. That, combined with the approach of early evening, had turned the heavens the colour of new denim.

'I rang all of her friends' houses and none of them have seen her, Frank,' Gina went on. 'None of them.'

'Who did you speak to?' he wanted to know.

'To the mothers. Who do you think?' she snapped.

'You spoke to all of them?'

'I just told you that.'

'Could she be with a friend we don't know about? We don't know all her friends, do we?'

'All her close friends. All the friends whose houses she goes round sometimes. Jesus, Frank, she doesn't even spend that much time at her friends' houses, does she? We know all her close friends. All the places she might have gone. I spoke to all of the mothers and none of them have seen Laura since school finished and that's now three hours ago. I'm calling the police.'

'And what are you going to say?'

'I'm going to tell them that our daughter is missing.'

'And what else?'

'What do you mean, what else? What more do I need to fucking say? Laura is missing, Frank. It's going to be dark in a couple of hours and she's not home. She's also not with any of her friends. What's wrong with you?'

'And the mothers were sure she hadn't been at any of the houses?'

'Jesus Christ,' she snarled. 'Haven't you been listening? If you were any sort of a father you'd come home now and help me look for her.'

'What's that supposed to mean?' Frank snapped. 'How the fuck is this my fault?'

'I didn't say it was your fault. I just said you should come and help me look for her.'

'If I could, I'd have come home the first time you rang me. I'm as worried as you are but I can't just leave work like that. They'd sack me.'

'You don't sound worried, Frank.'

'One of us has got to try and stay calm. If we both go to pieces that won't be any help to Laura, will it?'

Gina sucked in a deep breath.

'So I have to go out on my own to look for her?' she asked.

'Drive around the shops and past the school and anywhere else on the estate where she might be. She might be out playing with her friends.'

'I've just told you, none of her friends have seen her since she left them this afternoon.'

'It's worth a try.'

'She's eight, Frank, she's not a teenager. She doesn't stand around by the shops drinking cider. Not yet. She's a little girl and she's missing and I'm going to call the police because they need to know.'

There was a long silence at the other end of the phone.

'Are you still there?' Gina hissed.

'Yes,' he said quietly. 'All right, if you think that's the thing to do, then do it.'

'Thanks for the advice, Frank,' she said acidly. 'I should have done it an hour ago.'

'We had to check the other options first,' he intoned.

'We had to check? You mean I had to check.'

'If I could have helped I would have done, I've already told you that. How could I do anything? I'm here, aren't I? Ring me back when you've spoken to the police. I want to know what they say.'

Gina hung up.

She pushed the phone into the pocket of her jeans and remained at the window wondering what exactly she was going to say to the police when she rang. How would she bring herself to speak the words? Gina shuddered involuntarily and glanced up at the sky.

Was this, she wondered, some kind of punishment for her? Payback for her affair? For her infidelity and betrayal?

She shook her head. If God was punishing her why do something to Laura, she reasoned. Then, just as quickly as she'd begun to think about the possibility of this situation being in some way her fault, she dismissed the notion.

She pulled the phone from her pocket once again and prepared to dial the number she sought. Her hand was shaking.

Outside, the breeze was getting stronger. The leaves on the bushes in the small front garden were rustling softly. To Gina, it sounded like mocking laughter.

32

It was useless.

The lid of the coffin wouldn't budge. No matter how much pressure Paul Crane exerted on it from below, it didn't move one single inch.

That's it. Finished.

He could feel the sweat on his face and chest from his exertions.

'Game over, man.'

That was a line from a film, wasn't it?

No, fuck that. Don't start that shit again.

He lay there gasping, using up his precious oxygen but not caring for a moment. He was defeated. Beaten down. There was nothing else.

Paul tried to focus his mind once again. He attempted to cling to that shred of hope that he'd held earlier. He forced himself to think logically despite the voices that kept buzzing at his consciousness like angry wasps.

The lid of the coffin is sealed but you might still be

above ground. What if you're still in the chapel of rest or at the graveside? There might be people around to hear you. Taking heart momentarily from this thought he began to kick and pound at the sides and lid of the coffin, using reserves of strength he didn't know he had.

For what felt like a full minute he kept up this tirade, shouting at the top of his voice as well until finally he stopped and lay helpless on the satin, gasping for air.

No, that's it. You're under the ground. You're finished. If you were still above it someone would have heard that by now. Someone would have come.

'Jesus, Jesus,' he panted, wiping his eyes angrily when he felt the salty sweat stinging them.

Gradually he managed to bring his breathing under control and he felt his heart slowing down a little. He had to keep calm, mainly so that he didn't use up his remaining oxygen any quicker than he had to. Shouting and screaming would simply hasten the end.

Paul used both hands to wipe the sweat from his face then he lay perfectly still with his eyes closed.

What now? Just lie here and wait to die. What else can you do? You had a go. You failed. That's it. End of story.

What would Amy say when she found out? What would his mum say? He jerked his eyes open at the thought, not that it made any difference because he was still bathed in blackness. He saw a vision of Amy in his mind, standing at the grave crying. She had an arm around his mum who was also crying. His mum would say something about it not being right. That it should be her in the coffin, not her son.

No parent should have to bury their child.

That was a line of dialogue, too, wasn't it?

Every word circulating inside his head, he decided, was probably from some line of dialogue from some film or other that he'd seen. It didn't make any difference one way or the other, did it? Not any more.

No. It makes no difference to you, sunshine. You're worm food now. Ha, ha, ha.

Worm food. The very words made him shudder. An image filled his mind of his own face, the skin hanging off, the mouth filled with twisting, writhing shapes. Worms. It was the same in the holes where his eyes once were. Each socket was stuffed to bursting with slippery, engorged worms slithering over each other as they feasted on him. There were thousands to every square metre of earth, weren't there, and, even now, he could visualise them seething around the coffin, waiting to penetrate the wood when it rotted, eager to reach their feast within. And didn't slugs eat carrion, too? Big, black, bloated, slime-covered slugs that looked like lumps of cancerous excrement as they slid along on the trails of silvery slime that they exuded like noxious, gleaming phlegm. They would feast on him, too. Just like they did on people in horror books. Paul cursed his own vivid imagination and tried to drive the images away but, even as he did, another and far more terrifying one filled his mind and took root with alarming speed and determination.

He had read a story when he was younger called *The Graveyard Rats*. He couldn't remember who'd written it but it had given him nightmares for a week. It had been about some old guy who'd been a grave digger in a cemetery and who stole from the freshly buried corpses. He'd returned that night to remove a ring from one particular body and found that the large rats that inhabited the cemetery had stolen the body and dragged it off into their tunnels to eat. Instead of just leaving it, the stupid bastard had crawled in after them and ended up being devoured by them. Paul could remember the story with far greater clarity than he would have liked considering his predicament, but more worrying was the fact that rats did live in graveyards. Normal rats. Not huge, mutant ones the size of cats or oversized ones in cheap paperbacks, but just ordinary rats. The kind that burrowed into coffins and ate the soft parts of newly buried corpses.

The soft parts.

The eyes. The internal organs. The tongue and the brain.

He felt sick.

If he'd have been standing above ground with the sun on his face he'd have dismissed flesh-eating graveyard rats as the stuff of horror stories but now, stuck here in this coffin below ground, the idea seemed more horrifyingly plausible than most. What if they came for him now? While he was still alive.

Fresh meat. Fresh, sweating, screaming, writhing, blood-filled meat.

'No, no,' he panted, unable to banish this particular night-marish vision.

He could hear them outside the coffin now. Gnawing eagerly through the wood, desperate to get at the fresh meat that they could smell inside. If they came through the bottom of the coffin then they'd eat his feet first, he told himself. However, if they came through the lid they could drop straight on to him. On to his face. Paul shud-dered uncontrollably at the thought of their rank, furry bodies scurrying over his bare flesh. They would bite him immediately and they would be so happy when they saw blood jetting from the wounds. They'd probably fight over his eyes, desperate to be the first to bite into the bulging orbs. Would his eyes simply pop like overfilled balloons when they were punctured? Would he be able to hear the soft liquid sound as they were chewed or would the agony be so unbearable that he would pass out before he could suffer the supreme horror of being eaten alive?

The prospect of suffocation or a heart attack suddenly seemed quite pleasant in comparison to the fate he might suffer at the claws and teeth of the graveyard rats.

That was a story, nothing more. There's no proof to support the fact that rats eat into coffins. Nothing concrete. When bodies are exhumed they're not found eaten, are they?

Perhaps the warmth of his body would bring them running, he thought, unable to dislodge the nightmarish visions. All they ever had to eat normally was long-dead, cold flesh; perhaps that was why they only ate it as a last resort. But he was alive. He was fresh. He had warm blood coursing through his veins. They would want him.

You're a fucking delicacy, sunshine.

'Shut up, shut up,' he screamed, both hands clasped to his head.

But the images wouldn't fade this time and, now, the rats that were eating their way into his stomach, boring through his belly to reach his intestines, had been joined by the worms twisting and writhing in his eyes, one of which had burst as they ate it while several thick, stinking black slugs devoured his tongue and clogged his mouth with their slime and their bloated bodies.

Paul felt his stomach churning and he felt, for one terrifying second, that he was actually going to vomit.

He struggled to control himself, imagining what the consequences of such an action would be. He tried not to consider what would happen if he should throw up in such a confined space where the air was already beginning to smell sour and where the stink of his own rancid and acrid sweat was already becoming intolerable.

He clenched his jaws tightly together, praying that the spasms would pass and that his stomach would stop somersaulting. He felt hot then cold, as if he was suffering from some sort of fever. The sensations built then slowly faded away and he swallowed hard, relieved that he no longer wanted to be sick.

The thought of being a feast for all manner of creatures living in the earth of the graveyard, however, was one that persisted and he lay there for what seemed like an eternity, listening for any sounds of movement outside the coffin that might signal the onslaught.

He heard nothing.

It was silent.

As quiet as the grave in fact.

Oh, what a fucking comedian. The next stage leaves in half an hour, be under it. Ha, ha, ha.

Paul let out a long, almost painful breath. He lay still for a moment, his head motionless against the satin beneath. His lips moved slowly as if he were mouthing silent words. His breathing had slowed completely.

Have you accepted your fate? You know you can't do anything about it now.

Not now. Not ever.

A single tear welled up in his right eye and ran down his face.

33

Laura couldn't see the creature but she could hear it.

It was behind her somewhere, she was sure of that. She didn't need to be able to turn to watch it. She could hear it breathing as it moved about, preparing itself. For what she couldn't begin to imagine.

She didn't want to know what it was doing. She just wanted to go home.

Her mum had told her that if she was really scared in any situation singing to herself was a good idea. Pick a song that she liked and sing it until she didn't feel as frightened.

Now, as she heard the thing behind her moving about, Laura tried to think of a song that she could sing that would help her. She closed her eyes tightly, trying to think, screwing the lids together so hard that she wondered if she'd ever be able to open them again.

No songs came to mind. No catchy or comforting melodies that would soothe her and see her through this terrible time.

She tried again but still nothing would come. No words or

tune that she could hum (she couldn't sing, she told herself, because her mouth was still taped shut).

Laura wriggled her fingers. Her hands were starting to feel numb where she was bound. Her legs too were aching from where she was secured so tightly to the chair that the thing had put her on. She had stopped crying purely and simply because she didn't think that she had any more tears inside her to force out. Instead, she sniffed loudly, irritated by the two streams of mucus that were running from her nostrils and down over the masking tape that had been fastened around her lower jaw.

The thing had wound it around the back of her head, sticking her hair to the back of her neck in several places and Laura thought how painful that would be when it was removed. Like when she cut herself and her mum took the plaster off when the cut was healed. Her mum always said that it was best to pull the plaster off quickly, in one sharp tug. If you did it slowly then it would pull your skin and all the little hairs there would be torn out and it would hurt. So, it was best to just grab it and pull.

Laura wondered if the thing would remove the sticky tape around her mouth and jaw. Would it pull it quickly or would it take its time? Either way it was going to hurt. Laura didn't care about that, though. She didn't care if it hurt a lot. As long as the thing let her go afterwards then she didn't mind. However, the more she thought about it, the less likely that seemed.

Why had it taken her prisoner in the first place? What was it going to do with her?

One part of her mind, a large portion, didn't want to know at all.

In her mind she began to sing.

'Now I lay me down to sleep, I pray the Lord my soul to keep.'

It was all she could think of.

'If I should die before I wake.'

Laura suddenly didn't like that rhyme. She didn't like the word die. Not at this moment. It frightened her.

She tried to think of another song.

Behind her she heard another sound above the breathing of the thing. It sounded like a zipper being undone. A long, rasping noise that seemed to fill the room and Laura's ears.

Then she heard the sound of the metal on metal once more and, despite herself, she began to cry again. She surprised herself at how many tears she managed to produce. Perhaps, she thought, if the creature saw how upset she was it might let her go. It might go and get another little girl instead of her.

Laura knew that was selfish and cruel but she didn't care. She didn't want to be in this place with this monster, whatever it was. She didn't care who it took and who it strapped to a chair as long as it wasn't her. Or one of her friends, of course. She wouldn't want any of her friends to be in this position either. She wouldn't wish this on anyone, not even her worst enemy.

But she wanted so badly to be out of here and home with her mum and dad.

She heard the creature moving closer to her and she stopped crying for a moment.

When it stepped back in front of her again she saw what it was holding and, despite the tape that sealed her mouth, she tried to scream.

34

Paul Crane felt the tears flowing gently down his face as he lay motionless in the coffin and he wondered if he should try to control himself. He feared that once the first tears came he would be unable to stop those that followed. He wondered if this might be the beginning of the complete mental collapse he'd been expecting for some time. And not that it was surprising.

Was this the last straw? The final, unavoidable thread that had just snapped? Was there truly nothing left now other than to lie here and die?

He allowed the tears to flow freely, neither able nor willing to stop them. Why should he? What else should he do? Lie here stoically tasting progressively foul air until he choked and gasped on his final breath?

He wondered when his life would start flashing before his eyes; that was supposed to happen when you died, wasn't it?

How can people know that? The only ones who'd know would

be those about to die and they wouldn't be able to tell, would they?

Did you really get a full review of your life from birth through to the very end? Was it like a slide show or a video? Did it last longer if you were older? Could you pause it at the good bits and fast forward through the rotten parts?

You'll know soon, won't you?

He laughed humourlessly once again, surprised at how many times he'd managed that particular action in the past thirty minutes or so. Or maybe it wasn't that long. Time had become meaningless inside this box. It could have been a matter of minutes since he had been so enthused with the idea of escape and then so crushed by his latest defeat.

'*Shorter of breath and one day closer to death.*'

That wasn't a line of film dialogue. It was from a song. He was sure of that. It was unfortunately, wherever it came from, appallingly apt.

'*Dying time is here.*'

More meaningless words flooded into his mind and he tried to keep them out, tried to concentrate on anything else.

Like what? The fact that the air inside this box is definitely a little more bitter to the taste than it used to be or that it is also getting warmer inside here?

Both of those effects, he assumed, were due to the increasingly prevalent concentration of carbon dioxide inside the casket rather than oxygen.

If that's the case it won't be long until the end now then? Get ready for the film show.

Paul closed his eyes and wondered where his own recollections would begin. Where his mind would start replaying the memories like some kind of internal projector.

Would he see his own birth, he wondered, but from the inside out? Would he actually feel the slap when the doctor smacked him to ensure he was breathing?

All sorts of delights on the way, then?

His earliest memory was of a thunderstorm. He had been in his pushchair and his mother was pushing him down a narrow country lane with a canopy of trees over it and they had paused to shelter from the torrential rain. Paul could still remember the coal-black sky and the brilliant white flashes of lightning that tore across it. He tried to think how old he must have been then. It couldn't have been much more than three, he told himself but, if he was three, what was he doing in a pushchair?

Another mystery to be solved. Perhaps the rerun will give you the answer why.

If only life was like a video that you could rewind, fast forward and erase, he thought. Would he, he wondered, do anything differently? Would there be people he'd treat better (or worse)? Would there be things he'd do that he hadn't done? Things that he had done that he would never even contemplate a second time around?

It was all academic really, wasn't it, because he wasn't going to get a second chance. Not now.

He thought how he would grab that second chance if it came. He would enjoy every single moment of his life, savour every second of the good times and try to cope with the bad a little more competently. But there was to be no second chance, was there? All that remained was the

138

wait until the air ran out completely and death began to take a hold.

Paul shook his head, trying to force that ever-present thought away but finding it increasingly difficult. Perhaps, he reasoned, he finally had come to accept his fate. Could this be why the thoughts of his own demise wouldn't budge this time around? No matter what he did, had his unconscious mind finally taken over?

Think about some of the good times in your life. At least have a thought you want inside your head when the time comes.

'No,' he said, aloud and more tears began to flow. 'This isn't fucking right. This isn't fair.'

The words were spoken with a mixture of resignation, fear and anger.

Go on, cling to that anger. Use it. Better to be angry than resigned. Go out fighting.

He pushed against the lid again. He even managed to punch it.

'Fuck,' he rasped and he punched it again.

But he could get very little power into the blow from his current position and, instead, he tore at the satin above him with his nails.

There was a loud tear as a portion of the material came away.

Beneath it Paul could feel the bare, polished wood of the coffin lid.

He rubbed his fingertips against it, noticing how cold the wood felt to the touch.

That would be because of the tons of fresh earth that have been dumped on it. The earth that's keeping you pinned underground even if the coffin lid isn't nailed or screwed down.

Paul ran one thumbnail against the wood and managed to push into it slightly. He picked at the indentation like a teenager scraping the head from an acne spot.

Another idea struck him like a thunderbolt.

35

'What did they say?' Frank Hacket asked, taking a drag on his cigarette.

'They said they couldn't do anything yet,' Gina told him breathlessly.

'Yet, what do you mean yet?' he insisted.

'There's a time limit before they can list her as missing.'

'How long?'

'I can't remember.'

'What do you mean you can't remember? Gina. They told you something important, you've got to remember.'

'I can't fucking remember,' she shouted angrily, cutting him short. 'All right? I can't remember. If you want to know then you ring them and see if you can remember what they tell you. I've got other things on my mind, Frank. I just want to know where our daughter is.'

Hacket sighed wearily.

'So do I,' he reminded her.

'So what do we do now?' Gina demanded. 'If the police won't help us, what do we do? She could be anywhere.'

'I'm thinking,' he said distractedly.

'What do we do, Frank?'

'I told you I'm thinking,' he snapped.

'She's dead, isn't she?'

'No, she's not dead, Gina.'

'How do you know that? How can you be sure?'

Hacket clenched his teeth, wishing there was some way that he could feel as much conviction in his heart as he'd tried to put into his words.

'Tell me how you can be sure,' she persisted.

Hacket swallowed hard and tried to control himself.

'There's got to be an explanation,' he continued, as calmly as he could. 'She might be hiding somewhere. She might be scared to come home in case she gets told off. It might have started off as a joke and now she knows it's gone too far.'

'Laura wouldn't play a joke like that.'

'How can we be sure, Gina?' he said, trying to sound a little more jovial. 'She's a playful kid. She might.'

'She wouldn't play a joke like that,' Gina snapped.

'She might with some of her friends.'

'Then where are the friends, Frank? They're all at home, their mothers told me when I rang. None of them have seen Laura since they left school.'

'Perhaps she got lost somewhere.'

'Got lost walking home from school?' Gina interrupted. 'Got lost walking the same route she always walks? She isn't lost, Frank. She's missing. Our daughter is missing. It's nearly dark now and she's not home. God knows where she is.'

'Ring her friends' houses again.'

'What for?'

'I don't know what else we can do,' he admitted disconsolately.

'I'm going out to look for her again,' Gina announced. 'I'm going to walk around like I did before but this time I'll stay out until I see her.'

'You can't. What if she comes home while you're out?'

'Then you come and help me or you come home and wait while I drive around or you drive around while I wait. Help me, Frank. Do something.'

'Call the police again. Talk to them.'

'They won't do anything yet. How many fucking times? Look, I need you here now. I need you, Frank.'

He felt the sweat beading on his forehead.

'I've got another two hours before I can leave,' he told her.

'We're talking about our daughter, Frank,' Gina reminded him. 'Are you going to put your fucking job before her?'

'Don't you dare say that to me,' he snarled. 'I put nothing before Laura. She's all that matters to me. She's the most precious thing in my life. She's the only thing in my life.' He let out an angry breath. 'I'll be home in half an hour. I'll tell them what's happening. They'll understand. When I get back we'll decide what to do and where to go.'

'And what do I do while I'm waiting for you to get here?'

'I don't know, Gina,' he snapped. 'Try praying.'

He hung up.

36

If he could only pull the slivers of wood away then he could open a hole in the lid.

Paul Crane ran that idea through his mind over and over again as he felt his thumbnail sink into the wood of the coffin lid.

It was possible. It had to be.

Digging your way through thick wood and then up through earth. Go on then.

He pushed the internal voice to the back of his mind. Stifled its insistent interruption and continued picking at the coffin lid. It was more difficult in the pitch-blackness because he would not be able to see how much progress he'd made but he kept his thumb in position, moving it back and forth, occasionally withdrawing it slightly to feel the indentation he'd created. He used his index finger as well, eager to widen the gap as quickly as possible, trying to ignore the fact that the groove he'd managed to carve with his nails was less than a millimetre across. It was hardly an escape hatch, was it?

Nevertheless, he persevered, the perspiration pouring off him as he worked away. He realised that, as ever, time was his problem.

'Time is on my side.'

Or not, as the case may be.

Even if he managed to open a fist-sized hole in the box, how long would it take him to do that? An hour? Longer? He wondered if he had an hour's worth of oxygen left inside the box.

'Don't think about that,' he told himself, his voice echoing within the cramped confines of the coffin. 'Don't think about anything except getting out.'

He yelped as he bent his thumbnail backwards.

'Fuck,' he snarled as the sudden pain shot through the digit. He allowed his hand to drop to his side and he lay there for a moment until the discomfort subsided then, slowly, he raised his hand again, feeling across the lid for the small gash in the wood.

He couldn't feel it at first and his heart thudded a little faster against his chest. Had he imagined it? Had his scratching and clawing been worthless after all? He ran his fingertips over the wood, pushing through the rent in the satin until he finally found the gouged area of coffin lid. Paul let out a sigh of relief and concentrated on the gash once again, rubbing a little more quickly with his finger and thumb, becoming impatient when the groove didn't seem to increase either in depth or width. He scratched more aggressively at it, grunting in frustration in the process.

'Come on, come on,' he gasped.

He felt more pain in his fingertip. Sharper and even more severe than the first time.

A splinter had come free from the lid of the box. It had buried itself in the soft flesh behind the nail of his index finger as deep as the cuticle.

Paul was surprised by the extent of the pain. It felt as if the end of his finger had been dipped in boiling water. It was agony.

However, he dare not stop and he scratched frenziedly at the coffin lid, feeling something warm now running down two of his fingers. Another splinter speared into the pad of his middle finger and he shouted in pain once more.

It was another minute before he finally pulled his hand away, aware that at least one nail was hanging off and that he had sustained two deep splinters. His hand was shaking and he could feel the blood running from his fingers. He imagined it soaking into the satin beneath him. Staining the material as surely as the sweat that was pumping from his body.

He punched at the lid with his other hand, furious with the box now. He vented his rage and fear on the wooden casket as if it were a living thing, pounding against the lid and the sides, shrieking like a madman, ignoring the pain in his right hand and the blood that sometimes sprayed up on to his face or chest. He could feel the warm droplets landing on him as he thrashed about impotently. Paul kicked at the bottom of the coffin, too, until it seemed that every part of his body was fighting against the casket that held him captive.

When he finally lay back, exhausted, his face and the rest of his body was dripping with sweat.

The pain from his right hand seemed to have intensified

and his index finger was throbbing mightily. Paul lifted it slowly to his mouth and tasted the blood there. When he ran his tongue slowly over the digit he could also feel one end of the sharp splinter that had torn its way down behind his nail.

For a second he considered trying to remove it. If he could tease the end of the splinter with his tongue then he might be able to grip the sliver of wood with his teeth and pull it free. But, in the darkness, it would be all the more difficult. He allowed his hand to flop down uselessly beside him again and merely lay there, gasping for breath.

His situation had worsened considerably if that was possible. Now, no longer was he merely trapped in a coffin below ground but he had exhausted all his hopes of escape, his hands were bleeding and throbbing and his oxygen was running out more quickly than he'd imagined it would. The heat within the box was also building. The sweat was puddling around his sternum when he lay still and he could feel it soaking into the satin beneath him as well as slicking his face and neck. This, he guessed, was due to the change in the composition of the air inside the box. The concentration of carbon dioxide must now be higher than that of oxygen. Surely if that was the case then the end was much nearer than he feared.

He sucked in a breath and tasted the acidity on his tongue. The realisation made his heart thump faster. Paul was beginning to feel light-headed.

That knot of fear he'd felt in his stomach began to enlarge once again but this time it refused to be controlled.

He could feel it swelling and bulging like some out-of-control tumour, feeding on his terror and bloating him until he could barely move.

And then he heard the voice.

37

Gina Hacket looked at the phone, watching it as intently as a mongoose watching a cobra.

For what seemed like an eternity she had sat gazing at it. Wanting to pick it up but not daring to.

She had tried the police and they wouldn't help her. Her own husband had yet to return home. She was alone and helpless. She needed to speak to someone else, to tell them of the terrible fears she was feeling and to pour out her pain and longing. Gina wanted to tell someone else what was happening. She wanted to explain that her daughter, the one person she loved most in the world, was missing.

Gina swallowed hard, even the thought of the word making her shudder. She sat on the edge of the chair in her darkened living room, her body quivering slightly as if the house had been cold instead of filled with cloying heat the way it was.

With the onset of evening had come a cloaking humidity that had closed around her like a moist glove. She could feel perspiration running down her face and her back and she wasn't sure *that all of it was caused by the dull, unbroken humidity. She felt the sweat of fear as well. A fear that told her over and over again that her daughter was already dead. That she would never see her again and, no matter how she tried to fight those thoughts, they remained firmly planted inside her mind.*

She looked at the phone again, knowing who she wanted to call.

She wanted to call her lover. She wanted to tell him what was happening. She wanted to hear him tell her that it was going to be all right, that there was no need to worry any more. She yearned to hear those words from him but she knew that she wouldn't because she knew she could not call him, to begin with.

That was one of the rules.

Rules that they had both adhered to firmly during their illicit relationship. It was a game and every game had to have rules. They both understood that. No contact other than when they met. Of course there had to be the furtive phone calls to arrange their sordid little liaisons but nothing else. There were to be no impromptu chats over the phone. No passing of the time. Nothing. What they had didn't exist away from the grubby hotel rooms. There was nothing beyond the feverish fumbling and penetrations that they both enjoyed so much when they were in the sanctuary of their deceit.

That was the first rule. There were others that had to be strictly adhered to as well, but that was the first and the most important and they both realised it.

However, at this precise moment in time Gina cared nothing for the rules or for their consequences. She just wanted to hear his voice. To hear him say that he would help her. That he would be there for her. How badly she wanted to hear him tell her not to worry. That he would find her daughter and everything would be fine. That he would whisk them both away to a better life once all this was over.

Gina gazed blankly at the phone and reached for her cigarettes, cursing under her breath when she remembered that she'd smoked the last one ten minutes ago. She hoped that Frank would bring her more when he finally got home. She'd reminded him enough times, after all.

She reached for the phone, her hand shaking, but she swiftly withdrew it and clutched her hands together on her lap in a contemplative position.

She wondered what he would do if she did call him. Would he be angry? Or would the knowledge of her predicament override that? Would he tell her that he would help her find Laura? Gina shook her head, determined not to break that first cardinal rule that governed all adulterous relationships. If she did ring he might well decide that it was over between them and she couldn't face that.

Not now.

So she continued to stare impotently at the phone, her mind returning more fully to her missing daughter. She got to her feet and walked across to the bay window once more, peering out into the dimly lit street.

It was as she stood there that she saw the car headlights lance through the gloom beyond.

Only when the twin beams cut through the night in front of her house did she realise that they belonged to a police car.

38

Paul Crane knew nothing about how the human mind worked.

Not the actual chemical composition and how the thought processes functioned. He knew that there were things called neurons and synapses and that there were certain electrical charges that fired these components, but as to the actual composition of the physical parts of the brain he was ignorant. It was made up of a number of parts such as the medulla oblongata, the forebrain, the brain stem and others but what function each performed he had no idea.

He was, for instance, oblivious to which part of his brain controlled his hearing. But, whichever part it was he was beginning to think that it had deteriorated more quickly than the others due to his imprisonment inside this coffin. Perhaps, he reasoned, it was something to do with the lack of oxygen. Maybe that affected the auditory responses of the brain before anything else. He wouldn't know when his sight failed because it was so impenetrably black inside the box anyway but, for now, his concern was with his hearing.

At first he had imagined the gnawing and chewing of graveyard rats outside the coffin, the mucoid slithering of bloated earthbound slugs and worms determined to devour him while he still lived. That had been bad enough. But now, he was sure he'd just heard a voice inside the coffin.

And that was the crucial difference. The voice wasn't inside his head. It wasn't the internal voice that had taunted and challenged his thoughts and it wasn't the sound of his own fears and jumbled musings. This sound had been inside the coffin, he was sure of it.

Perhaps it was the voice of God, preparing him for his last journey.

Paul actually managed to smile at the thought. The possibility of some omnipotent being greeting him as he left this life was comforting. Or, if not God Himself, maybe one of His angels. Perhaps God didn't trouble Himself with personal visits to every single person who was about to die; He probably had people to do that for Him. What was the point in being God if you had to do all the little jobs yourself, Paul thought.

Why buy a dog and bark yourself, that kind of thing.

Again, he smiled thinly to himself.

He wondered what these angels would look like. Would they be seated on clouds carrying harps, as was expected, or would they assume a form more pleasing to the particular person they'd come to escort to eternity? After all, the Vikings had the Valkyries, didn't they? When they were killed in battle and escorted off to Valhalla they weren't taken by some scraggy-looking old hag dressed in an ill-fitting sack; they were taken to the home of the gods by beautiful maidens in gleaming armour. Paul wondered if his escorts would be slender blondes in skin-tight, short, black dresses teetering on high heels.

Each to his own, eh?

He was now convinced that his time was running out as quickly as his oxygen. Auditory disruptions. Hearing things. That must be a sign that the final stages were approaching.

For fleeting seconds he wondered if the voice might actually belong to someone who was standing next to the coffin. Someone who was going to undo the lid and free him. But the fantasy evaporated all too quickly. He knew and had known in his heart for a while now that he was going nowhere. This really was his last resting place and all the praying, positive thinking and fighting back wasn't going to change that.

Or was he just hearing the voices of those he was going to leave behind, he asked himself. Had the voice he'd imagined he'd heard (because, after all, how could he actually have heard a voice six feet below ground in a sealed coffin? It was impossible) belonged to Amy? Was he projecting his thoughts of her to the extent that they had become audible in the form of her voice? Perhaps this was part of his life flashing before him; maybe he would hear his girlfriend speaking to him. She might deliver some kind of eulogy about him. Then after that other voices might rumble into his mind to speak about him. He wondered who would be next. He wondered what they would say.

Would they say that he would be missed? That he'd been a good man or a bad man? Would they say he was reliable, trustworthy, respected, all the other epithets that people so badly hoped others would apply to them when they were gone?

Do you think you were a good man?

He exhaled slowly and tried to think if his life, the life that was ebbing away with every breath, had been worthwhile. Had he made his mark? Because, in the end, that was all anyone wanted, wasn't it? To know that they'd made a mark. To understand that people would know they'd been there. In five years' time would there be any tangible evidence of his presence on the planet? Would people remember him for something he'd done?

Paul struggled to think of anything. His work in advertising was there for all to see but how long would it remain and, besides, who would know that he'd been responsible for those adverts? It wasn't like being a writer and leaving loads of books behind that people could read for years to come. It wasn't in the same class as the achievements of a film star whose performances were there onscreen for others to enjoy for the foreseeable future. If he was honest with himself, there was very little to show that he'd ever been on the planet. It was a thought he tried hurriedly to dismiss. But *were* you a good man?

He'd never knowingly hurt anyone (had he?). Did that qualify as being good? What definition of good were we using here? Whose definition?

Paul coughed and tasted bitter phlegm in his mouth. He swallowed it and lay still, aware only of the silence and of the pain that still throbbed in his hand. The blood had stopped flowing from his torn nail but the splinter that was wedged into his flesh was still hurting.

Still, it won't matter soon, will it? Nothing will matter any more.

'Oh, God,' he murmured thickly.

When the voice spoke again, Paul Crane knew that he wasn't imagining it.

39

Gina Hacket watched as the police car cruised up the street, slowing down every now and then as if the occupants were checking the front doors of the houses.

Checking for what, she wondered.

She watched as the car moved further up the road then stopped for a moment.

Gina could feel her heart beating more quickly and she wondered if, after her earlier call, they had finally come to help find her daughter. Yes, that was it, she convinced herself. They had decided that they wouldn't wait the prescribed length of time before a search could be initiated. They had come with aid now. Taken pity on her. She actually managed a smile as she saw the police car gently reversing and she was sure now that the occupants were checking door numbers. That had to be the answer. The door of their house wasn't particularly well illuminated and they'd driven past it the first time; now they were rectifying their error.

There was a space next to her car and she watched as the police car reversed into it. It sat there for a moment, engine idling, then the driver turned it off and the stillness of the night descended once more.

Gina ran a hand through her hair, wanting to look presentable when she answered the door to the policemen. She wanted to look good for the men who had come to help find her daughter.

She felt a new belief flowing through her as she saw the two uniformed men swing themselves out of the car.

Now something would be done, she assured herself. Now Laura would be found and brought home safely. They would probably have her back in the house even before Frank got home. That thought buoyed her like no other that evening. She saw the two of them walking towards the house, heading for the short path that led to the front door and Gina headed for the hallway, ready to open the door and greet them.

She wondered if, at this very moment, another police car was arriving at the hospital where Frank worked to inform him of their involvement. He would be as relieved as she was.

Gina, now in the small hallway, heard two sets of footsteps approaching and she opened the door before either of the men could knock.

She smiled at them. One was in his thirties, the other older. His hair was greying at the temples and he had a thin moustache. It was this man who spoke.

'Mrs Gina Hacket?' he asked.

'Yes,' she responded. 'It's about my daughter, isn't it?'

'Yes, madam, it is,' the older man said. 'Could we come in, please?'

His voice was soft, even gentle, and Gina nodded enthusiastically and beckoned the men inside, closing the door behind them as she ushered them through into the living room.

Once inside they stood rigidly by the window, the older of the men looking evenly at her.

'You called earlier, didn't you?' he said.

'The man I spoke to said that there was some kind of time limit on how long a person had to be missing before you could start looking for them,' Gina announced. 'But I knew you wouldn't just leave a little girl out there without trying to find her. Not these days.'

'Would you like to sit down, Mrs Hacket?' the older man asked.

'I was going to ask if you wanted a cup of tea or coffee,' Gina continued.

'If you just sit down, please,' he said again. 'It might be best.' For the first time, Gina noticed weariness in his tone. She also noticed that the younger policeman was holding a clear plastic bag.

There was something dark inside it.

'What's wrong?' Gina wanted to know, her own tone darkening as surely as her mood.

She saw the older man nod to his companion and the other policeman reached into the bag and removed the dark object. As he unfolded it, Gina could see that it was an item of clothing.

It was a small cardigan.

She recognised it immediately and felt a coldness sweep over her. For a moment she thought she was going to faint.

'This was found about an hour ago,' the older policeman informed her.

Gina rose slowly to her feet, reaching for the cardigan.

The younger policeman allowed her to look at it but not to touch it. He had folded it over so that the nametag at the back of the neck was showing. Gina had known what it would say even before she saw it.

LAURA HACKET.

'Is this your daughter's, Mrs Hacket?' the older man asked quietly.

Gina nodded blankly, her eyes still fixed on the cardigan. There was blood on it.

'Can you hear me?'

Paul Crane froze where he lay as the words were repeated.

One part of his mind told him that he was hallucinating. The other that he dare not believe what he heard because to do so would have been to cling to hope and hope was something that currently had no place in his world. However, one tiny fraction of his tortured brain told him that he had heard those four words spoken before. That was what he'd heard. Not the gnawing of graveyard rats, not the projection of thoughts about Amy and not his own internal voice somehow made tangible. None of those things. What he'd heard was the voice of another human being. And they were the words of the person who was going to save his life.

'I know you can hear me,' the voice repeated.

Six words this time, he thought joyously. But where were they coming from? Who was speaking them?

Why? What? When? Who?

He exhaled deeply and waited, trying to focus on the sounds. They were distorted. It was even hard to tell if they were male or female at first.

'You can hear me,' the voice went on. 'Can't you?'

'Yes,' Paul said breathlessly, praying that he wasn't merely talking to himself. 'Yes, I can hear you.'

He spoke the words with a joy he had long forgotten. A surge of ecstatic relief that knew no bounds and that coursed through his entire body like a new and highly potent and benign drug. Forget the pathetic attempts to push the coffin lid open, banish the thoughts of picking a hole in the wood and somehow crawling out. Those were false hopes, fantasies that only came about because of desperation. This voice offered real hope. It offered the promise of release.

The promise of life.

'I can hear you,' he repeated. 'I can hear you.'

Paul wondered if shovels were already being driven into the ground as a team of eager rescuers dug down into the earth towards him. In his mind's eye he could see them toiling away above the surface, getting closer and closer. The earth would be flying as they dug, hurrying to reach him and prise the lid from the coffin. Or perhaps they were using one of those small JCB diggers that you sometimes saw on building sites so that they'd reach him more quickly. There'd be an ambulance waiting by the graveside, too, ready to whisk him off to hospital. Paramedics prepared to take away the searing pain in his hands and to give him some much needed oxygen. Someone had found out that he'd been buried alive and now he was going to be saved. He felt like crying again, but with relief rather than despair.

'Get me out of here,' he called, a smile on his lips.

There was a long silence.

Again Paul wondered if this was some kind of cruel hallucination. A last trick that his mind was playing on him before he entered his final moments.

'Help me, please,' Paul called. 'Please. Get me out of here. Can you hear me? I said, get me out of here. I don't know what happened but I shouldn't be here. Please, help me.'

Again there was silence.

Paul imagined that the diggers were more than halfway to reaching him by now. In fact, dependent on when they started, they might even be only inches from the lid of the coffin. Soon he would hear the clunk of shovel blades against wood and then they would be able to free him from the coffin for ever. He imagined someone kneeling on the lid of the box carefully removing the six screws that held the top of the casket securely in place. When all of them were removed the lid would be lifted and fresh, clean air would envelop him. He would drink in huge lungfuls of it as he was helped from the casket, embraced by his rescuers. And they would help him from the hole where he'd been placed and the nightmare would be over.

'I don't know what happened to me. I don't know how I got in here but I've got to get out. You've got to get me out. I don't know how much oxygen I've got left but it's getting difficult to breathe in here. Please help me.'

'Why would I want to help you?' the voice asked flatly. 'I was the one who put you there.'

41

Frank Hacket saw the police car as he rode up the street on his pushbike.

For a moment he didn't realise that it was parked outside his own house but, as he wheeled the bike off the road on to the path, he could see that the vehicle was indeed outside his house.

He could also see faces in the windows of the other houses in the street peering in his direction, similarly puzzled or concerned by the presence of the emergency services.

Frank headed along the narrow passageway that led to the back of the house, wedged his bike against the nearest wall and let himself in the back door.

He heard the sound as he walked in.

Loud crying punctuated by wails of pure despair.

It was Gina.

He could also hear a deeper voice. One that was trying to calm her but having little joy.

Frank blundered into the living room and saw the two policemen, both of whom turned to face him.

Gina got to her feet instantly and snatched the blood-spattered cardigan from one of them.

'Gina's dead,' she shrieked, holding up the garment as confirmation of her words.

Frank looked at the small cardigan and then at the face of the older policeman.

'Mr Hacket?' the older officer said quietly.

Frank nodded.

'Is this about my daughter?' he asked, his voice barely above a whisper.

'She's dead, Frank,' Gina interjected, tears rolling down her face. 'I told you. I said there was something wrong but you wouldn't believe me. I knew something had happened.'

The older policeman took the cardigan back from Gina and motioned for both her and Frank to sit down. They did so on either end of the sofa.

'The body of a little girl was found, Mr Hacket,' the policeman went on. 'She hasn't been identified yet so we don't know for sure that it's your daughter.'

Frank felt sick. He felt his stomach contract and he thought that he was going to vomit. He clenched his teeth together in an effort to prevent this.

'That's her cardigan,' Gina reminded him.

Frank nodded.

'Where is she?' he wanted to know.

'She's at the hospital,' the policeman told him.

'And you need someone to identify her?' Frank murmured.

The policeman nodded.

'I know this is painful,' he said.

'You don't know what it feels like,' Gina chided. 'How can you know what it feels like?'

'This isn't easy for us either, Mrs Hacket,' the older man told her apologetically.

'They're just doing their jobs,' Frank reminded his wife, his gaze fixed on his daughter's cardigan.

'We are going to have to ask you to come with us to the hospital,' the older man informed them.

'To identify the body,' Frank murmured.

'I'm sorry but it has to be done as soon as possible so the investigation can begin in earnest,' the policeman told him.

'We'll come with you,' Frank said. He got to his feet despite the fact that his legs felt distinctly shaky. He extended a hand towards Gina who merely looked at the outstretched limb dumbly.

'We've got to do it,' he told her, his hand still outstretched.

'I can't,' she told him.

'Then I will. But you don't want to stay here alone, do you?'

'No,' Gina said sharply. 'I'll come too. It might not be her. There might have been a mistake.'

Frank looked at the cardigan once more.

'I hope so,' he breathed, his voice quivering. 'Oh, God, I hope so.'

42

The words hit Paul Crane like a thunderbolt.

He felt his chest and throat tighten as they seemed to echo around the inside of the coffin. Spoken with such seething anger that they raised the hairs on the back of his neck.

The fear that he had come to know all too well during the preceding time inside the coffin now resurfaced with renewed ferocity and he felt himself shaking. He tried to control his breathing.

Just like at the beginning.

His heart was hammering against his ribs so hard he feared it might burst through the protective cage and explode before his eyes.

'Who are you?' he said slowly.

'I'm the person who put you in that coffin,' the voice told him triumphantly.

'But why? I haven't done anything to you.'

'You don't know who I am. How do you know you haven't?'

Paul tried to swallow but it felt as if someone had filled his throat with chalk. He licked his lips, feeling that they too were dry and cracked. As if he'd been trekking across a desert beneath a blazing sun.

'It's what you deserve for what you did,' the voice continued.

'What did I do?' Paul asked. 'Whatever it was it can't have been bad enough to deserve this. What am I supposed to have done?'

'I knew you'd do this. I knew you'd be like this.'

'Tell me what I'm supposed to have done.'

'You murdered my daughter.'

Paul heard the words as they seemed to echo around the inside of the coffin and he felt that all too familiar icy chill course through his veins again.

'I don't know what you're talking about,' he said quietly. 'I've never killed anyone in my life. Never even hurt anyone.'

'I knew you'd say that. I expected it. You must have thought you'd got away with it when the police didn't find you. I bet you were thinking you were so clever, weren't you?'

'Please. I honestly don't know what you're talking about.'

'Please? Is that what my daughter said before you killed her? Did she plead for her life? Well, now you're going to have to plead for yours but this time I'm in control. I decide whether you live or die, just the way you decided if my daughter lived or died. But you didn't give her a chance, did you? She never had a chance once you'd made up your mind.'

Paul tried to concentrate on the words he was hearing. Not just their content but their timbre and tone.

The voice that he heard was metallic, almost robotic. As if it was not only coming from far away but as if it was being spoken by some automaton. And then there was the question of how he was hearing the voice in the first place. The words that were being spoken became almost secondary to discovering their source.

'Tell me who you are,' Paul asked, anxious not to inject too much anger or fear into his voice.

You want to know how you can hear them. How about how they can hear you?

He extended both arms as far as he could, trailing them slowly over the satin there, not completely sure what he was doing or what he was looking for.

A speaker of some kind? It's got to be that. How else could you hear them?

And yet the voice still sounded androgynous. Neither male nor female. Was it, he wondered, being fed through some kind of audio filter?

Why would they do that? In case you get out suddenly and come after them? Get real. They've got you, whoever they are. You are completely at their fucking mercy. So just shut up and listen carefully.

'Can you hear me?' Paul went on when there was no response from his captor. 'I asked who you were.'

'I heard you,' the voice told him.

'Please tell me who you are.'

'I'm the mother of the girl you murdered.'

Paul exhaled deeply.

'I never killed anyone,' he said breathlessly.

'You'll be telling me next that you've forgotten her name.'

'How can I know her name when I didn't do anything to her? You've got the wrong man. I swear to God. This is all a mistake. It's not me you want.'

'Don't swear to God. He's not going to help you. No one's going to help you except me.'

'Then tell me what to do.'

'Admit you killed my daughter.'

'And then what?'

'If you admit it, I'll let you out.'

'No you won't.'

'You'll have to trust me. What choice do you have?'

'If I say I didn't kill her you'll leave me here to suffocate. If I say I did kill her then you'll leave me here as a punishment. You're not going to let me out, no matter what I say.'

'I told you, you'll have to trust me.'

'I'm not going to admit to something I haven't done.'

'Not even to save your own life?'

'I never touched your daughter. If I had the police would have arrested me, wouldn't they?'

'The police never found my daughter's killer.'

'So what makes you think that it's me? If the police couldn't catch the man who did it what made you come after me?'

'You weren't the only one. There were lots like you. People who could have done it.'

'Then why me?' he shouted, unable to control himself any longer. 'Why did you put me in this fucking coffin?'

'Because I want the truth.'

'Get me out and we'll talk.'

'We're talking now.'

'Face to face. I promise I won't press charges.'

'You won't press charges,' the voice said mockingly. 'Am I supposed to be grateful for that? You won't press charges. A murdering rapist won't press charges against me.' There was a sound like bitter laughter. A sound that raised the hairs on the back of Paul's neck. 'And another thing. Don't raise your voice to me like you just did. If you do that again I'll walk away and you'll die where you are now. Do you understand? Show some respect. But I suppose you don't know much about that, do you? Anyone who would rape and kill a little girl wouldn't know anything about respect.'

'Tell me what I'm supposed to have done,' Paul said, trying to stay as calm as possible.

'I told you, you raped and murdered my little girl.'

'When?'

'Eighteen months ago.'

'I didn't.'

'Liar.'

'All right, I did, now let me out. I killed her. That's what you wanted to hear, wasn't it? Now let me out. Call the police, let them come and arrest me and you'll have your revenge.'

'You think seeing you arrested will be enough for me after what you did to my daughter?'

'Well, you can't see me down here, can you?' he snapped. 'I would have thought that part of the fun, part of your revenge, would be to watch me suffer. How can you do that while I'm in this fucking box?'

'I told you not to raise your voice to me.'

'Where did you get the coffin, by the way?' he said

conversationally. 'I mean, coffins aren't that easy to come by without attracting attention. Where did you get it? Did you just wander into an undertaker's when they weren't looking and slip it in the back of your car?'

'That's a stupid question,' the voice said disparagingly. 'Really stupid. Does it matter? What use would knowing do you? All that matters is that you're inside it. And you're going nowhere unless I say so.'

'When are you going to kill me?' Paul laughed in spite of himself. It was a twisted, uncontrollable exhortation that made his whole body shake and caused him to cough when he'd finally finished.

'I warned you not to shout,' the voice said, reproachfully. 'I don't have to listen to this any more. I'm going.'

'No,' he shrieked. 'No, don't leave me.'

Silence.

'Please,' he roared, pounding on the lid of the box. 'Can you hear me? Are you still there?'

There was still only silence.

Once more, Paul Crane began to cry.

43

Gina Hacket sat on the end of the bed staring at the array of stuffed animals propped on the pillows there.

The teddy bears, the pandas, the dogs and the cats all gazed back blankly with their beady, blind eyes. Gina could see her own reflection in the blank glass orbs.

More stuffed animals and dolls stared down at her from the shelves on the wall beside her. On the floor near the bed there were more toys, board games and even some furniture from a doll's house. Gina bent and picked up the tiny table and chair and crossed the room to the doll's house itself where she gently placed the furniture inside, her hand shaking slightly. She moved back to the bed, this time sitting among the stuffed animals. Gina reached out and picked up the smallest of them.

It was a little Dalmatian. No more than four inches high.

Laura's favourite.

As Gina held it before her she began to cry softly, tears rolling down her cheeks and dripping on to her jeans.

She gently kissed the little stuffed dog.

Dummy dog, they had called it. Laura had christened it herself because, when she'd finally given up her dummy, she'd been bought the little animal as a reward. It had taken the place of her dummy so she had called it dummy dog. Gina felt more tears rolling down her cheeks and, when she held the dog close to her face, she could smell her daughter on it.

How she wished she could have held her in her arms now. She would have given her soul to be able just to look at Laura again. To see her smiling face and hear her laugh, but she knew only too well that joy was now to be denied to her for ever. For the rest of her life. The realisation brought fresh tears but Gina made no attempt to brush them away.

She got to her feet and crossed to the white chest of drawers close to the bed. Sliding the top drawer open, she pulled out a pink T-shirt and opened it up to display the design on the front. It was a cat with a top hat and the legend beneath proclaimed: COOL CAT.

Gina kissed it and held it against her lips, inhaling. Breathing in the scent of her child.

She took a step back and found the bed once more, seating herself on it and digging in the pocket of her jacket for a tissue. Finding one, she dabbed at her nose and sat motionless in the gloom of the bedroom.

Outside, she heard the floorboards creak and the door opened slightly. She looked up to see her husband standing there. He was holding a steaming mug in his hand and he advanced slowly into the room, almost apologetic that he had intruded upon her grief.

'I brought this up,' he said, holding the mug out before him as if it were some kind of offering. 'I thought you might want it.'

Gina let out a deep breath.

'We always think that things can be made better with a cup of tea, don't we?' she said, smiling.

Frank Hacket sat next to her on the bed and set the mug down on the bedside table.

'I just thought you might like one,' he went on softly 'I made one for myself.' He shrugged.

She nodded appreciatively.

'And did it help?' Gina wanted to know.

Frank shook his head almost imperceptibly.

'Can't hurt though, can it?' he whispered.

He watched as she reached for the mug and took a sip.

They sat in silence for what seemed like an eternity, surrounded by the paraphernalia of their daughter's life. A life that was now over. Taken.

'I just kept thinking that it was so unfair,' he said quietly. 'What the hell had she ever done to deserve that? What had we done to deserve it?'

'They say everything happens for a reason. God knows why this had to happen.'

'If He does I wish He'd tell us.'

Frank wiped a tear from his own cheek and sucked in an almost painful breath.

'I thought the police were very nice,' he added almost conversationally. 'It must be hard for them too, having to give people that kind of news. Having to go with them to the identification.'

Gina nodded.

They sat in silence for a little longer.

'People will have to be told,' Gina said finally, her voice little more than a whisper. 'About Laura. About what's happened.'

Frank nodded.

'Not now,' he murmured.

'Arrangements will have to be made, Frank.'

'It'll all be taken care of.'

Gina took another sip of her tea.

'Who's going to tell your mum and dad and mine?' she wanted to know. 'You never think about things like that, do you?'

'I told you, it'll be taken care of,' he said, tenderly taking the cup from her when he saw her hands shaking and some of the hot drink dripping down the sides of the receptacle.

Gina held the little stuffed Dalmatian in one hand, reluctant to let it go.

'What are we going to do without her?' she asked and the tears came again.

Frank put his arm around her and drew her closer, feeling her body racking as she sobbed.

He didn't answer.

He had no answer.

44

'Did my daughter cry when you raped her?'

The voice echoed inside the box once again and, despite the question it asked, one part of his tortured mind was glad to hear it. At least he knew he wasn't alone. As long as the voice was asking questions he had a chance, he told himself.

The voice repeated the question.

For a moment, Paul thought about ignoring it. There seemed little purpose in arguing with the owner of the voice. What was the point? Whatever he said he wouldn't be believed so he was beginning to question the sense of pleading his innocence any longer. However, he knew that his only hope of surviving lay in his ability to convince his captor that he was telling the truth. He sucked in as deep a breath as he dared and lay there motionless for a moment longer.

All his working life he had specialised in advertising. Basically selling people things they really didn't need. That was the single purpose of advertising and now he knew that those skills he'd honed for so long were the only weapon he had against whoever had imprisoned him below ground. He had to sell himself. Sell the belief that he was innocent and cause the owner of the voice to believe him.

This is your last chance. Maybe if those fuckers where you used to work could see you now they might even think about rehiring you. What do you think?

Paul managed to silence the internal voice for a moment, giving himself time to think.

If he told his captor what they wanted to hear he was doomed. If he continued to plead his innocence then he was still lost.

Damned if you do. Damned if you don't.

'Come on, think,' he murmured to himself, aware that whoever had put him in this box could hear his words.

'I asked you a question,' the voice persisted. 'Did my daughter cry when you raped her?'

'What makes you ask that?' he enquired.

'I heard you crying just now. It made me wonder.'

'Do you blame me for crying?'

'No. But why are you crying? Because you're sorry for what you did to my daughter or are you just feeling sorry for yourself?'

'I think it's a reasonable reaction considering the situation, don't you?'

There was a moment's silence then the voice returned.

'You still haven't answered my question,' it said.

'What difference is it going to make if I tell you or not? It's not going to bring your daughter back, is it? It isn't going to make you feel any better. Didn't the police give you details about the way she died?'

'Not much. They didn't think there was any need. But I insisted.'

'Why put yourself through that?'

That's good. A little empathy. Catch them off guard.

'I remember when my dad died,' Paul continued. 'I couldn't even bring myself to look at his body in the chapel of rest. My mum wanted me to but I just couldn't.'

'Why not?'

'What good would it have done? It wouldn't have brought him back to life, would it? And he couldn't hear me saying goodbye or how much I'd loved him. I wanted to remember him when he was alive, not when he was embalmed in a coffin.'

'What did he die of?'

'He had a stroke. He'd been ill for a while. I felt so helpless looking at him in his hospital bed. It was like he was just waiting for the end.'

'Did he wake up after the stroke?'

'No, he never regained consciousness. My mum stayed beside his bed from the time they took him into hospital until the day he died. Six days. I thought she was going to die, too. I remember thinking that I could lose both my parents in the space of a week.'

'Why did you think she was going to die? Was she ill?'

'No, but you know sometimes when one half of a married couple dies the other one follows pretty quick. It's like they can't survive without each other. And they were very close.'

'But she didn't die?'

'No.'

There was another long pause.

Paul licked his lips.

Well done. If you can make them think about you more as a person then they might find it harder to let you die. Keep going.

'I visited my daughter in the chapel of rest,' the voice said finally. 'Of course, they'd used make-up to cover the worst injuries. I remember thinking that she looked like a little doll with her face all covered in powder. It wasn't right that a child of her age should have powder on. Then again, it wasn't right that she was dead to begin with. But that's your fault, isn't it?'

'No, it isn't,' Paul said wearily.

'You still haven't answered my question,' the voice went on.

'Which one?'

'The one about whether she cried when you raped her. You must be able to remember.'

'If you let me out of here and we talked face to face I'd remember a lot more. Lying in a coffin six feet below the ground isn't a great aid to memory.'

There was defiance in his voice that he couldn't suppress.

Fuck it. Why should you? Don't keep your feelings to yourself. You might not be around for much longer to use them. Get everything off your chest.

'So where do you think we should talk?' the voice enquired.

'I don't mind. Anywhere. You take me where you like,' Paul offered.

Had he sowed a seed of doubt in his captor's mind?

'I'll tell you everything I can,' he continued. 'But not

180

while I'm in here. I'm running short of oxygen. That affects memory.'

Does it really? Nice touch.

Paul waited nervously for the response.

'You've got enough oxygen to last you another hour,' the voice told him flatly.

'How can you be sure?'

'By the time you were put into the coffin.'

'And how did you get me in here in the first place? Or, more to the point, how did you get me out of my flat without anyone seeing? It's impossible. Someone would have seen you. People around me know my friends. They would have seen you. They'll be wondering where I am. Someone's probably called the police. They'll be looking for me.'

'No one saw you and even if the police are looking for you they won't find you. How will they know where to look? They're not just going to think that you're in a grave-yard somewhere and start searching for newly dug earth, are they? Who's going to think that someone who's gone missing is buried alive?'

'But they'll come looking for me.'

'They won't find you. Not before you've told me what I want to hear.'

'If you let me out I won't press charges. Just let me out and walk away. I don't even have to see your face.'

Paul heard a sound coming into the coffin that he couldn't identify at first. Only after a moment did he realise that it was laughter.

'You're trying to bargain with me,' the voice said. 'You arrogant bastard. You think you can get me to let you out on your terms.'

'I was just suggesting.'

The voice cut him short.

'Shut up,' it rasped. 'You get out of that coffin when I decide you're telling me the truth. That's the only consideration. And you'd better start talking now.'

45

Gina Hacket didn't know how many times she'd counted the sympathy cards. It might have been nine. It might have been ten. It didn't really matter.

There were twenty-eight of them. From relatives and friends and neighbours and there were even six from complete strangers who had been touched by their situation. It had been the same at the cemetery. There had been bouquets and wreaths from friends, family and neighbours, naturally, but there had also been a number simply left at the cemetery gates as a mark of respect. Some had names on the cards, others didn't. The smell of so many flowers had made Gina a little nauseous but she still appreciated the gesture.

The sympathy cards were displayed all around the living room of the Hackets' house. They stood there like silent apologies, some of them on the speakers of the stereo, others on the bookcase and the rest all propped up where they could be seen. Gina had wanted those who had come to the house after the funeral earlier that day to see them. She wanted people to know how loved Laura had been.

She and Frank had been pleased to see so many of Laura's little friends at the funeral although she doubted that they actually realised the full enormity of the ceremony they were witnessing, just as they probably didn't realise the true meaning of the words that the vicar had spoken so expertly over the grave.

They would have understood the tears and the sobs, though.

Standing there at the graveside with their parents, most of them in their school uniforms, they had all behaved immaculately. A number of them had cried, too, especially when the coffin appeared.

It had taken all of Gina's remaining self-control to prevent herself grabbing at the tiny white coffin as it was carried to the grave. She didn't want it lowered into the ground. She didn't want her only child to be hidden from her beneath six feet of mud and earth. She wanted her back but she knew that was not to be.

Now she got slowly to her feet and wandered through to the kitchen where her husband was washing the last few plates in the sink. He set each dripping piece of crockery on the drainer carefully then wiped his hands on a tea towel and prepared to dry the waiting plates.

'Leave them,' Gina said quietly, sitting down at the kitchen table.

'There's only a couple left,' Frank said softly. 'Otherwise they've got to be done in the morning.'

'Does it really matter, Frank? I mean, what else have you got to do in the morning?'

He considered the question for a moment then nodded and replaced the tea towel on its hook next to the back door.

'Do you want a drink?' he asked, filling the kettle.

'I'll have a brandy if we've got any left,' she told him.

'Do you think that's a good idea, Gina?'

'I think it's the best idea I've had all day. I think it would be an even better idea if you joined me.'

Frank hesitated for a moment then he crossed to the cupboard behind her and removed a bottle of Hennessy and two glasses that he set down on the table in front of Gina. He poured each of them a measure then pushed one glass towards his wife. She took it and swallowed the contents in one, the alcohol burning its way to her stomach.

She looked at Frank and saw something close to recrimination in his eyes but he didn't speak and, when she pushed the empty glass towards him he refilled it immediately.

'How many's it going to take?' he asked quietly.

'To stop what I'm feeling now?' she wanted to know. 'A lot more than two.' She took a sip from the glass. 'What about you, Frank? What's it going to take to make you feel better?'

'I don't know,' he admitted. 'I feel numb. I can't think of any other word to describe it. It's like there's a big hole inside me. A big black hole. I feel as if I'm walking around with a crash helmet on. I hear things, smell things and see things a fraction of a second later than everyone else. I don't feel as if I'm part of this world any more. When we were in the funeral car on the way back from the cemetery this afternoon it was as if nothing outside was real. I didn't belong to that world. Do you know what I mean?'

Gina nodded.

'Anyone in our place would feel the same way,' she offered. 'I appreciated people coming to the funeral, and the things they said were thoughtful, but I didn't want to speak to any of them really. I just wanted to be here, away from everyone else.' She smiled bitterly. 'The vicar said something about celebrating Laura's life rather than mourning her death. How are we supposed to do that? She hadn't had a life. Eight years isn't a life. It's nothing.'

A note of anger had crept into Gina's tone. 'He stood there talking about how his God was taking care of her now when it should be us taking care of her. She should be here with us. What kind of God allows an eight-year-old to be raped and murdered?'

Frank had no answer. He merely sat gazing blankly at the brandy bottle.

They sat in silence for a long time then Frank reached out and touched her hand.

'When I looked at those other parents today, standing there with their kids, I hated them,' Gina said softly. 'I hated them because I envied them so much. They'll get to see their kids grow up. We won't, Frank.'

'I know that,' he admitted, taking a sip of his own drink. 'But it's not their fault. We shouldn't blame them for what happened.'

'I don't blame them, I'm just saying, it's hard not to hate them just a little bit.' She held up her thumb and index finger, the digits about an inch apart. 'While we sit here tonight, they'll be tucking their kids up in bed, kissing them goodnight and thinking about how they'll be seeing them again in the morning, but we won't do that again. We'll never do that again.'

Frank bowed his head slightly and wiped his mouth with the back of his hand. He waited a moment then poured himself another brandy. It seemed the right thing to do. It seemed the only thing to do. He wanted to get drunk. He couldn't remember the last time he'd done that. The last time he'd surrendered himself to the oblivion of inebriation. That option seemed highly desirable at the moment.

Frank prepared to take a sip from his refilled glass. He paused and raised it in salute, glancing at a school photograph of Laura that stood on the window ledge nearby. The image smiled back happily at him.

'Here's to Laura,' he said. 'Our little girl.'

The words faded as he stifled a sob, clearing his throat.

Gina leaned forward and kissed him on the cheek, wiping a tear from his face.

'You don't have to be strong all the time, Frank,' she told him. 'Not any more.'

He looked at her and saw his own devastation mirrored in her expression.

They both put down their glasses and held each other. And they wept uncontrollably.

46

'You haven't told me yet how you managed to get me out of my flat last night,' Paul said.

'Does it really matter?' the voice taunted him.

'You must have broken in.'

'It wasn't difficult.'

'How did you know where I lived?'

'We'd been watching you.'

We. So there's more than one of the bastards up there.

Paul frowned, stretching his mind to try and consider who might be capable of carrying out such a monstrous act.

'For how long?' he enquired.

'Who cares?'

'You had no reason at all to take me. No evidence against me.'

'We thought we did. And now we'll be proved right.'

'What if you left fingerprints back at my flat? You must have left some evidence behind.'

'We were very careful.'

Paul felt his mouth drying up and tried to lick his lips but it felt as if his tongue was stuck to the roof of his mouth. After a moment or two he managed to manufacture enough saliva to enable him to moisten his lips and he spoke slowly.

'Listen, I'm very, very sorry about what happened to your daughter,' he said. 'But I swear to you that I had nothing to do with it. I'm not that kind of man. I've got a girlfriend. I'm not interested in kids. I'd never hurt a little girl. Never.'

'Prove it.'

'How can I do that when I'm in this fucking box?' he snarled angrily.

Paul punched the right-hand side as hard as he could and the coffin was suddenly filled with an ear-splitting, high-pitched whine.

'Jesus,' he hissed through clenched teeth, the sound jabbing into his ears.

'Don't do that again,' the voice told him reproachfully.

'What the hell was that noise?' Paul wanted to know.

'There are two microphones in the coffin, one on each side about a foot from your face. That's how I can hear you. There are two small speakers as well. That's how you can hear me. You can't reach them even if you wanted to because you can't move your arms far enough. They were placed out of your reach deliberately in case you tried to damage them. Any impact against the coffin could have caused that sound.'

'So you're an electronics expert as well as being a burglar and kidnapper,' Paul exclaimed angrily.

'It didn't require that much expertise,' the voice told him.

'You still haven't told me how you got me from my flat to here.'

'And I said it wasn't important.'

'Tell me. I need to know.'

'Why? It won't help you get out.'

'I know that.'

'You were drugged. Is that enough for you?'

'You broke into my flat, drugged me, kidnapped me and buried me alive.'

'I told you.'

'And I told you that I didn't touch your daughter, so why don't you just let me out of here? If I die the police will find you and you'll go down for murder. There's no two ways about it. What you're planning to do is murder me. If you let that happen there's no way you'll be able to escape, nowhere you'll be able to hide.'

'No one will ever find you. How will they know you haven't just run off somewhere?'

'Because I've got family and friends who will miss me and who will report my disappearance. Sooner or later someone will realise I'm not at home and they'll contact the police, then they'll start looking for me.'

'That will all take time. Days. Weeks even. You'll be dead long before that. I told you, you've got about an hour before your oxygen runs out. That's it. After that it won't matter. I don't care if the police come looking for you. They're not going to save you. Only one person can save you and that's yourself, by telling me the truth about what you did to my daughter. And if you don't do that in the next hour you'll die. You'll suffocate. It isn't a nice way to die.'

'There's no such thing as a nice way to die,' Paul snapped.

'It starts with a tightness in your chest,' the voice went on evenly. 'You know when you try to hold your breath and you're at the point where you can't hold it for much longer? Apparently it's like that. It feels as if someone's sitting on your ribcage, pressing down harder all the time until it feels as if your lungs are being squeezed. You start to feel light-headed. The pain in your chest gets worse.'

'What are you, a fucking medical expert now?'

'Some people have a heart attack before they run out of breath. Did you know that when you die all your muscles relax? You'll die lying in your own piss and shit. I think that's very fitting in your case.'

'You're insane.'

'Grief can do that.'

Paul screwed his eyes tightly shut and allowed his head to relax back on to the satin at the base of the coffin.

You're not going to talk your way out of this one, sunshine. Not like you did with Amy.

He swallowed hard, wondering why those thoughts in particular had resurfaced, especially now.

You talked your way out of it with Amy, didn't you? You know the time. What was that other girl's name? Trish, wasn't it? Or was it Claire? Which one was it that you managed to persuade Amy you weren't having an affair with? You used your charm and your bullshit on her, why not just do the same with the person who put you in here?

'I'm sorry,' he whispered.

'What did you say?' the voice enquired.

'Nothing,' Paul lied. 'Nothing you'd want to hear.'

How long ago had it been now? Two years? Longer? You still miss her, don't you?

And the memories came hurtling back into his mind.

47

'Penny for them.'

Paul Crane heard the voice beside him and turned his head slowly towards their speaker.

Trisha Bennett moved a little closer to him, one of her hands resting on his chest, her fingers grazing the flesh there as she stroked them back and forth.

'I didn't hear you,' Paul said, smiling.

'You looked like you were deep in thought,' Trisha told him. 'I wondered what you were thinking about.'

'Nothing important,' he confessed. 'My mind was a blank. Like it usually is.'

They both laughed and she kissed him lightly on the lips.

'Your mind never stops working. That's why you're so good at your job,' she told him, straightening up in bed and reaching towards the nightstand beside her.

'Flattery will get you everywhere,' he smiled, studying her with approval.

With just the night light on behind her, the soft glow seemed to create a halo around her head. It made her shoulder-length blonde hair look almost luminescent. The sheet that had been covering her breasts slipped down, exposing the pert globes and swollen nipples. She made no attempt to cover herself, knowing that he was watching her.

She took a sip from the glass of Bacardi and Coke and rattled the ice in the empty receptacle.

'Refill?' he asked and she nodded.

Paul took the glass from her and tipped more rum and Coke into it before handing it back to her. She smiled and drank a little more before setting it down once again.

'It needs more ice,' she commented. 'We've run out.'

'Call room service for some more,' he offered.

'I'll survive,' she told him, settling down beside him again.

'No, go on,' he insisted. 'Then you can answer the door dressed in just my shirt like they always do in films.'

'I could answer it naked,' Trish grinned.

'Give the room service bloke a treat.'

'He might be young and cute. I might fancy him. I might want to shag him.' She giggled.

'As long as I can watch,' he laughed.

'You dirty sod,' she said, punching him playfully on the arm. 'Would you like that? Watching me get a good seeing-to by another guy? He might be better at it than you.'

'No chance,' Paul said, shaking his head.

They lay close and he kissed her lightly on the forehead.

'What time have you got to be at work in the morning?' he wanted to know.

'I'll get in for about half-nine,' she told him. 'How about you?'

'I've got a breakfast with a client at nine. If we get the alarm call for eight then you and me can have coffee here before I have to leave.'

'I hate the mornings,' she confessed. 'I hate it when we have to leave the hotel separately. I'd just like to be able to walk out with you. Just once.'

'I'm sorry, too, Trish, but that's the way it goes.'

'You mean that's how it goes when you're having an affair.'

'I thought you didn't like calling it an affair.'

'I don't.'

'So what do we call it? We meet up at a hotel once or twice a month, go out for dinner, spend the night together during which time we fuck each other's brains out. Sometimes we get to have lunch together. I talk to you on public phones so the calls can't be traced and we don't send each other e-mails to our personal computers. It certainly looks like an affair.' He smiled almost apologetically.

'We're friends.'

'Friends who sleep with each other.'

'You know what I mean.'

'I know what you mean but I don't think anyone else would. It certainly looks like an affair from the outside.'

'What would Amy say if she found out? Would she finish it with you?'

'Let's hope it never comes to that.'

'Do you think she would?'

'I don't know. I don't think so, but you can't tell with something like that, can you?'

'Sometimes I feel bad for her. For your girlfriend. I wonder what I'd feel like if my boyfriend was cheating on me.'

'You haven't got a boyfriend,' he reminded her. 'You did have but you dumped him because he was emotionally unstable. Like most of the guys you go out with seem to be.'

'You know what I mean,' she continued, slapping him playfully on the stomach.

'Where's this come from?' he asked, turning to look at her more sternly. 'One minute you're asking for another drink, the next you're trying to make me feel guilty for being here with you.'

'I wasn't trying to make you feel guilty,' she told him, resting her head on his chest. 'I was just thinking aloud.'

'If that was what you were thinking then perhaps you'd better stop,' he told her, his left hand now gently caressing her shoulder beneath her hair.

'Don't you ever worry about Amy finding out about us?' Trisha wanted to know.

'I don't think about it. As long as we're careful, there's no reason why she should ever find out.'

They lay in silence for a moment and he kissed the top of her head as she nestled against him.

'Can I tell you something?' she said finally.

'Of course you can,' he told her.

'I'm not sure I should.'

'You're pregnant.'

'Fuck off,' she chuckled. 'No, nothing like that.'

'Go on then, tell me.'

She raised her head and looked at him.

'I'm falling in love with you,' she breathed.

48

Paul could see her clearly in his mind's eye and he wondered why that particular image had forced its way into his consciousness at this precise moment.

Perhaps it's part of your past life flashing before your eyes. It was quite a big part of your life, that affair with Trish. How long did it go on? Three years, wasn't it?

Paul rubbed his face with both hands, hissing in pain when he felt the splinter jab deeper beneath his nail as he accidentally caught it against his jaw. He was suddenly aware of the relentless throbbing in that finger once more.

'Didn't you ever feel guilty about what you'd done?'

The voice seemed to fill the coffin as it filtered through the speakers.

'Guilty?' Paul said, confused.

They're talking about the murder, not your affair with Trish.

'Why should I feel guilty?' he asked. 'I haven't done anything. Not to your daughter.'

'I wouldn't be able to live with myself if I'd done something like that.'

'If you let me die will you be able to live with yourself?'

'Why shouldn't I? Letting you die would be fair. It would be justice that my little girl never got.'

'It'd be revenge, that's all.'

'What's the difference?'

'Revenge is a kind of wild justice. Someone famous said that.'

'I don't really care who said it.'

'But you care about revenge on me.'

'For what you did. It's what you deserve.'

'What about a trial with a judge and jury. Shouldn't I be entitled to that? That's the law.'

'The law doesn't always work.'

'You mean I might be found not guilty. Then you wouldn't get your revenge. It won't bring your daughter back. Killing me. It just makes you as bad as me.'

'So you admit it.'

'No, but if you kill me then the people who love me will want revenge on you. What if they come looking for you and kill you?'

'So someone loves you, do they? Who?'

'My girlfriend. My mother.'

'Your mother will know what I feel like when she loses her child.'

'She doesn't have to know what that feels like. You've got the power to stop her feeling like that. You can't wish that on someone else, surely. Not when you know how painful it is.'

'You didn't think about how much pain I'd feel before you murdered my daughter, did you?'

'I didn't murder your daughter. How many times do I have to say it?'

There was a long silence then the voice came again.

'What's the worst experience of your life?' it asked finally.

'Apart from this one, you mean?' he snapped irritably.

'Whatever it is, it can't compete with sitting in a room in a hospital with a policewoman, waiting to identify your dead child. That's what I had to go through. Because of you.'

Paul thought about protesting, then considered it useless.

'Have you ever had to identify a dead body?' the voice went on.

'No.'

'You're lucky.'

'I've seen one. When my dad died.'

'That's different.'

'He was my father.'

'I had to sit in this little room and all the time I kept saying to myself that perhaps someone had made a mistake and that it wasn't my daughter who was dead. Perhaps it was someone else's child. I wished that. I prayed for it. I know that's awful, wanting someone else's child dead, but I didn't care. I just didn't want the body I had to look at to be my daughter.'

Paul could hear low breathing coming through the speakers.

'It seemed to take ages,' the voice told him. 'It was like I was sitting there for hours and the policewoman didn't say anything. She held my hand every now and then but what else could she do? Nothing she could have said or done would have made me feel better. Even now I can see that room if I close my eyes. There was a little wooden table in the middle of it with a couple of magazines on it. There were five chairs. Plastic ones. And there was a water cooler. You know, those things where they have the little triangular paper cups in a holder next to them. The floor was lino and it was dirty. Scuffed. It was like hundreds of people had been in the room before me. I wondered if they'd all had to go through later and identify bodies or hear bad news. It was like this was the bad news room in the hospital. They brought you here to give you the worst news. I wondered if they took people there to tell them they had cancer. And there were posters on the walls about swine flu and meningitis and HIV, but all I could think about was my daughter.'

Paul listened to every word, each passing moment convincing him more intently that he was truly never going to get out of this coffin. Whoever had put him here would never release him. Not a chance.

There is a chance. It's a slim one but slim is better than none.

Paul exhaled slowly.

'Someone came into the room in the end,' the voice continued. 'Another policeman. He was in plain clothes, though. I think he was a detective. He said could I follow him so I walked through into this other room with him and the policewoman and there was some glass and some white curtains. Not like net curtains but really thick white ones and they said I had to look through the glass. So, when I was ready, someone on the other side pulled the curtains back and I could see that there was a body lying on a sort of metal table in this other room. I could see straight away that it was my daughter. I remember screaming and the policewoman put her arms around me but I tried to get away from her. I just wanted to hold my daughter again. I must have thought that if I touched her she'd come back to life. I don't really know what I was thinking. Then I must have passed out because I woke up back in the other room again. The first room where they'd made me wait.'

'What did the police say to you?' Paul enquired.

'They tried to be understanding. I suppose they couldn't do anything else really. They were just doing their jobs. It wasn't their fault and I actually felt quite sorry for the policewoman who had to stay with me. I asked her if she had any kids and she said she had. She was probably trying to imagine what she'd have felt like if she'd heard that kind of news and had to identify her dead child.'

'Did they tell you how she died?'

'I wanted to know but they said it was best that I didn't know the details. I suppose they were trying to protect me.'

'Why did you want to know? I mean, why did you feel as if you had to know every single detail of the way she died?'

'I don't know. Don't the Americans call it closure or something? Perhaps I thought that if I knew every single detail of how my daughter had died then I'd be able to get over it. Move on, or whatever they say. I'm not sure I want to move on.'

There was a long silence. Something Paul was becoming accustomed to.

He wondered what the owner of the voice looked like. How old? How tall? How fat or thin? If she was a woman he tried to imagine what colour hair she had. Brunette. Red-head. Blonde.

Like Trish?

Paul wondered why those thoughts were flooding his mind again. Why here? Why now? Why her?

She was part of your life. She was also part of a lie. You should be thinking about Amy now, not about your mistress. What would the owner of the voice say if she knew you were a cheat and a liar? That wouldn't look very good when it came to defending yourself, would it?

'Shut up,' Paul hissed.

'Did you say something?' the voice demanded. 'I thought I heard you speak.'

'No. It must have been static,' he offered.

Again the memories filled his mind.

49

'What makes you think that?' Paul Crane asked, gently kissing the top of Trisha's head. 'What makes you think you're falling in love with me?'

'How does anyone know when they're falling in love, Paul?' Trisha asked. 'The greatest poets and writers in history haven't been able to define what love is and now you want me to tell you.'

'I just asked. I'm curious.'

She moved closer to him, looking into his eyes now.

'When I'm not with you all I can think about is the next time I'll see you,' she said softly. 'When you ring me at work my hands shake when I answer the phone. My heart beats quicker when I hear your voice. When I know I'm going to see you I'm like a kid just before its birthday. And when we're together I never want that time to end. Does that sound like I'm falling in love?'

'Falling or fallen?'

'Does it matter? I can't stop the way I feel even though I've tried.'

'Why have you tried?'

'Because I'm going to be the one who gets hurt. You're never going to leave Amy. I know you love her and I wouldn't want that. I wouldn't want to break you two up.'

'But if I did leave her?'

'You won't.'

'Listen, Trish, I'm very flattered that you're falling in love with me. Thank you.' He kissed her lightly on the lips.

'That's not the answer you're supposed to give,' she told him, a note of reproach in her voice.

'What do you want me to say?' he challenged. 'That you're stupid? That you should have kept better control over your feelings?' He reached out and touched her cheek with one open hand. 'You're a beautiful woman; why shouldn't I be flattered that you're falling in love with me?'

'But where does that leave me? Where does it leave us?'

'It's not going to frighten me off, if that's what you think. You don't want it to end between us, do you?'

'No, of course I don't but I don't want to get hurt.'

'I'd never hurt you, Trish, you should know that.'

She looked at him for a moment longer then lay down again. Paul looked down at her.

'Tell me you know that,' he persisted. 'That I'd never hurt you.'

She looked up at him then nodded almost imperceptibly.

'Tell me,' he insisted.

'I know you wouldn't,' she confessed. 'Not knowingly.'

'Not ever.'

They regarded each other evenly for a moment then Paul broke the silence that had descended.

'Do you want to finish it?' he whispered.

'No,' she murmured. 'Even though I know that would be best for me in the long run. If you weren't in my life then I could concentrate on finding a man who would actually be with me and just me.'

She smiled wanly.

'I'm sorry,' Paul said quietly.

'For what?'

'For any pain I've caused you.'

'I don't think it's anything compared to what's to come. But I'll take that chance for now.'

She snaked one arm around his neck, pulling him closer to her, kissing him hard this time. Paul responded, his eager tongue flicking out to meet hers, his hand gliding across her flat belly and up to her breasts.

He gently slid his fingers over the right one, feeling the stiffness of her nipple. She moved nearer to him, parting her legs and pushing against his thigh.

'Make love to me,' she whispered breathlessly.

'I thought that was what we did earlier,' he told her, smiling.

He tensed as he felt her hand close around his hardening shaft.

'I want you,' she breathed, her fingers encircling his penis strongly now.

She parted her legs wider and he moved between them, the tip of his erection now nudging her moist sex. Trisha lifted her feet from the mattress and placed them on the small of his back, urging him to enter her. He did so with one deep movement that made them both gasp.

For long moments they lay motionless, just breathing heavily and gazing into each other's eyes as if one or both of them were awaiting the precise moment to begin. Trisha kissed him lightly on the lips and he began moving gently inside her.

Less than thirty seconds later the phone on the nightstand rang.

50

The shrill ringing of the phone cut through the stillness inside the bedroom. *A stillness punctuated only by the soft moans and sighs of two people deeply engaged, ensnared within their own pleasure.*

Paul slowed his pace as he heard the sound.

Trisha put one hand on the small of his back, her slender fingers tracing a path to his buttocks.

She looked up into his eyes and then shook her head very slightly.

He glanced across in the direction of the phone, the ringing now apparently more strident.

'No,' Trish gasped.

He stopped moving inside her completely and lay there between her legs, still deep inside her.

'No,' she said again. 'Leave it.'

'I've got to answer it,' he said.

Again she shook her head.

'It could be Amy,' he insisted.

'She wouldn't be ringing at this time.'

He pulled free of the grip of her slippery muscles, sliding his penis out of her reluctantly.

She looked at him irritably and rolled over towards the phone, reaching for it.

'What the hell are you doing?' Paul snapped, trying to reach it before Trish. 'It might be Amy.'

She picked up the receiver and lifted it off the cradle, holding it towards him by the mouthpiece.

Paul took it from her and pressed it to his ear, seating himself on the side of the bed beside Trish who, after reaching for her cigarettes and lighting one, had now settled herself in an upright position against the pillows at the bed head. She kicked the duvet off and sat there naked, one slim leg bent at the knee. Paul looked at her disdainfully and found the look returned.

'Hello,' he said softly into the receiver.

Trish took a drag of her cigarette and looked at him again.

'I didn't expect you to call this late, babe,' he said into the receiver. 'Is everything OK?'

It was fine, Amy told him at the other end of the line. There was nothing for him to worry about; she just couldn't sleep and she wanted to hear the sound of his voice.

He smiled awkwardly and shrugged in Trisha's direction.

Amy asked if she'd woken him.

'No, I couldn't sleep either. I never can in hotel rooms,' he told her.

She asked what he'd been doing that night.

'Just that business dinner I told you about,' he explained. 'Nothing exciting. The usual bullshit but it has to be done, unfortunately.'

Trish blew a stream of smoke in his direction, her expression impassive but something dark in her eyes.

'You go back to bed now,' Paul said into the phone. 'You'll drop off soon enough.'

She told him she loved him.

'I love you, too,' he said softly.

Trish swung herself off the bed and crossed to the window. She peered out at the night, her back to Paul now.

'See you tomorrow,' he murmured into the phone. He waited a moment then hung up.

'What did she want?' Trish asked without turning around.

'Does it matter?' he said a little sharply.

'Why was she ringing so late?'

Paul got to his feet and crossed to where Trish was standing. He slid his arms around her waist and pulled her close, pushing himself against her shapely backside. She didn't respond but merely stood there, still smoking and still staring distractedly out into the darkness of the night.

'I suppose it was better than sneaking off to the bathroom and talking to her on the extension like you usually do,' Trish breathed.

'And you never normally complain. What's the problem this time?'

She merely shook her head.

'I'm sorry, right? I didn't know Amy was going to call,' he said defensively.

'Was she checking up on you?' Trish chided and he wasn't slow to catch the derision in her voice.

'No. Now, will you just forget it? And if the phone rings again, I'll pick it up.'

'Sorry. My mistake. I'll try to remember that next time.'

He kissed the back of her head, the scent of her perfume strong in his nostrils.

They stood there motionless for what seemed like an eternity, both of them staring at the blackness of the night. Thick banks of rain clouds had been gradually building during the night and somewhere in the distance there was a muffled rumble of thunder.

When Trisha finally spoke, her voice was low.

'It just reminds me of the way things are when she rings,' she said softly. 'It reminds me that I'm just a bit on the side. That your real girlfriend is waiting for you back home.'

'Don't be stupid,' he said, squeezing her more tightly to him. 'It's not like that.'

'Not to you, Paul, but you don't know how it feels from my point of view. I never wanted to be thought of as your mistress or as just another notch on your bedpost.'

'I don't think of you like that.'

She turned to face him, her breasts pressing against his chest. She felt his hands slip to her buttocks as he held her.

'How do you think of me?' she wanted to know. 'What makes me different from the others?'

'What others?'

'Come on, Paul, I'm not stupid. You've had other affairs. Christ, we've even talked about them.'

'I told you, you're different.'

'I bet you said the same thing to them.'

He kissed her lightly on the forehead.

'Do we really have to have this conversation now?' he asked softly. He put an index finger beneath her chin and lifted her head so that she was looking at him.

He could see something close to pain in her eyes.

'I would never hurt you,' he breathed.

'You might not mean to but that doesn't mean you wouldn't,' she told him.

He kissed her on the lips, one hand stroking her long blonde hair.

'I would never hurt you,' he repeated.

'Promise me,' she asked.

'I promise,' Paul told her.

There was a light pattering against the window and they both turned toward it.

It had begun to rain.

51

Why these thoughts? Why now?

Why should this particular episode of your life come hurtling back into your mind at this, of all times?

Because you're dealing in lies and this was the biggest lie that you lived through, dummy. It's logical really.

Paul didn't want logic. He wanted his mind clear. He certainly didn't want it filled with memories like these.

But they were good memories.

But not now. These were memories to be sifted and dwelt upon in quieter, more pleasant times, not at the point of death.

'I'm not going to die,' Paul murmured. 'Not yet.'

You seem very sure of that.

Paul sighed, expelling more carbon dioxide into the air that was already thickly tainted by the continuous exhalations. He closed his eyes tightly, trying to force the images of Trisha from his mind, still wondering why this particular episode of his life had entered so force-fully into his consciousness at this particular time.

Because it was a time of your most elaborate and intricate lies. And lies are the only thing that is going to get you out of this coffin. You proved when you had that affair that you could live quite comfortably with lies and that you could bend and manip-ulate the truth to your own ends. Christ, since when has anyone in the advertising business had a problem with lying? If there were no liars in that business then the fucking business wouldn't exist.

Paul tried to force the image of Trisha from his mind but it stubbornly refused to go. He could even see her now. Slender, despite her small build, her honey-blonde hair brushing her shoulders.

Inside his mind she was smiling at him.

What would she say now if she could see you? Would she think it was poetic justice for the way she'd been treated? Would Amy think the same if she knew?

Amy had never suspected his infidelity. Never questioned him because, he reminded himself, he'd never given her any reason to.

She never questioned your infidelities. Plural. There was more than one, don't forget.

Paul wasn't proud of that; in fact he had agonised about telling her about one or two of the one-night stands when she had asked him. He would have been economical with the truth, of course; he would have told her that the one-night stands happened in the early stages of their relationship, that they'd been the result of too much drink and too much overfamiliarity with women he felt nothing for. The usual excuse that anyone who has strayed from the path of unerring monogamy uses and believes is justified. His relationship with Trish had been different. It had been more than sex. And that was what had made it dangerous. They had a lot in common besides the physical attraction. He had cared about her. And caring was a major drawback in situations like that. He had cared about Trish and he cared about Amy.

But did you love them? Either of them? Have you actually got the capacity for real love? If you had, would you have cheated on the woman you knew loved you? Amy loved you unquestioningly but that never seemed to make a difference, did it? She would have given her life for you but would you have done the same for her?

'For Christ's sake,' he snapped at himself. 'Get a grip.'

He shook his head, as if to physically shake the thoughts from his mind. They had no place there. Not now. Not in this direst of hours. There were other things that should be considered and mulled over, not past infidelities.

But those things were important. Your feelings during those times were important. For instance, you fantasised about Amy being dead. Was that the act of a man in love?

Paul could still remember those recollections. He knew that he would never leave Amy. He knew that he could never be with Trish and, if he was honest, he wasn't even sure if he had wanted to be. Not on a full-time basis. And yet, it hadn't stopped his fantasies. He had pictured the two of them living together and going through the same routines as he and Amy. But he wasn't sure if he wanted that. Trish gave him things that Amy didn't and vice versa.

You wanted your cake and you wanted to eat it. Simple as that.

And that was precisely what he'd been doing. In an act

of flagrant selfishness he had done exactly that, taking from both women in different ways but giving little back. He had often wondered what it would be like if Amy died. There was no malice in his ponderings. He didn't want her to be dead; he just mused on what life would be like if such a scenario came to pass.

It would have been easier for you if she'd just died, wouldn't it? Then the responsibility would have been taken away from you. You wouldn't have had to make the decisions. You wouldn't have had to think about the rights and wrongs of leaving her. She would have died and you would have been free.

Paul felt those same feelings of shame that he was coming to recognise all too easily now. He wondered how he could ever have entertained thoughts like that. And yet they had persisted. He didn't think about Amy being ill and going through a long period of suffering. He just thought what life would be like if she was no longer on this earth. Surely he wasn't the only person ever to have done that? People wished death on others every day of the week. He wasn't wishing it on Amy, merely considering the impact it would have on his life and the way that such an event would change his existence. Was that so appalling?

These thoughts, he told himself now, had resurfaced because of his own closeness to death. Had he been sitting safely in his flat he would not have thought of those recollections, but here and now, surrounded by stale air and confronted by the images of his own end, it was only natural to re-examine thoughts that centred on death and its consequences.

That's probably enough of the split-arse psychology for now. Don't try to excuse yourself and the thoughts you had.

Paul attempted to ease his conscience by reminding himself he had never *wished* Amy dead. Never actively *wanted* her to be gone. He had only imagined what his life would be like without her.

Oh, that's all right then.

He swallowed hard and clamped his eyes closed for a full twenty seconds.

Clear your mind. Concentrate. Think about what you're doing, where you are and how the fuck you're going to get out. You haven't got a hope unless you focus.

'I know,' he murmured under his breath.

The internal voice was retaining its annoying tendency not only to be logical but also to be right. Paul knew that he must concentrate when he spoke to his captors.

Even though you're probably wasting your time anyway?

'I'm not wasting my time,' he told himself, the words directed at his inner voice even though he knew that no amount of remonstration would silence it. 'I can do this.'

You honestly believe that, don't you?

Paul knew that he had to believe it. He had to cling to the hope, however vague, that he could turn this appalling situation in his favour. To think otherwise was to accept death and he promised himself that he would not do that until it was beyond question.

'Come on, think,' he told himself. 'Get yourself out of here.'

He licked his lips, feeling the cracks on them where they'd dried. Paul rubbed them with one index finger and took a couple of deep breaths.

The time had come.

52

Gina Hacket slammed the phone down and stood motionless, gazing angrily at it. She waited a moment then blundered back into the living room and slumped heavily into her chair.

'Useless,' she exclaimed, looking blankly at the television set on the other side of the room.

'Who was it?' Frank Hacket wanted to know, seeing the anger on her face.

'The police,' she informed him. 'I rang to find out how their investigation was going but they still haven't got anyone.'

'Give them time, Gina, they're doing their best.'

'Well, it doesn't look as if their best is good enough. Jesus Christ, when are they going to find Laura's killer?'

'They told us they didn't have much to go on from the beginning. You can't expect miracles. They'll find whoever did it, you'll see.'

'When, Frank? When will they find him? It's already been two months since she was killed. They'll never find who did it.'

'And perhaps you should stop bothering them with phone calls all the time. They'll contact us when they've got something worth-while to tell us.'

'I won't hold my breath.'

Gina got to her feet and crossed to the window where she peered out into the gloom of the early evening.

'They said that the success rate was pretty good with cases like this,' Frank reminded her.

Gina nodded.

'Great,' she chided. 'I feel so much better now.'

Frank rose and crossed to where she stood. He slipped an arm around her waist but she pulled free of him.

'They don't care, Frank,' she said dismissively. 'We're just another job to them. Another statistic.'

'That's not true,' he offered. 'They're doing their best to find Laura's killer.'

'And even if they get him, what then?' she rasped. 'It's not as if he's going to be hung, is it? Even if they catch him what'll he get, Frank? Ten or fifteen years? Twenty at a push?'

'He'll get life.'

'Life is thirty years. If the bastard's in his twenties he'll be out before he's sixty. He'll have plenty of time left to live his life when he gets out. That isn't justice, Frank. Justice would be that he loses his life, too. Why should he have the right to live when he took Laura's life?'

Frank regarded her evenly for a moment then he retreated to his chair and sat down again.

'Even if he was executed it still wouldn't bring Laura back,' he offered.

Gina turned to face him, an expression of fury on her face.

'What are you saying, Frank?' she snarled. 'That life would be good enough? Have you forgotten what he did to our daughter?'

217

'I'm saying that whatever they do to him isn't enough,' Frank snapped. He sat back in his chair and exhaled wearily. 'If we still had capital punishment, and he was caught and sentenced, what's the worst they could do to him? He'd have been hung. It would have been over in seconds. A quick and painless death. What I'm saying is that I wouldn't have wanted him to die quickly and painlessly.'

Gina's expression softened.

'What would you have wanted?' she pursued.

'I'd have wanted him to suffer,' Frank announced. 'I'd have wanted him to go through agony for hours, the way Laura did before he killed her.'

Gina sat down again. When she spoke, much of the anger had gone from her voice.

'But that won't happen to him,' she breathed. 'Even if he's caught. He'll be in prison, in a single cell, locked away for twenty-four hours a day but he won't suffer. Not the way we do every day. Every time I look at a picture of Laura it's like someone's sticking a needle in me. I can't even enjoy my memories because all I'm thinking about is that there won't be any more. Once he's caught, that's it. It's over for him. All he has to do is serve his time and wait until they let him out. And they call that justice.'

'If there was anything we could do, I'd do it,' Frank said flatly.

Gina looked evenly at him.

'He's an animal, Frank, he doesn't deserve to live,' she continued. 'He deserves to suffer. He deserves pain. As much pain as anyone can give him.'

Frank nodded almost imperceptibly.

'I often think about what I'd do to him if I got the chance,' Gina mused. 'People would think I was sick for some of the thoughts I've had.'

'What kind of thoughts?' he wanted to know.

'I'd break his legs with an iron bar,' she said quietly. 'Every bone in his body. I'd beat him until he was begging to be put out of his misery and then I'd cut his balls off. One at a time. And I'd stuff them in his mouth.'

Frank watched her expressionlessly.

'Or I'd cut him,' Gina continued. 'Very slowly. Every part of his body. I'd ram splinters under his nails and push my fingers into his eyes until they popped like balloons. I'd use a drill on his kneecaps and then on his elbows. I'd rip his teeth out one by one with pliers. I'd cut out his tongue.' She bowed her head as if ashamed at the extent of her fantasies.

'I want him dead, Frank. I want him to suffer.'

'I know. So do I.'

'But that's not going to happen, is it?'

Frank didn't answer. He was momentarily lost in his own thoughts. And if he was honest with himself, the nature of them terrified him.

53

'Was she your only child?'

Paul surprised even himself with the question.

'Your daughter,' he repeated. 'Was she your only child?'

Very clever. Try to make them think you care. Catch them off guard.

'Yes,' the voice told him.

Paul wished he could hear more clearly. The sound of the voice was still so badly distorted that he was still unsure as to even the sex of the owner. He wondered if the reception was as bad at the other end.

The other end.

Where was the other end? Where was his captor listening to him? If there were microphones and speakers they would have to be hooked up to receivers somewhere.

And what good is knowing going to do you?

'Did you have anyone who you could talk to about what happened?' Paul asked.

Silence.

'Hello,' Paul said sharply. 'I asked if there was anyone.'

'I heard you,' the voice cut in. 'Who did you talk to after your father died?'

'I spoke to my mum sometimes but otherwise I didn't like to bother people with the way I was feeling.'

'No, because people aren't really interested, are they? They think that there should be a time limit on how long you grieve for. People tell you that life goes on and that time's a great healer and all that sort of shit. And then, when you don't start perking up within their time limit they tell you not to dwell on the past. They tell you to look forward. How can I look forward when I know my daughter is dead? I'll never see her get older. Never meet her first boyfriend or see her get married. There won't be any grandchildren for me. All the things that other parents look forward to I can't. There's nothing for me now. There hasn't been since she was killed.'

'I can't imagine what it's like.'

'No, you can't.'

'I had a friend whose brother was in the army. He was killed in Iraq.'

'Killed doing his job. He wasn't murdered.'

Paul had no answer.

'That morning when I dropped her off at school she was talking about the summer holidays,' the voice went on. 'About what she was going to do when she broke up. How she was going to play with her friends and how she was looking forward to going to the seaside to stay with her grandparents. You should have seen the effect it had on them. I'm surprised they didn't die, too. If having to identify my daughter was the worst thing in my life then having to tell her grandparents she was dead was the next one. Having to tell them that she'd been murdered and raped by some fucking animal who should be punished.'

Paul swallowed hard as he heard the building rage in the voice.

'It must have been terrible,' he offered. 'I'm really sorry.'

'No, you're not,' the voice said flatly. 'Because if you were sorry, you wouldn't have done it in the first place. You would never have killed her.'

'I didn't kill her,' he said despairingly.

'Liar.' The word was shouted and it echoed inside the coffin, throbbing inside Paul's ears.

'All right,' he shouted back. 'All right. If you want me to talk then I'll talk. I'll tell you what happened. I'll tell you what I did to your daughter. Every detail. But I want you to swear that when I've finished you'll let me out of here. I want you to swear on the soul of your dead daughter.'

'You bastard.'

'Tell me you'll release me if I let you hear what you want to hear. Swear, otherwise I'm saying nothing.'

'You're not in a position to bargain.'

'You've already told me that. Now you've got a decision to make. You want to hear the truth? Well, the only one who can tell you that truth is me. The only one who can tell you what happened is me. Make your decision.'

54

'Gina, it's impossible.'

Frank Hacket lay on his back gazing at the ceiling of the bedroom, his own words echoing inside the small room as well as inside his own head.

'But our daughter was the one who was murdered. Why shouldn't we be informed of how the investigation is going?' Gina insisted, moving closer to her husband. 'If they've got a man in custody then we should be told.'

'They won't give us that kind of information,' Frank went on, looking at her.

'How do you know that?'

'Because that's not the way things work.'

'Why won't the police give us information about the man who killed her? We have a right to know.'

'They're not going to give us details about a man who they might only have taken in as a suspect. That's not how the police work in these cases.'

'How do you know that, Frank? How come you're the expert all of a sudden?'

'I didn't say I was but I'm telling you that they won't give us details of every person they bring in for questioning. Chances are this guy isn't even the one who did it.'

'And what if he is?'

Gina's words hung in the air like cigarette smoke.

'If he's the one then the police will find out,' Frank went on. 'They'll find out while they're questioning him and if they charge him then they'll inform us and that'll be it.'

'Yes, it'll be over. He'll be locked up. Locked away without ever really paying for what he did to Laura.'

'There's nothing else we can do, Gina.'

'We talked about this, Frank.'

'Yes, we did, and what we talked about was ridiculous. It was crazy. We weren't thinking clearly. We're crazy even to think about it now.'

'If wanting justice is crazy then you're right: I'm completely insane.'

She lay motionless, gazing questioningly at Frank.

'You wanted it as much as I did when we spoke,' Gina reminded him. 'Why have you changed your mind?'

'I haven't changed my mind,' he told her. 'But what we talked about doing and what we can actually, physically, do are two different things.'

'Why?' she demanded. 'You said there would be some way. You said we could do it.'

'In theory. I was talking about something that could be done in theory. It's too risky.'

'Have you forgotten why we'd be doing it?'

'Don't start, Gina,' Frank snapped. 'Don't try and make me

224

feel guilty. I know this would be for Laura. It was always going to be for Laura.'

'Then why the hesitation?' she insisted.

Frank swung himself out of bed.

'We need to think things through,' he told her, pulling up his pyjama bottoms as he headed for the bedroom door and the landing beyond. 'We need some kind of plan.'

'So let's talk about it now,' she continued, sliding out of bed and following him out of the room.

She saw him enter the bathroom, saw him push the door shut behind him. She heard him urinating.

Gina stood on the landing facing the bathroom door. She heard water running, the toilet flush and then, moments later, Frank emerged once again.

'Gina, forget it,' he said, raising a hand dismissively.

'Do you know what I did today?' she asked him, allowing him to pass and make his way back to the bedroom.

Frank shook his head and clambered wearily back into bed. Gina sat at the small dressing table opposite him. She glanced at herself briefly in the mirror there, noticing the dark smudges beneath her eyes. Her hair needed washing and she hadn't worn more than a touch of make-up for days.

'What did you do?' Frank asked her.

'I sat in Laura's room wondering what to do with her things,' she told him quietly. 'Her clothes, her books, her toys.'

'I'm not with you.'

'Eventually we'll have to decide what to do, Frank. We'll have to decide whether we keep them or get rid of them. If we keep them then that room will be like a shrine to her but if we sell them or give them away then it'll be like betraying her. It'll be as if we don't want any reminders of her in this house any more.'

'No, it won't, Gina,' he said tenderly. 'Even if we give every-thing of hers away we'll never lose the memories of her that we have.'

Gina sat silently in the gloom, gazing across at her husband.

'I read somewhere that the first thing people forget about dead loved ones is how they sounded,' she said sadly. 'They forget what their voices were like. How their laugh sounded. Stuff like that.'

'We won't forget,' he assured her.

'How can you be so sure?' she said challengingly.

Frank shook his head.

'Then after that you start to forget what they looked like,' Gina continued. 'You can remember their features but you forget little things like how they smiled and cried. Little by little they fade in your mind, like old photos and then, in the end, all you've got is old photos.'

'That won't happen with us,' Frank insisted. 'We'll never forget her.'

'Because if we did, that would be betraying her, wouldn't it, Frank?' Gina said.

Again he nodded.

'Just like letting her killer escape would be betraying her,' she added.

'It's not down to us to catch her killer. That's the police's job,' Frank reminded her.

'But it should be down to us to punish him.'

Gina's words came at him in the darkness of the room like stones fired from a slingshot.

'We should have that right, Frank,' she went on. 'We should be able to decide the way he lives or dies. If we want to make him suffer then we should have that option.'

226

'But we can't.'

'We could if we did what we talked about.'

'It's not possible. No matter how much we might want it. It can't be done.'

'Why not?'

'Because if we went after the man who killed Laura that would make us murderers, too.'

'Not unless we took his life. Just trying to find him wouldn't be wrong. We'd be helping the police.'

'We're not detectives. Where the hell would we start?'

'The police told us the kind of man they were looking for. His approximate age, his build.'

Frank listened silently.

'They said he probably lived alone. That he was strong.'

'That's hardly a description, is it?' Frank murmured.

'But it's a start, Frank,' she told him, her voice more animated than it had been for a while. There seemed to be genuine enthusiasm in her tone and her words. As if someone had pumped her full of adrenaline. It was a side of her that he hadn't seen for longer than he cared to remember. 'If we could just find out things like his hair colour, any distinguishing marks he might have, then we'd be able to find him.'

Frank shook his head and exhaled.

'That's what you want, too, Frank, I know it,' Gina said. 'You want to find him as much as I do. You want him to suffer as much as I do. You want him dead as much as I do.'

Frank Hacket didn't answer.

He merely sat in silence, the thoughts tumbling through his mind.

'I'm right, aren't I?' Gina added.

Frank nodded.

Gina crossed to him and kissed him lightly on the cheek and, as she drew back, there was a smile of triumph on her face.

55

The woman sat back in her chair, breathing heavily.

The arrogant bastard. How dare he dictate to her? How dare he try and bargain for his worthless life?

Her eyes were fixed on the speaker before her. The speaker through which she could hear Paul Crane's voice. It was distorted to the extent that she sometimes had difficulty hearing everything he said but she heard enough.

She wondered what he looked like. He'd had a pillowcase fastened tightly over his head when he'd been brought to the car and dumped unceremoniously in the boot the previous night. That, and the fact that it had been so dark, had made any kind of identification impossible. Not that she really cared what he looked like, but there was part of her that wanted and needed to see this man who she had been interrogating. She had felt the burning desire to look upon the face of the man she was convinced was responsible for the death of her daughter. She had wanted to look at him before he was put into the coffin but she'd been denied that pleasure. There was no need, she'd been told. Besides, they had to get this over with before dawn. The coming of the daylight would leave them exposed and they couldn't allow that to happen. They couldn't allow themselves to be caught.

It had all happened so quickly she'd barely had time to take it in.

She had driven the car the previous night. She had been the one who had ferried them to this place where they now were. This place of confession, possibly of execution, too. The thought of a man dying by her hand didn't bother her. Why should it? He deserved to die for taking her daughter's life. It was a simple equation. An eye for an eye and a tooth for a tooth, even the Bible said that. There was nothing else to it. No room for moral dilemmas and questions of right and wrong. He had been untroubled by those things when he'd raped and murdered her child. Why should she be bothered by them now? The only thing she did find a little troubling was that she wasn't going to see his face before he died. There was a part of her that would have relished looking into his eyes as he got closer and closer to his final moments on this earth. She wanted to see him suffer. Hearing him beg for mercy was all right but it didn't match actually watching him die.

The woman wondered if she should be feeling this way but every time she had doubts about her right to end his life she imagined what her own child must have gone through at his hands. When she considered that, there was no room for doubt at all.

Wouldn't any parent who had lost a child secretly take

this kind of justice, she wondered? Any parent whose offspring had been raped and murdered would want this for the killer, wouldn't they? If they were honest. She'd seen people on the news emerging from court saying that vengeance wouldn't bring their kids back and that they were satisfied with the court's decision. But were they really? Wouldn't they have preferred to know that the one who had ended their child's life was going to lose his own life, too? And how much better that they should be the controllers of that fate as she herself now was.

For all that, she wished she could see him.

She reached for the bottle of Coke beside her and took a swig. The beginnings of a headache were gnawing at the back of her neck and she fumbled in her handbag for some painkillers and swallowed two with another mouthful of Coke, tasting their bitterness as they stuck briefly in the back of her throat.

The speakers and microphones that had been set up inside the coffin were simple, crude, even, but they did their job. The woman knew nothing of how they worked and cared even less. They ensured that her daughter's killer could hear what she was saying to him and that was the only thing that mattered even though she would have appreciated being able to hear him with a little more clarity.

She herself now sat in a bare-walled Portakabin listening to the sound of his breathing as it rasped through the speakers. It was cold inside the small hut and it smelled of damp and wet earth in there. There were several shallow puddles on the floor and, when the wind blew strongly it felt as if the entire flimsy structure was going to either collapse or be blown away. But the woman realised that she would only be inside for another hour or so. It would do until this was over with, one way or the other.

If she was honest with herself there was only one possible outcome.

The man in the coffin would be left to die.

If he was guilty of murdering her child then that was his just and deserved fate.

If.

For a fleeting second, for only the first time since she'd arrived at this place, did she pause to consider that he might not be guilty of the crime.

She was still considering this fact when the door to the Portakabin opened.

Gina Hacket turned to greet the newcomer.

56

Paul gritted his teeth.

He wanted to shout to his captor that he was ready to speak again. Ready to tell them whatever they wanted to hear.

Don't provoke them. You're in deep enough shit as it is. If you provoke them they might just walk away and leave you. Just for the hell of it.

But he knew that wasn't the case, or hoped it wasn't. He'd been put in this coffin for a reason. Someone didn't go to these lengths just to walk away.

So, basically, you've played your last card.

Paul wondered if he should have bargained for the right to be let out of the coffin before he started speaking again.

No, don't push it. One step at a time. Take it easy and you might just talk your way out of this.

He knew it was going to take all his strength and will to come out of this situation alive but, as earlier that night, he felt that energy surging through his veins once again. Paul had almost convinced himself that he could escape this wooden prison simply by using his powers of persuasion.

And lies.

He sucked in a warm, bitter breath and coughed.

His captors had told him that he had enough oxygen left to last him an hour. What if they were lying?

They want a confession before they leave you to rot. What would be the point in letting you die now?

But if they didn't intend to let him out anyway, then why bother about the time limit?

Just concentrate on getting them back on that fucking microphone. Keep them talking.

Even though talking was also using up the oxygen quicker.

Damned if you do. Damned if you don't.

Or just damned.

Oh no, not back to that. Not the Heaven or Hell scenario. Not now.

Paul felt light-headed. He tried to hold his breath for a moment, attempted to inhale while he counted to three, hold it and then exhale to a count of three or more. It had, he reminded himself, worked earlier on when he was attempting to calm himself down and limit the number of deep oxygen-draining breaths he'd been taking. Perhaps it would work again. He put his hands to his face, cupped them over his mouth and nose and exhaled. He did this five times in succession and some of the terrible light-headed feeling of unreality began to subside a little.

You've got to keep your mind sharp now. Now, more than ever. If you're going to persuade them to let you out you've got to be one hundred per cent focused on what you're saying.

But this person only wanted to hear one thing. All they wanted to hear was that he had killed their daughter. They wouldn't settle for anything other than a full and frank confession.

Then give them one.

Paul closed his eyes, his heart thumping a little harder.

Confessing isn't normally your strong point, is it, but then again, your life doesn't normally depend on it. Christ, asking someone in the advertising business to be honest was a bit like asking Hitler to become a rabbi.

'Very funny,' he murmured to himself, his eyes jerking open again despite the fact that it was still pitch-black within the box.

Had they heard him? He strained his ears to detect any sounds at all coming from the speakers but he could hear nothing.

What about other sounds like the squealing of the graveyard rats or the slithering of those big, fat flesh-eating slugs? They'll still be coming for you, no matter what happens.

Paul shuddered involuntarily and stretched his left hand down the side of the coffin, fumbling at the satin there. Perhaps trying to reach the speaker or the microphone that had been inserted. And yet they had told him it was pointless.

Even if you find one, what are you going to do? Even if you find the microphone and you can disable it, what good is it going to do you?

The thought struck him like a thunderbolt.

There *was* a way out.

57

'Tell me you don't want to do this, Frank.'

Gina Hacket looked at her husband who was seated in his living-room chair, his head slightly bowed.

'Look me in the eye and tell me you don't want to do it,' she repeated.

'It's not that I don't want to,' he said evasively.

'But?' she challenged.

'The risks are incredible,' he stated, finally looking at her in the darkened room.

'Not if we're careful and not if we do things the way we said we'd do. The way we planned.'

'More intelligent people than us have tried to do things like this over the years and got caught,' he said, managing a smile. 'It isn't always down to organisation. Sometimes it's down to luck and we haven't exactly been blessed with good luck during our lives, have we?'

'So what do we do? Forget about it? Let it go?'

Frank shook his head.

'No,' he said flatly. 'We do what we said we'd do.'

Gina smiled.

'When?' she wanted to know.

'Everything should be ready by tomorrow,' he informed her. 'I found a perfect place. Isolated. Nothing for miles around. We won't be disturbed.'

'How long do you think it will take?'

Frank shook his head again.

'I don't know,' he confessed. 'I really don't know.'

Gina got up and moved towards him. She knelt beside his chair like a supplicant before the throne of a king.

'We've got to stick together, Gina,' he told her. 'Once this is done there's no going back.'

'I know that,' she admitted. 'It's what I want. I don't care about the risks.'

'Perhaps you should,' Frank snapped.

'I'd do anything for Laura,' she told him softly.

'Even spend time in prison?'

'If that's what happens. At least I'll know that her killer has got what he deserved.'

Frank sucked in a deep breath.

'Are you sure about the dosage to give?' Gina wanted to know.

'I spoke to someone in the pharmacy,' Frank said. 'Just a hypothetical conversation. We were talking about some cop programme on the TV and I asked what kind of chemicals would be needed and how much. That kind of thing.'

'And no one saw you take it?'

'I was very careful.'

They sat in silence for a moment, then she reached out and rested one hand tenderly on his thigh.

'You know how much this means to me?' she murmured.

'I'm doing it for my sake too, not just yours,' he said quietly.

'We're doing it for Laura,' she said.

'Is that how we're going to justify it to ourselves, Gina? Is there anything we couldn't excuse by saying it was for Laura?'

'You're having second thoughts.'

'No, I'm not,' he snapped. 'I just don't want any mistakes.'

'And I'm not going to make any. Just make sure that you don't. Don't give him too much of the sedative or you'll kill him.'

'I told you, I know what to do and how much to give.'

Again silence descended. Gina got to her feet and moved back to her own chair. The television was on in one corner of the room but the sound was muted. The only light inside the room was from the flickering images on the silent screen. They both stared blankly at the set. The ticking of the carriage clock seemed thunderous in the stillness.

'What's his name?' Gina wanted to know.

'Does it matter?' Frank sighed.

'I was just curious,' she persisted.

'Then you ask him when you get the chance.'

'I won't see his face either.'

'Is it that important to you?'

'I would have liked to look into his eyes. Just once.'

'There's no need.'

Another long silence fell upon them, finally broken by Gina.

'Tomorrow night,' she murmured.

Frank nodded in the gloom.

They both continued staring at the soundless television set. The insistent ticking of the clock filled the room.

58

'Where have you been?'

Gina Hacket glanced questioningly at her husband as he closed the door of the Portakabin behind him. Frank Hacket took a deep breath and shrugged.

'Walking around,' he informed her. 'Trying to clear my head.'

'You should have been here.'

Frank didn't speak. He merely slumped down in the seat next to his wife and dug in his jacket for his cigarettes.

'Has he said anything?' he wanted to know.

'Only what I expected him to say,' Gina informed him. 'That he's innocent.'

'What else did you expect him to say?'

'You should have been here with me. If he'd confessed you would have missed it.'

'I'd have heard it on the tape later.'

Frank lit a cigarette and drew heavily on it.

'I can't hear him very well,' Gina complained. 'There's

so much distortion and interference coming through these speakers.'

'They were all I could afford,' Frank snapped. 'Besides, it'll be the same for him. He won't be able to recognise your voice either.'

'Well, he couldn't do that unless he knew me, could he?' she chided.

'If he got out he might be able to identify it later.'

'He's not going to get out though, is he?'

Frank took another drag on his cigarette and nodded towards the microphone.

'So, what did he say?' he wanted to know.

'He says he'll confess if we release him,' Gina murmured.

'That's what you expected, wasn't it?' her husband enquired. 'I thought that was the idea, to get him to confess.'

'It was, but not to release him.'

'He's going to know that, Gina. He must know that he's fucked, no matter what he says.'

They regarded each other silently for a moment then Gina exhaled wearily.

'How did you know it was him?' she asked quietly. 'How did you know it was this man? Out of all the ones it could have been. What made you pick him?'

'I told you,' Frank informed her. 'I had my reasons. You didn't care what those reasons were when I said I could get him. What's wrong? Are you starting to think this was a bad idea now?'

Gina shook her head.

'He's the one, Gina, I'm telling you,' Frank insisted. 'Do you think I would have risked going to these lengths if I wasn't sure? What we're doing, we're doing for Laura. For our dead daughter. Our murdered daughter. If you start having second thoughts just remember that.'

'I know why we're doing it,' she snapped. 'And I want him dead. I want him to suffer.'

'So what's the problem?'

'We don't even know his name.'

'He fits the description that the police gave us. He's the man who killed our daughter. That's all we have to know.' Frank blew out a stream of smoke and closed his eyes.

'Do you want to talk to him?' Gina asked.

'Not yet,' he told her. 'I'm sure you can handle it.'

Frank massaged the back of his neck with one hand and sat forward slightly in his chair.

'Don't you want to hear what he's got to say, Frank?' Gina said challengingly. 'Don't you care how our daughter died?'

'We know how she died, Gina.'

'Well, I want him to tell me.'

'How is that going to help?'

'I want to know what she said. I want to know if she called for us before he killed her.'

'Why torture yourself any more? Just leave him where he is and have done with it.'

'Not until I've got all the facts. I want to hear from his lips what happened and why. That's what I really want to know. Why he did it.'

'I'm not sure I do.'

'Then leave now,' Gina snapped.

Frank regarded her silently for a moment then took another drag on his cigarette.

'I'm going to speak to him again now,' Gina told him. 'Do you want to hear or not?'

Frank hesitated for a moment longer then nodded gently.

59

They wanted answers to their questions, Paul Crane thought. Well, he'd give them answers.

Too fucking right he'd give them answers.

And they'd hear them when he decided. Not when they decided. No longer would his captors dictate to him. From now on, he was the one making the decisions.

Paul actually managed a smile. For the first time since waking inside the coffin that night he forced his lips to crease upwards in that unmistakable expression. Surprised by his own audacity, he lay still in the coffin feeling relatively composed. His breathing had slowed and his heart was beating relatively normally. The air still tasted stale and acrid to him and it was uncomfortably warm inside the box, but Paul was able to consider all those factors with uncharacteristic calm at this precise moment. He felt that, despite his situation, he was gaining some measure of control. Or at least he would be.

Now all he needed was for his captors to begin speaking

to him again; then he would give them exactly what they wanted.

Again he smiled.

You're very smug for a man who's still buried six feet below ground. What if this master plan doesn't work? The others haven't exactly been roaring successes, have they?

This plan would work. He felt it in his bones. Despite the seemingly inescapable surroundings he found himself in, and the sheer soul-crushing hopelessness of the situation, Paul had almost convinced himself that victory was just a short time away. He would be getting out of this coffin. He had decided.

And then?

He felt pain from his injured hand and he flexed the fingers slowly.

How he wanted to drive that fist into the faces of his captors. How he wanted to make them suffer when he finally got out of this wooden prison. He gritted his teeth, visualising himself standing triumphantly before them at the graveside. They would cower from him as he loomed furiously above them, desperate to make amends for the agonies they'd put him through. But their entreaties would do them no good.

He would grab one of the shovels that had been used to bury him and he would smash the metal across their heads and faces.

And he would keep swinging until their heads split open and their twisted, febrile brains spilled out on to the earth of the cemetery where they'd buried him.

'Fuckers,' he hissed aloud.

He could see himself standing over the first of them,

driving the blade of the shovel down on to an outstretched neck, pressing down with all his weight, cutting through the flesh, muscle and, finally, through spinal cord. He wouldn't stop until the head was severed. And, when it was, he would prop it on the headstone of the grave in which they had buried him. That would be fitting, he decided.

The other one he would disembowel.

Paul could see himself using the shovel again like some massive blunt but deadly scalpel. Cleaving the torso of his other tormentor from sternum to pelvis. Then he would pull the intestines free with his bare hands, holding the slippery lengths like bloated worms before him. He would hope that the owner of the vital organs was still alive so that he could see his own viscera being held before him.

He would then be drawn. That was what the next part of the process was called, wasn't it? Hanging, drawing and quartering? He would dispense with the first step, preferring the spade as his weapon of destruction. But he would use the second phase of that execution so feared in days gone by with relish.

He would hold the dripping entrails before the bulging eyes of his captor, watching as the flickering light of life gradually diminished and then disappeared in those orbs.

He would make him pay.

And then what? Call the police and calmly give yourself up?

Paul hadn't thought of what would come next. He didn't care. All that mattered was getting out of the coffin, and now he was sure he had a way. Whatever happened after that he would deal with in due course. Things had to be taken one step at a time and this was the first step.

So your plan's foolproof, then? You've thought through every single eventuality and you're still satisfied that it's going to work? Is that why you're still smiling?

The smile faded from his lips but Paul was still sure that what he planned to do would be enough to get him free. It had to be.

'Come on, you bastards,' he murmured. 'Talk to me.'

And what if they've gone? What if they didn't appreciate being shouted at and given ultimatums? What if they've just thought, fuck it, let's leave him where he is? Then what, genius?

But Paul was sure that he wouldn't have been abandoned to his fate. Someone had gone to a fair amount of time and trouble to kidnap and imprison him inside this coffin; they weren't just going to walk away without the answers they wanted, were they?

You seem very sure. I hope you're right. Trying to call someone's bluff from six feet under doesn't seem like a very good idea to be honest, but I suppose you know what you're doing. After all, the success of this venture depends on your ability to lie convincingly, doesn't it? And no one would want to diminish your skills as a liar.

Paul shook his head irritably.

Sorry, that same raw nerve keeps getting touched, doesn't it? Liar, liar, pants on fire. Ha, ha.

'Yeah, very funny,' he whispered.

There was a sound inside the coffin. Something like a dull thud.

Are you sure it was inside? Maybe the graveyard scavengers have turned up early for their feast.

Paul heard the same noise again and he recognised it. It was the sound of someone breathing close to the microphone. He was sure of what was going on now. It wasn't the graveyard rats or anything ridiculous like that. It wasn't something that had forced its way from his imagination through to his consciousness and it wasn't the product of his tortured mind and an atmosphere now badly short of oxygen. The noise he'd heard meant just one thing.

His captor was about to speak to him again.

60

'Can you hear me?'

Paul heard the muted, distorted voice and experienced that familiar feeling of defiance flowing through his veins.

Come on, you fucker, bring it on.

'Yes, I can hear you,' he said, not sure whether or not to disguise the newly found strength in his tone. He knew he had to play this carefully. He couldn't antagonise his captors too much or they would merely leave him to rot in his subterranean container. However, so convinced was he of the possibility of success that he was struggling to control that confident edge to his voice.

Just calm down and play it by ear.

Paul took a breath.

One step at a time, remember?

'Have you thought about what I said?' Paul asked, wondering instantly whether or not he should have taken the initiative.

There was a long silence during which he feared he might have lost his final chance for freedom.

'Are you saying that you're prepared to admit murdering my daughter?' the voice asked.

'I'll tell you what you want to hear,' Paul answered.

'I'm taping this conversation. I'll play the tape to the police. You'll be arrested. You'll go to prison for killing her.'

Fuck you. Go and fetch the law now. Let them dig me out of this fucking grave. At least I've got a chance of getting out now. Prison is better than a slow death by suffocation.

'I don't care if you tape it,' Paul said.

'But you might lie.'

'I won't. I'll tell you just what you want to hear.'

There was another long silence. Paul clenched his left hand into a fist as he waited for it to be broken.

'You want to know what happened to your daughter, don't you?' he offered. 'I said I'd tell you.'

'I know what you said. And I know the conditions you made. Don't try to play games with me. I'm still the one in control here.'

'I know you are. That's why I'm prepared to say what you want. I know that my life is in your hands. I'm going to have to trust you, though.'

'And about me swearing on my daughter's soul?'

'I want you to do that. It's the only way I'll be able to believe that you're going to release me once I've told you what you want to hear.'

'Tell me.'

'Swear.'

Silence.

'You want to hear, don't you?' Paul said. 'You want to know what happened to her? Swear.'

'Tell me.'

'Do it or I'll say nothing. I'll die in here, I know, but everything you've done to me will have been a waste of time.'

'All right, I swear I'll let you go if you tell me the truth.'

'On your daughter's soul.'

'I swear on her soul, you bastard,' the voice snarled. 'Now talk.'

Paul licked his lips and took another muggy breath.

'What did the police tell you?' he wanted to know.

'How she died. When she died,' the voice informed him.

'Then what can I tell you that you don't already know?'

'Details. The police wouldn't give details.'

'Like what?'

'Just tell me what happened from the beginning. From the time you picked her up in your car. And don't lie, I'll know. I'll sense it.'

Yeah, right.

'I still don't know what you expect from me,' Paul said, his voice lower now.

'A confession and a reason why you did it. I need to understand that. Why my daughter and not someone else's? I have to know.'

Paul nodded to himself. He swallowed hard, licked his lips again and prepared himself.

After this there was no going back. No more chances. Nothing else.

'All right,' he began. 'Turn your tape on.'

61

'I picked her up after school,' Paul began as confidently as he could. 'I thought about doing it outside the school. I'd driven past there a couple of times before I stopped but then I thought that there might be parents around who would recognise my car or me.'

'Did you know you were going to kill her when you picked her up?' the voice interrupted.

'Are you going to let me tell the story or not?' Paul snapped.

He waited a moment then took another breath.

'Are you listening to me?' he said. 'If you keep inter-rupting me I'll stop talking and then you'll never know what happened.'

'Go on.'

'I saw lots of kids going home, on their own and in groups. I knew I had to wait until one of them was on their own. If I went near one who was in a group then the other kids would see me and be able to recognise me. I knew I had to wait until one was walking alone.'

'Why did you pick that school?'

'Does it matter? It could have been any school that day. Once I'd decided what I was going to do it was just a matter of which one I came to first.'

'And which kid you took?'

'Yes.'

'So you didn't have any idea about which child you wanted?'

'No. I knew I'd decide when I saw them.'

'Had you ever done it before?'

'Never. I'd fantasised about it. I think more men have than would like to admit it. I'm not saying it's common but a lot of men have fantasised about raping a woman or they've wondered what it would be like to have sex with a relative. A sister or cousin or something. It's not the kind of thing you talk about, though, is it?'

'So you'd fantasised about having sex with a child?'

'Yes.'

'And then murdering them?'

'I knew that if I did one I'd have to do the other. Once I'd had sex with them, they'd be able to identify me. I know paedophiles don't kill their victims but this was different. I'm not a paedophile.'

'You raped my eight-year-old daughter. What the fuck are you if you're not a paedophile?' the voice snarled.

'I was experimenting. I knew that it would probably be a one-off. I wasn't interested in kids as sex objects normally. I told you I've got a girlfriend.'

'So why didn't you just rape a woman? A grown woman?'

'At that time I didn't want to. I wanted to see what it would be like with a child.'

Paul closed his eyes and drew in more of the stale and humid air. He could feel sweat running down his face now. Tiny droplets tickled his hot skin as it dripped off him and soaked into the satin beneath.

'Laura wouldn't have got into a car with a stranger,' the voice challenged. 'She knew not to do that.'

'I knew that, too,' Paul went on. 'I had to force her in. Once she was inside I knew there was no way she could get away.'

'You bastard. She must have been terrified.'

'I didn't ask. I just drove.'

'Where to?'

'Around. I drove around for about an hour trying to decide where to go and what to do. I hadn't planned everything, you see. I wasn't a hundred per cent sure of what to do once I'd got the child I wanted.'

'Why did you pick Laura?'

'She was on her own. She . . . looked as if . . . I don't know. She was just the one. She was in the wrong place at the wrong time. That was all. There was no design and selection in my choice. I just grabbed the first child I could.'

'Where did you take her?'

'To . . . to just outside the town centre. An estate. They're building a new estate. I knew the houses were finished but I knew they were empty. There were no workmen around. I knew no one would see us.'

'But the houses would have been locked up.'

'Some were. It didn't take much to break into one.'

'Where was Laura while you were doing this?'

'Still in the car. I broke into one of the houses then went back and fetched her.'

Every word that Paul spoke seemed to be amplified now by the tight confines of the coffin. Every syllable seemed to fill the small space, turning the air itself more noxious with every passing second. It was as if imparting the words was darkening and poisoning the atmosphere itself.

'The whole place smelled of fresh paint,' Paul continued. 'And there were still dust covers on the floors. I thought they might come in useful for later. After I'd finished with her. Did the police tell you what was done with her body?'

'They said that she was found by a roadside just outside the town centre. Nothing else.'

'I knew that she'd be found pretty soon, wherever I dumped her, so I didn't think there was much point in trying to hide her body. No point taking the time to dig a shallow grave when some prick walking his dog was going to find it. That usually happens, doesn't it? The best-laid plans are undone by something as stupid and trivial as that. I thought just dumping her body was as good a way to get rid of her as anything.'

'You must have known that you'd left DNA behind.'

'I didn't think about it at the time.'

'So what happened after you got her out of the car?'

'I took her inside the house.'

'She must have screamed or something. How did you keep her quiet?'

'I gagged her.'

Paul heard something snarled through the speakers but he couldn't make out what it was. He shifted uncomfortably, trying to change position slightly. The cramp that he'd felt gripping his calf much earlier was beginning to bite once more and he flexed his toes in an attempt to prevent the muscle contraction from taking too serious a hold.

'Go on,' the voice said finally.

'She was gagged,' Paul went on. 'Once she was like that I knew she couldn't make a noise.'

'Had you tied her up too?'

'Yes. In case she tried to get away.'

'What would you have done if she'd tried to run?'

'Hit her. I'd have hit her. I wasn't going to let her get away from me once I'd got her inside that house.'

'When did you decide to rape her?'

'I suppose I always intended to do that from the time I picked her up. From the day I decided to take a child I suppose I was intending to do that. That's why I took one. Like I said, it was just an experiment. Something I wanted to try.'

'Laura was eight. What did you want with an eight-year-old?'

'I'd been thinking about doing it with an older girl, a teenager. One about fifteen or sixteen. That was what I really wanted to do. I wanted to fuck a teenage girl. One of those mouthy ones that wear their school skirts up around their arse. The ones that you see in little groups around the shops smoking and laughing. They know how good they look to men and they love it. They tease men and when men look at them or talk to them they call them perverts and dirty old men. It was one of them that I really wanted to fuck. I wanted to get one of them alone and see if she was still as mouthy then. I wondered if she'd give me a load of attitude when I was lying on top of her but then I thought that some of them might enjoy it. They might like me fucking them.'

'Wouldn't you have wanted that? Would you have wanted them to resist? Isn't that what makes it more exciting for you?'

'She might have resisted at the beginning but what I'm saying is that after I got started she might have liked it. I've seen them on the internet on web cams. Sometimes they do them alone from their bedrooms. All made up and dressed in their bras and knickers. Showing off for the camera and anyone who'll watch because they know that blokes like that. They're doing it for men. That's what makes me think that they might actually enjoy being fucked by some stranger who's grabbed them off the street. I imagined getting one of them into my car. I'd even have bribed one to begin with. They'd have taken the money. Any of those cheap, tarty-looking girls with the platinum-blonde hair and the skirts up to their arses would have taken it. The ones with the big mouths who think they're so fucking experienced and grown up. The ones who have those tattoos on the smalls of their backs. They call them tramp stamps, don't they? I'm not surprised. They'd have got in my car for twenty quid just to prove how tough they were. I know they would. And once I'd got them in there that would have been it. I'd have talked about sex to the one I picked. Asked if she had a boyfriend and if she was a virgin and all that. She'd probably have told me what she did with her boyfriend. How she sucked his cock and let him fuck her. She'd have thought she was turning me on, talking dirty like that. And when she wasn't expecting it I'd have pulled over and that's when I'd have done it. And when I'd finished I would have pushed her out of the car.'

'Why do you hate girls like that?' the voice wanted to know.

'I don't hate them,' Paul offered.

'You sound as if you do. Did you have a bad experience when you were a teenager? Couldn't you get a girlfriend?'

'I had no trouble getting a girlfriend.'

'Then why do you hate the kind of girls you're talking about?'

'I don't like the way they behave. I don't hate them all.'

'But you wanted to punish one of them?'

'Not punish. I just wanted to teach one of them a lesson. They're always so sure of themselves. So arrogant.'

'You think that raping one would have taught her a lesson?'

'It wouldn't have been rape, that's what I just said. She might have pretended to struggle at the beginning but I bet she would have enjoyed it by the end.'

'Is that another of your fantasies? To rape?'

'Look, I thought you wanted to hear about what happened to your daughter.'

'I want to know what else goes through that sick mind of yours.'

'Well, now you know.'

There was a moment's silence and then the voice spoke once again.

'So why didn't you go after a teenager that day?' it asked. 'Why pick on my little girl?'

'She was easier. A teenage girl would have been harder to get into the car. She would have been stronger. She might have fought back. She could have scratched me or hurt me. There might have been signs of the struggle and I didn't want that. I wasn't ready for that. I thought that taking a smaller kid would make things better for me. That's why I picked your daughter.'

There was another long silence and Paul could feel his heart thudding more rapidly against his ribs.

Keep going. You're doing well. Tell them everything. That's what they want.

He cleared his throat and prepared to speak again.

62

'You're sick.'

The words echoed inside the coffin. They throbbed in his eardrums like angry wasps and refused to budge.

'You deserve to die in that coffin,' the voice went on.

'You kidnap me and put me under the ground then let me suffocate and you call *me* sick?' Paul countered.

'There must be something seriously wrong with you mentally if you had thoughts like that. You're an animal.'

Paul waited a moment.

Gone too far? Made their minds up for them?

'You said you wanted to know what happened,' he reminded the owner of the voice. 'I'm telling you why it happened. I'm telling you what I was thinking that day. That's what you want to know, isn't it? You said you wanted to know everything.'

'About what happened to my daughter, not about how your sick fucking mind works.'

'I think you're the one who's sick for wanting to know.

Your daughter was raped and murdered. What kind of parent wants to know details about something like that?'

Careful now. Don't overstep that line. Not now.

'Did you ever want children?'

There was softness to the tone of the voice that startled Paul. It seemed suddenly devoid of the venom and anger that had infected it since he'd first heard it. He paused as if to reassure himself that the words were being spoken by the same person.

'What did you say?' he enquired.

'I asked if you ever wanted children,' the voice went on. 'You and your girlfriend. Hadn't you ever talked about starting a family?'

'What the hell has that got to do with what I'm saying?'

'I'm curious.'

'And I'm running out of oxygen. Let me tell you what you want to hear and then let me get the fuck out of this box.'

There was another long silence.

'Are you listening?' Paul prompted.

'Get on with it.'

'I took her inside the house and I raped her.'

'How?'

'What do you mean, how? I raped her. You know that.'

'I want to know everything. Was your cock hard when you took your trousers off? Were you ready to fuck her?'

'What?'

'You heard me. Did the thought of fucking an eight-year-old turn you on?'

'Yes.'

He spoke the word through gritted teeth.

'Was she conscious when you did it?' the voice asked.

'Yes.'

'Did you take off all your clothes or just your trousers and pants?'

'All of them.'

'And what about Laura? Did you undress her?'

'Yes.'

'Did you strip her naked?'

'Yes.'

'Did Laura have any idea what you were going to do to her?'

'She was eight. How could she have known?'

'Yes, she was eight. That's all. Did she struggle when you undressed her?'

'I told her not to. I said that I'd hurt her if she didn't do what I wanted.'

'Did she cry?'

'To begin with.'

'You mean when you started undressing her?'

'Yes.'

'What did you take off her first?'

'For Christ's sake,' Paul gasped.

'Tell me, you fucking animal,' the voice roared.

'I took off her school uniform. Well, I made her take it off while I watched.'

'And you were already naked?'

'Yes.'

'You had to untie her hands to let her strip off?'

'Yes, but I told her not to try and escape otherwise I'd make her sorry.'

'And when she was naked?'

'I tied her hands again. Then I raped her.'

'Did she cry when you put it in her?'

'Yes.'

'But that didn't make you want to stop?'

'No.'

'Did she say anything to you?'

'Like what?'

'Did she ask you to stop? Did she say it hurt?'

'I think so.'

'You *think*?'

'Yes, she did. She asked me to stop and a couple of times she said that she wanted to go home.'

A single tear ran slowly from Paul's eye, mingling with the sweat that still coated his face.

63

'I've heard enough.'

Frank Hacket got to his feet, shaking his head, his breath coming in gasps.

'Where are you going?' Gina asked him irritably.

'I told you, I've heard enough,' Frank snapped.

'But this is what we wanted. He's confessing. That's why we brought him here and put him in that coffin, to make him confess.'

'I know it is.'

'He's telling us what he did to Laura.'

'We know what he did, Gina. You might want to hear it but I don't.'

'She was your daughter too, Frank.'

'That's why I don't want to hear it,' he snarled. 'Him giving us all the gory details isn't going to bring her back, is it?'

'Nothing's going to bring her back.'

'Then just leave it now. He's confessed. He's admitted what kind of thoughts he had. We've heard how warped he is. No normal bloke has thoughts like that. How much more do you need? It's Frank who doesn't want to hear any more details. I certainly don't need details. He killed her and he's confessed to that. That's all I need. That's all I ever needed.'

'Well, it's not enough for me.'

'Then you listen to what else he's got to say. I don't want to hear it.'

'What kind of man are you?'

The words were said with a sneering contempt that Frank wasn't slow to detect.

'The kind that doesn't want to hear how his eight-year-old daughter was raped and murdered,' he roared at her. 'If this is what you want. If this is what you need to get over Laura's death then that's fine. You deal with it your way and I'll deal with it mine. It's enough for me knowing that the bastard's dead.' He stood with his back to her, his breathing gradually slowing down. The veins on his neck and at his temple had been throbbing madly and he could still feel them pulsing. Frank kept his teeth clenched, his jaw muscles as tight as fists.

'If that makes me less of a man in your eyes, Gina, then I'm sorry,' he said finally, almost apologetically. 'What would you rather I did? Dug him up and beat him to death in front of you? Is that a more fitting punishment?' He turned to look at her once more. 'I did this for you. I kidnapped a man and buried him in a coffin for you. I stole the drugs from the hospital where I work, broke into his flat and brought him out. I found this place. I set up the microphones and speakers. I buried him. I took the risks.'

'I drove the car,' she reminded him.

He nodded.

'Sorry. I didn't mean to overlook your part in all of this,' he sighed.

'You were supposed to be doing it for Laura, for your daughter,' she chided.

'It was for Laura, too,' he told her, battling to keep his temper in check. 'But you were the one who wanted this. You wanted him to die this way.'

'So did you, Frank,' she reminded him. 'Don't try to blame me for this. You wanted him to suffer as much as I did.'

'Yes, I did and he has suffered and he will suffer more before he dies. But that's it, Gina. Once he's gone, he's gone. It has to stop somewhere.'

'What's that supposed to mean?'

'We can't do this again.'

She looked at him evenly.

'You said you were sure he was the one,' she snapped. 'You said you knew it this time. You knew that he was the one who killed Laura. What if he isn't? What if we have to do this again? What if we have to keep doing it until we find the man who actually killed her?'

'I told you, it stops tonight.'

'Why were you so sure it was him, Frank?'

'I know it's him.' He turned away from her again, his voice low. 'I know it. You've got to trust me. He's the one. He's been right so far, hasn't he? He's told you details that only the murderer could know.'

She nodded almost reluctantly.

'Then why do you doubt that it's him?' Frank insisted.

'Because we've been wrong before,' Gina breathed. 'Because of the others.'

64

It was silent inside the coffin.

Paul wiped his face and waited for the sound of the voice to invade the solitude yet again but that distorted, unnatural and indistinguishable vocalisation didn't begin again as he'd expected.

'Hello,' he called.

There was no reply.

'Can you hear me?' he said, raising his voice but trying not to sound too challenging.

There was still no sound from the speakers.

This is not good.

Perhaps there'd been a fault at the other end, he thought. Perhaps they weren't speaking to him because there had been some kind of electronic failure. Maybe the equipment wasn't working at this precise moment.

Never considered that, did you?

And if it was broken? If they couldn't hear him or speak to him then, he realised with a shudder, he was finished.

Fucks your plan and you, doesn't it?

Paul shook his head. It couldn't be that. The silence couldn't be down to some kind of electronic failure. If someone had gone to the trouble of kidnapping him from his flat and imprisoning him in a coffin for the purposes of forcing a confession from him, then they would have checked and double-checked the quality of the equipment they were using to monitor such an event.

Wouldn't they?

But what if the kidnappers weren't technical wizards? What if this failure in communication was as much a surprise to them as it was to him?

'What we have here is a failure to communicate.'

Another line from a film that he couldn't remember the name of. It popped into his mind as unwelcome as the others before it.

Focus.

If there were a technical problem, some kind of mechanical hitch, then his captors would be trying to repair it. That was only logical. They'd put him in this place for the express purpose of communicating with him and hearing him speak, so they wouldn't just leave it as it was, would they? He could imagine them, even now, rushing around to make good the fault so that they could continue their interrogation. The thought comforted him a little.

But what if the problem is not that easy to put right? What if they get fed up with waiting and just decide to leave you here and now?

Paul wouldn't entertain that eventuality. Instead he focused his mind on visualising his captors above the ground somewhere, desperately attempting to repair the microphones and speakers that were their only connection to him and him to them.

He found it difficult to picture them, though, because he had no idea at all of what they might look like. He knew there was more than one of them. That much had been revealed when the voice had repeatedly said we, our, and any other word that indicated more than just a singular presence.

They told you there was more than one of them because it isn't going to matter in the long run. You're not going to get out of this fucking box to do anything about it anyway. It doesn't matter if there's one of them, two of them or an entire bloody gang. They're up there and you're down here. That's it. That's why it doesn't matter how much information they give you. They could tell you their fucking names and it still wouldn't make any difference. Christ, you already know the name of their daughter. Why not just ask them for their names? You could ask for their addresses and phone numbers while you're at it.

Paul tapped gently on one side of the coffin, wondering if the sound would galvanise his captors into some kind of response.

If they can't hear you then it's not likely to work, is it?

But, Paul reminded himself, he didn't know that there'd been some kind of electronic failure. He was just telling himself that to try and explain the uncomfortably long and rather worrying silence. He was humouring himself, he thought.

Or clutching at straws, depending on your viewpoint.

He tapped the coffin again, beginning with the sides then transferring his attention to the lid, particularly the area above him where he'd torn the satin away. The sound was louder when he hit it there. The material didn't muffle the impact the way it did on either side of him.

He continued with his knocking for a moment longer, then allowed his arms to flop back to his sides once again.

'I haven't finished,' he called. 'There's more you need to hear.'

There was still no answer.

Paul swallowed hard and waited.

65

'We can't think about them now.'

Frank Hacket reached for his cigarettes and lit another, sucking hard on it.

'That's in the past. We thought we were right at the time. We thought they were the ones. That's all that matters.'

'We've done the same thing to two other men, Frank,' Gina reminded him. 'Two others who we've left to die in the holes we put them in. Two other men who we were sure were Laura's murderers. What happens if we're wrong again?'

'It's a bit late for second thoughts,' he reminded her.

'It's not that,' she insisted. 'I'm not complaining. I'm just saying. If we're wrong then that's three innocent men who are dead because of us.'

'No one's innocent in this world, Gina.'

She looked at him and held his gaze.

'What did the others tell you?' Frank wanted to know.

Gina looked puzzled for a moment.

'What did the other two say?' Frank went on. 'About Laura?'

'The first one didn't say anything about her,' Gina informed him. 'He just kept saying over and over again that he was innocent and that he hadn't done anything. He begged for his life. So did the second one but he said that he'd help us find her killer if we'd let him out.'

A thin smile creased Gina's tired features.

Frank nodded.

'But you were sure it wasn't either of them,' he muttered.

'They didn't give the right answers,' she reminded him.

'Exactly. They made out they didn't know anything about what had happened to her.'

'So did this one to begin with.'

'Isn't that what you expected?'

Gina nodded.

'He's given you more information than you could ever have hoped for,' Frank observed. 'Doesn't that prove to you once and for all that he was the one who killed Laura? How could he know the kind of details he's given us if he hadn't been there?'

Gina regarded her husband evenly, her nails absently scratching the top of the desk where she sat.

'Why wouldn't you let me see his face?' she enquired. 'You let me see the other two?'

'Does it matter?' Frank intoned.

'I suppose not.'

'The man who raped and killed our daughter is lying in a coffin out there. What the hell does it matter if you saw his face before I put him in there?'

She had no answer.

'It's him, Gina, I'm telling you,' Frank insisted. 'I can feel it this time. I just know.'

'Then why won't you listen to him?'

Frank sighed.

'I told you,' he said. 'I've heard enough. And you should have, too. How much oxygen has he got left?'

'Thirty minutes, perhaps a bit more.'

'Then get it over with, Gina. If he's got more to say then let him say it and let's go. Let's get out of here. Let's leave this once and for all.'

There was a bone-crushing weariness in his tone that she hadn't heard before. He looked drained. His face was pale and there were dark rings beneath his eyes. When he lifted the cigarette to his mouth she noticed that his hand was shaking.

'What will happen to us, Frank?' Gina said finally.

He looked at her with an expression of bemusement on his face.

'No one will find the bodies,' he began. 'There's no reason to think the police will link us to the three disappearances.'

'No,' Gina said, cutting him short.

'After this is over. There'll be nothing left for us. We'll have done what we wanted to do. We'll have avenged Laura's murder. Not the police but us. That's what you wanted, isn't it?'

'But what will be left for us? What is there in the future for us? For you and me?'

'Not much. But there never was, was there?'

She looked at him expressionlessly.

'We're the same as a lot of couples, Gina,' Frank went

on. 'We see time passing and we can't do anything to stop it. We don't try to change the way we are. Life just passes us by. It's something that happens to other people. At least when this bastard is dead I'll feel as if I've done something. As if I've made a mark. My life won't have been wasted. I couldn't stop my daughter being murdered and that will haunt me for the rest of my life but at least I can comfort myself with the knowledge that the bastard who did it will be dead as well. Dead, thanks to me. Dead, because of what I did. If there is a Heaven I hope Laura's looking down at us now and I hope she's happy with what we've done for her.'

'Do you think she will be?'

He could only shrug.

'We can only hope,' he murmured.

'Hope,' Gina breathed. 'We haven't got too much of that either, Frank.'

He got to his feet and nodded in the direction of the small microphone on the desk before her.

'Let him say what else he has to say,' Frank offered. 'It's time to finish this.'

'Are you going to listen?' Gina wanted to know.

He remained motionless for a moment then, very slowly, he seated himself once more.

66

'I said, there's more for you to hear,' Paul called, raising his voice.

His words reverberated inside the coffin for a moment and he tensed, preparing himself for the silence that would signal his doom.

'I can hear you,' the voice said. 'Carry on.'

It was a joyous sound for Paul and he relaxed instantly in the knowledge that his captors were still present. They had not deserted him yet. And while they were still there he had a chance.

'I thought you'd left,' he said.

'Not until you've finished,' the voice reminded him.

'How long have I got?'

'What do you mean?'

'It's very warm in here. It's getting harder to breathe.'

'Just keep talking. There's enough oxygen, if that's what you mean.'

'How much did the police tell you about the condition of your daughter's body?' Paul enquired.

'Why?'

'You said you saw it in the morgue at the hospital,' he added quickly. 'I wondered if you knew details of her injuries.'

'Why don't you tell me? What did you do after you'd raped her? Was that when you cut her up?'

Paul hesitated for a moment, putting one hand to his chest. It really was getting more difficult to breathe inside the box. The air had been muggy and uncomfortably warm for a while now, and he had to suck in really deep breaths now to feel as if he was anywhere close to filling his lungs.

Please don't let me die now, he thought. Not when I'm this close to possibly getting out. Not after everything I've been through. Don't let it end like this.

And who are you talking to? God? You're wasting your time. The only ones who can get you out of here are the ones who put you in. If you can convince them. And if you can trust them.

'Why did you cut her?' the voice wanted to know. 'Wasn't raping her and then strangling her good enough for you? Or was it some other sick fucking fantasy that you'd had that you wanted to live out?'

Paul swallowed hard.

'What did you use to cut her?' the voice insisted.

'There were some workman's tools in the empty house when we first arrived,' Paul explained. 'They were in a big bag like a rucksack. There were hammers, saws and chisels. That kind of thing. I used those.'

'Why?'

'Because I wanted to. I thought about hiding her body. I was going to dispose of it. I considered cutting it up into pieces and dumping each one in a different place to make it more difficult to find but I knew that would take too long.'

'So you just cut her throat instead?'

'Yes.'

'Was she already dead when you did that? Was she dead after you put your hands around her neck?'

'I didn't check. I thought that cutting her throat as well would finish her for sure.'

'What about the blood? Didn't you have to be careful not to get covered in blood?'

'I was already naked. I just made sure that my clothes didn't get splashed. I wiped most of the blood off myself with a handkerchief. There wasn't as much as I thought there'd be. I had a shower when I got home.'

'And then you just dumped her body?'

'What else was I going to do? I'd finished with her.'

A bit of bravado in the voice there? Be careful. Don't let them mistake it for arrogance or gloating. They could still change their minds about letting you go.

There was a long silence then the voice spoke once more.

'When you raped her did you come inside her?' it asked evenly, almost gently.

'For Christ's sake,' Paul grunted.

'I want to know.'

'Yes.'

'How long did it take?'

'What?'

'How long did it take you to come?'

'I didn't time it,' Paul rasped.

'How long?'

276

'Four or five minutes, I suppose.'

'Is that how long it takes you when you're with your girlfriend?'

'What the fuck does that matter?'

'I'm curious. Does it take you longer to come when you're fucking your girlfriend?'

'This is bullshit,' Paul snapped.

'Does it take you longer to come when you're fucking your girlfriend than it did when you were raping my eight-year-old daughter? Answer the question, you sick bastard.'

'Of course it takes longer,' Paul roared.

'I wondered if you might be a bit inadequate in that department,' the voice chided. 'Perhaps that's why you had to rape an eight-year-old because you can't satisfy a grown woman. If you come after four or five minutes when you're fucking your girlfriend then she can't be very impressed with you in bed.'

'It takes longer with her.'

'Do you satisfy her? Do you make her come when you're fucking her?'

'For God's sake.'

'Do you?'

'Yes.'

'Then why did you come so quickly with my daughter? Was it more exciting with a little girl?'

'She was tight, it felt good,' Paul snarled. 'Is that what you want to hear?'

'You sick fucker.'

'You said you wanted to know everything and that's what I'm telling you.' He knew he was dangerously close to losing control of his temper. 'I came quick because it felt good. If she'd had tits I'd probably have wiped my fucking dick on them when I'd finished. How's that? Are you getting all of this on your tape recorder? This is what you wanted to hear. This is why you put me in this fucking coffin so I'd tell you everything, and now, when you hear it, you can't take it.'

'I hope you die in fucking agony.'

That's it. You've pushed them too far.

'I did as you asked,' Paul added quickly. 'I've co-operated with you. I've told you everything.'

'Then you're no good to me any more. You've served your purpose.'

Paul felt a chill envelop him.

They're going to leave you. Just like they always intended to. It wouldn't have mattered what the fuck you told them. You were never getting out of this coffin alive.

'You wanted all the details,' he said, his voice as even as he could keep it.

'What else do I need to know?' the voice chided. 'Did you honestly think that we were going to let you go after you told us what you'd done? You fucking idiot. You believed that? You actually thought you had a chance? As if we were ever going to let vermin like you carry on living. You'll die where you are now, you bastard.'

'And if I do you'll never know what I did with what I took from her.'

67

That's it, Paul thought. Trump card played. Now you have to wait.

And pray.

And what if they don't go for it? What if they don't swallow it? Don't want to play ball? Or any other cliché that you care to use? Then what? Death inside this coffin, that's what.

But that was always going to be the outcome, wasn't it? Why not try one last, desperate gamble?

And this was really desperate.

'What are you talking about?' the voice enquired. 'What do you mean, what you took from her?'

'I took something and kept it,' Paul insisted. 'Something that belonged to your daughter.'

'You're lying.'

'Am I?'

'The police would have told us something like that.'

'Perhaps the police didn't know what I took either.'

'What was it?'

'I'll tell you when you let me out of this coffin.'

'Tell me what it was that you took from her.'

'When you let me out. That's the deal. If you leave me here you'll never know.'

Paul allowed his head to rest against the satin. Inside the box he could smell the acrid odour of his own sweat mingled with the dampness of the wood that he'd come to know so well. He felt hot and sticky and he knew that the tainted air he was breathing was running out by the minute, but at last he felt a strength he hadn't experienced before. A belief that he hadn't dared embrace up until this moment. A belief that he was actually going to escape this wooden prison. Through his own wits and bravery he was going to get out. He was sure of it. Not just optimistic or misguided in his confidence. He was sure.

Don't get cocky. Not now. Not when you're so close.

'Tell me what you took from her,' the voice insisted.

'Let me out first,' Paul challenged.

Be careful.

'You can't dictate to me,' the voice told him.

'You wanted to know all the details. I'm willing to give you the last detail when you release me. Not until.'

'This is a trick.'

'No, it isn't. I took something from your daughter after I killed her. I kept it and only I know where it is. I'm the only one who can show you where it is. Let me out and I'll take you to it.'

'Why would you take something?'

'I wanted a memento.'

'You bastard.'

'Something to remember her by. Something to look at when I felt like it.'

'I don't believe you.'

'The police will tell you. Murderers usually keep something that belonged to their victims to help them relive the crime or to help them remember what they did.'

'No. I don't believe you.'

'You'd never forgive yourself for not knowing. For not letting me show you.'

'You could still be lying.'

'After what I've told you? How much more detailed could I have been?'

'Then tell me what colour school uniform my daughter was wearing when you took her.'

Paul felt as if his body had been injected with iced water. He shuddered involuntarily, his chest tightening.

'I can't remember that,' he said, trying to retain the bravado in his voice.

'You remembered everything else,' the voice reminded him.

'I can't remember.'

'Then you're lying. You were making everything up. The whole time you've been in there you've been lying to me. You've been telling me what I want to hear just so I'd let you go. You haven't been telling me the truth, you've been telling me what you thought I wanted to hear to try and save yourself.'

'No one could know what I've told you unless they were there.'

'Then what colour school uniform was she wearing when you picked her up?'

'If you didn't believe me then why didn't you stop me earlier? You knew I was telling the truth and you know that now. You want to know what I took from her?'

'What colour was her school uniform'

'Fuck that,' he snapped angrily. 'Let me out of here now or you'll never find what I took from her.'

68

'He's bluffing,' Frank Hacket snapped. 'If he'd taken something from Laura the police would have told us.'

Gina looked at her husband questioningly.

'What the hell does he mean anyway?' Frank persisted. 'What could he have taken? It wasn't an item of clothing. The police returned all her clothes. There isn't anything else he could have taken. I don't believe him.'

'What did you take from her?' Gina asked, leaning closer to the microphone.

'How many times do I have to tell you?' Paul Crane snapped back. 'I'm not saying until you let me out of this coffin.'

Gina sat back in her seat once more and looked at Frank.

'What are we going to do?' she wanted to know.

'Leave him there. He's lying,' Frank insisted.

'And what if he's not?'

Frank reached for a cigarette and lit it.

'Let's think about this logically,' he murmured, glancing

at the microphone. 'What could he have taken and kept? You saw her at the hospital morgue. We both saw her in the chapel of rest.'

Gina swallowed hard.

'We can't take the chance that he's lying, Frank,' she said meekly. 'We've got to get him out.'

'No way.'

'We've got to. If that's what it takes.'

'And what are we supposed to do with him when we let him out? What do you think he's going to do, Gina? Just climb obediently into the car and tell us where to drive him? And then what? He's going to try and escape and if he does that we're finished. If he gets away and reaches the police we'll both spend the rest of our lives in prison. We can't let him out.'

'But we could drug him again. You could use the same stuff you used on him in the first place.'

'If he did really take something from Laura then he's got to show us where he hid it. Drugging him's no use.'

'So what do we do?'

'Leave him in there. I told you, he's bluffing.'

'You can't know that, Frank.'

'I know. I can tell. He'd say anything to get out of that coffin. I'd do the same in his position. He's trying to trick us into letting him out.'

'I'm not willing to take that chance.'

'Then you dig him up,' Frank roared. His voice reverberated inside the Portakabin.

Gina saw the fury in his eyes but she wouldn't be dissuaded.

'I haven't come this far to give up now,' she said.

'Give up what? It's over, Gina. He'll be dead in fifteen minutes. His oxygen will run out and he'll suffocate. He'll be as dead as our daughter. The daughter that he killed.' His voice rose steadily in volume and vehemence as he spoke.

'How can you be so sure?' she challenged.

'Sure of what? Sure he'll be dead? Of course he will.'

'No, I mean that he's lying. I'm not taking that chance. I want him out of there, Frank. I want to know what he knows.'

'Then you dig him up.'

Gina looked at her husband with a look of bemusement. She'd never seen him so enraged before and she knew that, over their years together, he'd had plenty of opportunities to vent that anger. His eyes were wide, his lips slicked with white spittle as he barked the words at her, almost daring her to speak again.

She regarded him evenly for a moment then got to her feet.

'If it means finding out the truth,' she breathed. 'I will.'

She took a step towards the door of the Portakabin but he grabbed her arm and pulled her back towards her seat.

'Sit down,' he snarled.

'Leave me alone, Frank,' she rasped. 'I'm going to dig him up. I want to know what he knows. Even if you don't.'

'This is what he wants. Can't you see that? He wants us to believe him. That's his only way out.'

Gina was on her feet now.

'We can't give in. Not now,' Frank reminded her. 'We've come too far and done too much. If we let him go now then he wins.'

She hesitated.

'Is that what you want?' Frank went on.

Gina was standing midway between the chair and the door, unsure of what to do next. Not certain what her next move should be. She felt dizzy as the thoughts swirled around inside her brain.

'Just think about it,' Frank persisted, his tone even now, his voice calm.

She nodded gently then returned to her chair.

Frank smiled and reached out to touch her hand. It was a gesture of comfort that she appreciated and one that she had not experienced for too long now.

'Let me talk to him,' Frank offered.

69

A combination of the acoustics and the inferior quality of the speakers inside the coffin had made it impossible for Paul even to determine the gender of his captor. However, when the crackle of static heralded more distorted syllables, Paul was sure of one thing. The voice that came through the speakers this time was different from the one he'd been hearing so far.

Like the first it was reedy and strained due, he guessed, to the poor quality of the speakers, but it had a different timbre and convinced him that it belonged to a newcomer.

'You're lying,' the new voice told him. 'Nothing was taken from our daughter when she was killed. The police would have told us.'

Paul lay motionless for a moment, listening to this new voice. He tried to picture its owner, as he'd tried to picture the source of the first voice. Man or woman? Tall, short, fat, thin?

Did it really matter?

He was beginning to wonder how many of them were actually up there but, logically, his mind told him there were probably two. He was accused of killing a child so it was safe to assume that both of her parents had seized him. Two people had kidnapped and imprisoned him.

And killed him?

He forced the thought from his mind and concentrated instead on this second voice.

'You're bluffing,' the voice went on. 'I don't think you've got anything else to say. You're playing for time.'

'Why the hell would I do that?' Paul laughed and he was surprised at himself.

Why laugh? Why now?

'What do you think I'm stalling for?' he continued. 'Do you think there's someone waiting to come and rescue me? I'm running out of oxygen in this fucking coffin. Why would I want to be in here any longer than I have to be?'

Silence greeted this observation.

Paul waited a moment then continued.

'Can you hear me?' he called.

'Yes, I can hear you,' the second voice informed him.

'Then you should be able to understand what I'm saying.'

'The police report didn't mention anything about something being taken from our daughter. What kind of thing do you mean?'

'I'll tell you that when you let me out of here.'

'That's not going to happen.'

'Then you'll never know everything. You buried her but you buried her incomplete.'

'What the hell are you talking about?' Frank snapped.

'Not until you let me out of here. Once you do that I'll tell you. I'll even show you where I hid it.'

'Hid what? I'm warning you. You'd better tell me what you're talking about.'

'Or what? What are you going to do, kill me?'

Paul laughed and the sound echoed mockingly inside the Portakabin.

'This is bullshit,' snarled Frank Hacket.

'And what if it's not?' Gina demanded.

'If we get him out of there then we're going to have to kill him,' Frank told her. 'No question about it. If he sees us and can identity us to the police then that's it. There's no going back if we let him out. He has to die.' He looked at his wife. 'Are you going to do it, Gina?'

'If I have to,' she told him.

'It'll be different from sitting listening to him suffocate. He'll struggle. It'll be messy. There'll be blood. Evidence to get rid of.'

'I don't care, Frank. Get him out of that coffin.'

'And how are we going to do it? Strangle him? Smash his head in with a hammer? Stab him to death?'

'We'll do whatever we have to do.'

Frank shook his head.

'We kidnapped him so we could force him to tell us the truth. He's going to tell us the truth, Frank. The whole truth.'

'And nothing but the truth, so help him God?'

'What?'

'The truth, the whole truth and nothing but the truth, so help me God. It's part of the oath that you swear in court, isn't it?'

'Well, he's in a court. He's in our court and he's been condemned as far as I'm concerned. His evidence has been heard and he's been convicted. Now he's going to be executed. The only question is how. We were happy enough to let him suffocate; what does it matter if we have to kill him some other way?'

Frank exhaled deeply but he didn't speak.

70

Paul was beginning to feel light-headed again.

He felt faint and the nausea that he'd experienced earlier was now returning but more vehemently.

Was this the end? The beginning of his last few moments on earth?

Or below it, more to the point.

He felt the sweat on his body and he wiped it away with one hand as if removing the moisture would somehow make a difference.

They *had* to believe him. His captors had to go for this, he told himself. His last throw. The final roll of the dice in a game that had been stacked against him from the very beginning. Please don't let me come so close and then fail, he thought.

And if you get out, what then? Are you going to dedicate your life to being a good man? Are you going to seize the second chance with both hands?

There wasn't even any point in thinking that far ahead,

Paul told himself. The first and most important thing was that his lie had worked on his captors. He had sown the seeds of doubt, that much he was sure of, but now he needed all his powers of persuasion to secure the final step and release from this coffin.

If they take too much longer making up their minds it won't matter. You'll be out of oxygen.

The irony of that situation wasn't lost on him. How dreadful to have persuaded his captors to release him only for them to dwell too much on their task and leave him in the rancid, unbreathable air for too long. Even now they would be discussing the pros and cons of letting him out, but what if that conversation went on for so long that when they eventually reached him he was dead anyway?

A fresh wave of panic swept over Paul.

His options, he realised, were becoming more limited by the second.

If they decided to leave him where he was, then the end he had feared for so long was merely minutes away. However, if they decided to free him, if they went for the lie, there was the question of how long it would take them to dig him up.

Never thought of that, did you, genius?

That thought had not crossed his mind and now it filled him with terror. How long would it take to dig him up again?

Well, let's consider the situation, shall we?

He was six feet below ground in a sealed coffin. If they were exhuming by hand using shovels and spades then it could take anything up to an hour or more.

And you haven't got an hour, have you?

That was an hour at least to uncover the coffin. It then had to be opened. That might take another ten or fifteen minutes depending upon whether it was sealed with nails or screws. Normally six screws or nails were used to keep the lid down (that was what they always showed in films, anyway) but these bastards might have used more than that and, if they had, every single one had to be removed before the lid could be lifted and fresh, clean air came flooding into his nostrils and lungs.

He tried to think about it logically. Tried to find some shred of hope in what was swiftly turning into a hopeless situation. It had always been a long shot, this master plan, but to fail now at so late a stage and so near to triumph would be even more intolerable. Hope had been dangled before him as if it were suspended on fishing line and now, it appeared, that hope was to be yanked out of his reach. He could feel his heart beginning to beat faster with a combination of fear and anger. This wasn't fair. It just wasn't fair. He'd found a way out. He'd plotted and schemed inside his subterranean prison, and he'd found a way to escape, but now it appeared that he was to be undone by time.

'Oh, God,' he murmured, wanting to weep.

Even if they had a mechanical digger he was probably looking at somewhere close to fifteen or twenty minutes before they got him out. Even that wasn't long enough.

Or was it?

Paul had no idea exactly how much oxygen he had left. He'd gleaned some information from his conversations with his captors but the taste, smell and feel of the air inside the box were now telling him that time was running out. At best, he guessed, he had half an hour. At best.

If they had a digger then he might just make it, but if they were using shovels and spades he was done for.

But how the hell could he get them to speed up? He couldn't even persuade them to get him out. They were still deliberating over that and might well be for some time to come. So, if they did decide to release him how could he convince them that they had to do it fast? He had played his trump card with the story about the hidden item. Could he now play it again?

'What's your answer?' Paul shouted.

He had to force their hand. He had to make them react more quickly or everything would be lost. Everything he'd gone through would be for nothing.

'Let me out and I'll take you to the place where I hid it,' he called more insistently.

Silence.

'There isn't much time left,' he reminded them. 'You don't want to let me suffocate before you can get me out. That wouldn't help you, would it?'

No response.

'You've got my confession,' he reminded them. 'As soon as I've shown you where I hid it you can turn me over to the police. I won't try and escape, I promise. There'd be no point. You know where I live; you know what I look like. You could lead them straight to me if I managed to get away. Whatever happens, you've won. You've got what you wanted. You wanted justice for your daughter. You wanted a confession. You've got them.'

A hiss of static came from the speakers but nothing more.

Paul took another tainted breath, thinking how bitter

the air tasted. He tried to take a deep breath but it was becoming more difficult to fill his lungs. He coughed and felt a burning sensation at the back of his throat.

'There isn't much time,' he called, trying to remind his captors of a fact that he himself was becoming all too aware. 'What's your answer?'

And still from the speakers inside the box there was only silence.

71

'What are we going to do?' Gina Hacket asked. 'He's right about the oxygen inside the coffin. If it runs out and he dies before he can tell us what he took from Laura then what's the point of all this?'

Frank didn't answer.

He got to his feet and began pacing the Portakabin slowly, his feet beating out a tattoo on the damp floor.

'Frank,' Gina persisted.

'I'm thinking,' he snapped.

He continued to pace.

'What could he have taken?' he murmured. 'How do we know he's not bluffing?'

'We don't. We'll just have to trust him.'

'Trust the man who raped and murdered our daughter?'

'We haven't got any choice.'

'At the moment he's under our control. It's in our hands whether or not he lives or dies. He knows that. The only way he can change that situation is by getting out of that coffin, and the only people who can get him out are us.'

'And if we leave him then we'll never know what he took from Laura. He'll have won, Frank, because he'll have that knowledge and we won't.'

'Just think for a minute. When you picked up Laura's clothes from hospital was everything there? Every single item of clothing?'

'Socks, skirt, blouse, tie and knickers. Yes, it was all there. I already had the cardigan.'

'So it wasn't an item of clothing that he took and kept.'

'A body part?'

Gina put a hand to her mouth.

'Oh, my God,' she murmured.

'What else could it be?' Frank asked, still pacing.

'So he took a part of her away, cut it out or hacked it off and he kept it?'

'That's what it looks like.'

Gina clamped her jaws together hard. For a moment she thought she was going to be sick.

'What kind of man does that to an eight-year-old girl?' Frank mused. 'What kind of monster?'

'What do you think it was, Frank?' Gina wanted to know.

'I don't know,' he sighed tearfully. 'A finger? An ear? A toe?'

'But I saw her body in the morgue. I would have noticed.'

'In the state you were in? Gina, you wouldn't have noticed if one of her arms had been missing. What mother would? And that's what he's banking on now.'

'But if he'd cut part of her away it would have been in the police report, like you said.'

'Not necessarily. They might have thought it was one of the injuries that caused her death. There were quite a few wounds on her body, weren't there?'

Gina nodded slowly, tears welling up in her eyes.

'So, do you think he's bluffing or not?' she wanted to know. 'Why tell us so much about what he did to her? He couldn't have made that up, Frank.'

Still he paced the small area, his face now set in hard lines, the knot of muscles at the side of his jaw pulsing.

'What if it's at his flat?' Frank said finally. 'What if the thing he took from her is at his flat?'

'I'm not with you.'

'Murderers keep mementos of their crimes but they'd want to keep them nearby, wouldn't they? If he took something from Laura then he'd want it close to him, so he could look at it when he wanted to. I bet it's in his flat.'

'Even if it is you couldn't get back there in time to find it. It might take hours and he's running out of oxygen.'

Frank hesitated.

'We've got no choice, Frank, we've got to let him out,' Gina insisted.

'I told you what has to happen if we do.'

'He has to be killed.'

'And we both have to do it. For every time I hit him you have to hit him. For every time I stick a knife in him you have to.'

'I don't care. I'll do it. For Laura's sake I'll do it.'

Frank stopped pacing and stood motionless in the middle of the floor, his head bowed as if in thought. Or prayer.

'Once he's dead we just put him back in the coffin and bury it again,' he said evenly.

298

Gina nodded enthusiastically.

'It'll be the way it was meant to be in the first place,' Frank went on. 'With him buried the police will never find him. They still won't know where he is. It'll be days before he's even reported missing. As long as we make sure we clean everything afterwards and don't leave any footprints or fingerprints or any kind of evidence, then we'll be all right.'

'Are we going to let him out?' Gina asked, the question hanging in the air.

Frank had his back to her now, his head still bowed.

'He could still be lying,' he told her. 'But we have to know. And if he's telling the truth, and he did take something from Laura, then we've got to get it back. For her sake.'

Again Gina nodded.

Frank crossed to the microphone and leaned close to it.

'Can you hear me?' he said.

'Yes,' Paul's voice came back.

'If you're lying I'll kill you. I swear to God I'll kill you,' Frank rasped. 'And I'll take my time doing it. I'll make you suffer like you can't imagine.'

'Get me out, I'm running out of oxygen,' Paul told him.

Frank stepped away from the microphone. He looked at Gina.

'I'm going to get him out,' he said flatly. 'I'm going to dig him up.'

72

'I'm coming to get you.'

Paul heard the words reverberate inside the coffin and it was all he could do to stifle a shout of triumphant relief.

It had worked. His final gambit had been successful. He'd talked his way into release.

But it only begins now. You've still got to get past whoever's up there. You've got to get away from them and they'll be ready for you. Anyone who goes to these lengths to punish the man they think has murdered their child will be prepared for all eventualities.

But the first step was accomplished. The initial and most difficult aspect was taken care of. He had secured a way out.

Paul tried to breathe more slowly, knowing that time was now more his enemy than the maniacs who had imprisoned him. He lay still and began to consider what he could do next. He thought of each option, running it through his mind with the kind of consideration he'd become all too familiar with during his time below ground.

On the assumption that they actually manage to free you before you suffocate, what is your next move?

What if they're armed?

Paul had considered the possibility but the prospect of facing a loaded gun seemed insignificant compared with what he'd already gone through. At least if his captors did have guns then he would have a chance to fight back in a way that he hadn't had before. It didn't matter what weapons they carried. At least, once he was freed from the coffin, he would have the chance to use his strength and power against them. This was no longer a battle of wits (which he felt he'd already won) but now it was to become a physical contest and he was confident of his own abilities in that area.

Why so confident? Your body's stiff from lying in this fucking coffin for so long. Your right hand is virtually useless where you tore the nails and got that splinter jammed in it. In a fight you've only got one good hand.

But, Paul comforted himself, he had the strength that rage and desperation brought with them.

So you don't think that their rage at losing a child matches that? They went to the bother of kidnapping you and putting you six feet under in a coffin. I'd say that you didn't have the monopoly on rage.

He lay still, hoping to hear some sound from above. The beginnings of excavation or exhumation. The beginnings of his release.

So far there was nothing.

Now, think this through. Once they start digging you've got to have things clear in your mind. You've got to know what your course of action is.

Would they, Paul wondered, bother to haul the coffin from its hole in the ground? That was, he told himself, unlikely. It would take too much effort. Once the lid was off he could be dragged free, pulled from what was beginning to look like his final resting place. They wanted him out now as much as he wanted to escape. They wouldn't waste time.

So, once the lid was prised off, what then? He wondered if he should just lie still and pretend to be unconscious so that they moved closer to him. If they did that it would make them easier targets. He could just grab them.

Both at once? How do you fight two people at the same time? You're not exactly well versed in the art of brawling, are you? How many times have you ever hit a man, or been hit, for that matter? This isn't the movies where the good guy knocks out his tormentor with one lucky punch.

If only he had some kind of weapon with which to fight back. A knife or a piece of wood. Anything.

If they're armed it won't matter.

But it was a big if, Paul told himself. Perhaps they weren't. Perhaps they didn't have weapons of any kind. They hadn't needed them to begin with and they hadn't expected they would. He might be lucky and find them even more bemused and off balance than he himself had been at the outset. This was not in their original scheme, he would have bet money on that. Digging him up again hadn't been part of their plan. They hadn't expected him to turn the tables on them psychologically; there was no reason to think they'd been anywhere near ready for the developments that were now taking place.

Don't get cocky, for Christ's sake. Just because you might have

*outsmarted them once doesn't change things that much. They're
still in control at the moment. They're in control until the time
you're standing over them ready to call the police. Or kill them.*

Paul lay perfectly still, the thoughts tumbling through
his mind.

They deserved to pay for what they'd put him through.
Maybe calling the police on them wasn't retribution
enough.

*So what are you going to do, hard nut? Kill them both? Beat
them to death? Stab them? Bury them alive?*

For one insane but deliriously ironic moment that
thought stuck in his mind and refused to budge.

Yes, that would be so achingly poetic and just. To bury
them in the hole that they'd buried him in. Push their
unconscious forms into this very hole and then shovel the
earth on top of them. Once that was done he could stand
there beside the grave for as long as he wanted, knowing
that his tormentors were beneath him. Knowing that
revenge had been exacted in the most apt and pleasing
way. Paul even managed a smile. A smile of victory and
anticipation.

*No. You're getting overconfident again. Cocky bastard. It'll be
your downfall. Don't underestimate these fuckers. To go to the
lengths they've gone to they could quite possibly be mad and
madmen don't play by the rules.*

He nodded to himself, aware that the knowledge of his
impending release was overriding any other thoughts inside
his head. He knew that he had to control his elation no
matter how hard that was. The struggle so far had been
psychological. From the time the coffin was opened, it
would become physical.

Or would it?

His hands and feet weren't tied. Once the lid was lifted, he told himself, he could burst free, clamber out of the grave and run like hell. It wouldn't matter where or in which direction as long as it was as far as possible from the grave and his captors.

He could take them by surprise. They wouldn't be expecting that. There was no need for a fight. No need for physical confrontation if he could run quickly enough. The idea appealed to him more than a battle with his captors but he considered he might have no other choice but to fight.

Then use everything you've got. Your strength, anger and frustration. Channel it all into fighting back. Show these bastards what a mistake they made messing with you in the first place.

He clenched both fists, wincing when he felt the pain from his right hand. However, that pain was rapidly overshadowed by the continued thoughts of freedom. Surely it couldn't be long now.

He took another mouthful of thick, bitter, reeking air and prayed that he was right.

73

'You stay here,' Frank Hacket said, turning towards the door of the Portakabin.

Gina was already on her feet.

'But you said I had to help you,' she protested.

'I've got to get him out of the coffin first,' Frank reminded her. 'I'll come back when I'm ready. When it's open.'

'I want to help, Frank.'

'It won't take me long.'

As he spoke he dug his hand into one pocket of his jacket and pulled out the pillowcase he'd stuck there when they'd first arrived. He'd removed it from the head of Paul Crane just before he'd closed the coffin lid.

'What are you going to do with that?' Gina wanted to know.

'We can't let him see our faces.'

'If we're going to kill him what does it matter if he sees us?'

'Do you want him looking into your eyes when you

push a knife into his throat? Do you want him staring at you when you're smashing his head in with a brick?'

Gina held her husband's gaze for a moment then shook her head.

He brandished the pillowcase before him.

'Talk to him,' he instructed.

Gina looked vague for a second then she sat down at the microphone, but her eyes were still on her husband as he stood by the door of the Portakabin.

As she watched he pulled a hypodermic needle from his other pocket. It was already filled with clear fluid.

'There's enough here to subdue him,' Frank said. 'Not as much as I gave him when I broke into his flat but enough so that we can keep him under control once we get him out of the coffin.'

He slipped the needle back into his pocket and headed out of the door, closing it behind him.

Gina sat motionless for a moment, hearing his footsteps die away the further he got from the small building. It had been raining outside and his feet sploshed through the mud as he walked. She wondered if it would make disinterring the coffin more difficult and if it would take longer.

She turned back to the microphone.

'This doesn't mean you're going to get away with what you did,' she said quietly. 'If you try and trick us we'll kill you.'

'You were going to kill me anyway,' Paul answered.

Gina sat silently for a moment, gazing at the microphone as if it was somehow a conduit into the coffin. She wished she could see this man's face. She wanted to look at him. She would have preferred to look into his eyes.

At first she wanted to see his fear as he realised that he was caught like a rat in a trap. She had wanted to enjoy his terror and his knowledge that he was going to die.

'Tell me why,' she murmured.

'Why what?' Paul asked.

'Why it had to be my daughter?'

'I've already told you. She was unlucky. It could have been anyone's daughter.'

'What makes you think you've got the right to take a life the way you did? No one but God has a right to do that.'

'Do you still believe in God after what happened to your little girl?'

Gina actually managed a bitter smile.

'I've never been very religious,' she confessed. 'I did like most people, I suppose. I only went to church for christenings, marriages and funerals. I always said I believed in God because I didn't know what else to say. I believed in something. Not the old man sitting on a cloud looking down at everything from Heaven. Not that kind of God, but I always thought that there was something there. Some kind of all-powerful thing, you know, like a sort of superhero.' She laughed but it had a hollow sound and echoed around the Portakabin like an afterthought. 'I prayed to God when Laura was missing. I prayed that she'd come home safely. When I saw the police car pull up outside the house I prayed that they weren't coming with bad news. When they took us to the hospital I prayed that it wasn't her on the slab. I prayed that it was someone else's daughter.' She paused contemplatively. 'Do you think I was wrong to do that? To wish that kind of suffering on someone else?'

'No,' Paul answered. 'Anyone in your position would have done the same.'

'Did you ever think about how what you did would affect the family of that child?'

The question was asked almost matter-of-factly, conversationally.

'No,' Paul murmured. 'You never think of the pain you're causing others when you do something wrong.'

'That's true,' Gina agreed. 'You never think about it until it's too late and they've already been hurt, and by that time there's nothing you can do to make things better. No matter how hard you try you've still caused the pain and there's no way to stop it hurting.'

'Have you hurt people?'

Silence greeted the question and it remained unbroken for more than a minute.

74

Paul Crane shifted uncomfortably inside the coffin.

He could hear a slight hissing coming from the speakers but other than that there was no sound at all.

Now you've done it. You've pushed too far.

He took a small breath, feeling a growing pain in his chest.

'Hello,' he called tentatively.

There was still no answer.

You've fucked it up. This late in the day, when you actually had a chance of getting out, you've fucked it up.

Paul clamped his jaws together tightly, that all too familiar feeling of icy coldness spilling through him yet again.

'Hello, can you hear me?' he repeated, his tone more insistent this time.

'I didn't hurt them in the way you have,' the voice suddenly intoned and Paul let out an audible sigh of relief.

'Thank God,' he whispered.

'Not physically,' the voice went on. 'But I've hurt them emotionally.'

'How?' Paul enquired.

'I've done things I'm not proud of to people I love.'

'So have I.'

'Who?'

'My girlfriend,' he said, his voice cracking. 'I've lied to her about things. I've betrayed her trust.'

'I've done the same things to my husband and I'd do anything to change it. I wish I could start my life over again and not make so many mistakes.'

'Don't we all.'

'They say that as long as you learn by your mistakes then it's all right. I wish I could believe that.'

'I swore to myself that if I ever got a second chance I'd grab it with both hands.'

'People don't get second chances.'

'They do sometimes.'

'Not people like me. I think my life was mapped out for me from the beginning and there's no way I can change it.'

'What's so wrong with your life?'

'No money. No future. No dreams, not any more. My marriage is a disaster. My life is a mess.'

'Thanks to me.'

'I wish I could blame it all on you but I can't. My life was worthless even before you did what you did to my daughter.'

'And will killing me make your life better?'

'It'll make me feel better for a little while and a little is better than nothing.'

Paul wanted to disagree but couldn't find the words.

'My girlfriend will be devastated when she knows I'm missing,' he said at last.

'It's a bit late to expect any sympathy,' the voice warned.

'Avenging angels shouldn't ask for sympathy from their victims, is that it?'

'What does that mean?'

'It's a line from a film. I can't remember which one. It seemed appropriate. All sorts of lines from films have been going around in my head. Stuff from films and from songs, things I thought I'd forgotten. Memories from childhood and other times of my life.'

'Good memories?'

'Some of them.'

'Better than mine, I bet.'

'Is your life that bad?'

'Bad enough.'

Paul could hear the despair in her voice despite the distortion imposed on her voice by the speakers.

'Your girlfriend will know how I feel when you're dead. She'll know what it's like to lose someone she loves.'

'But she wouldn't even have known I was dead, would she? Not if you'd left me to rot in this coffin. My body might never have been found. People would think I'd just disappeared.'

'I used to think that was what I would have wanted with Laura. You know, that she'd just disappeared. I thought I would have been able to cope better if there was just the slim chance that one day she'd be found. But then I thought it was better to know than not to know. That's the only reason we're letting you out. That's why I need to know what you took from her and where you hid it. Then it really will be over.'

'And you'll kill me?'

Gina didn't answer. She merely stared blankly into space, tears coming to her eyes. She ran a hand through her auburn hair, her fingers shaking slightly.

'Wouldn't you do the same in my position?' she asked. 'If someone had done the same thing to your girlfriend, wouldn't you want to hurt them? Kill them?'

'Yes,' Paul said without hesitation.

There was a long silence finally broken by Gina.

'You said you hurt her, lied to her,' she reminded him. 'What did you do?'

'I cheated on her.'

'Who with?'

'With some other women. There were two or three one-night stands but she forgave those. She never found out about the affairs. If she had I think she'd have finished with me.'

'Do you blame her?'

'No, I don't. I would have deserved it.'

'How many affairs were there?'

'Two.'

'Are they over now?'

'One is.'

'And the other one?'

'I see her a couple of times a month.'

'Do you love her, this woman you're seeing?'

'No.'

'So it's just sex.'

'Yes.'

'So you're using this woman, too?'

'We're using each other. I get what I want and she gets what she wants.'

'Do you even know what she wants? Do you even care?'

'We have a good time together. I like her.'

'Is she good in bed?'

'I'm not an expert.'

'You've had plenty of women by the sound of it. Were they good in bed? Were they better than this woman you're seeing now?'

'They were different. All of them were different.'

'Every woman's the same, isn't she? I thought men like you looked at them all in the same way. Three holes to use and not much else, is that it?'

'No, it's not. That's not how I look at women.'

'Really?'

'Your husband might be the same as me. How do you know he doesn't think of women like that?'

'I know him. He's not like that. He's got more respect for women.'

'But you haven't got any respect for him, have you? If you had you wouldn't have hurt him the way you said you have.'

'I didn't mean to hurt him. I didn't want him to find out I was cheating on him.'

'So you had an affair?'

'Yes.'

'Why?'

'Because I wanted something more out of life. Some excitement. Anything other than the usual drudgery and disappointment.'

'And your husband found out about it?'

'He did the first time. He doesn't know about the affair I'm having at the moment.'

'Are you frightened he'd throw you out?'

'I know he wouldn't.'

'You seem very sure.'

'He obviously loves you. He was willing to kill for you.'

Paul found himself surrounded by silence once again. He could hear the sound of his own heartbeat. The pain in his chest was still there but he tried to ignore it, fearing that the extra stress might bring on the heart attack he was so terrified of. He stroked his chest with one hand and hoped that the pain would diminish.

'Don't try and judge me,' the voice offered.

'I'm the last person to judge anyone,' Paul conceded.

'You don't know anything about me.'

'I know something. We've been talking for long enough.'

'Long enough for you to confess.'

'That's what you wanted. I told you what you wanted to hear.'

'I wanted to hear the truth.'

'The truth hurts.'

'Very funny. You think you're so clever, don't you?'

'If I was that clever I wouldn't have let myself get caught by you and your husband.'

'You would have been caught eventually,' she told him.

'But not by you,' Paul murmured, his words muffled by the thick and oppressive atmosphere inside the coffin. Every breath now tasted bitter to him. It was as if the air was solid and he was trying to digest it rather than inhale it.

Then, above him, he heard something.

75

Paul strained his ears to try and pick out the exact nature of the sound.

There was a dull thud followed by a sound that reminded him of a dog's low growl.

It was almost rhythmic.

The thud then the growl. Always the same.

No, not a growl but a scraping. A thud then a scraping. As if someone was digging.

'Oh, God,' he said aloud.

That was it. It was digging. They were getting closer to the coffin. The initial thud must have been the sound of the shovel hitting the earth and the scraping was the mud being removed from it.

His entire body began to tingle. He even momentarily forgot the pain in his chest.

He wondered how far away the digger was? Two feet or less? He guessed that it could be only a matter of minutes now before he was released.

'Come on, come on,' he said encouragingly.

The impacts from above seemed to increase in speed and volume. Paul tried to picture the grave being dug into, the shovelsful of earth being tossed aside wantonly. He could barely control himself he was so overcome with the thought of being freed from this place.

Out of the frying pan into the fire?

Perhaps: but at least once the lid was off he would have a fighting chance.

Paul wondered why he hadn't heard the impact of shovel on earth earlier. Surely, he reasoned, he would have been able to detect the passage through the earth. It was deathly silent inside the coffin; the slightest noise reached his ears easily and they must have been digging for at least twenty minutes or half an hour to be as close as they were.

You don't know how close they are. They might just have started. Sound carries down here.

No. He told himself that was impossible. For the impacts to be so loud, they must be close. The two feet or less that he'd estimated.

You've got absolutely no way of telling. They could be another half an hour or even longer from getting you out. And you haven't got enough oxygen for that kind of delay.

Paul's feeling of elation receded slightly. Had time indeed run out for him? The irony of the situation was almost unbearable. To come so close to release only to die of suffocation or heart attack. What a stupid way to die, he thought, as he tried to concentrate more on the sound of the shovel in the earth above him rather than his own imminent demise.

The pain in his chest was still there and he placed one

hand on his sternum as if that simple act would remove the discomfort.

It didn't.

Above him the impacts were growing louder, Paul was sure of that. He wondered if both of his captors were digging, eager to release him from the coffin, desperate to free him so that he could tell them the information they so desperately sought.

And what then? What are you going to tell them?

Paul hadn't thought about that. All that had occupied his mind since he'd been told he was to be released from the coffin was the thought of breathing fresh air again. He wanted to feel the rain and the wind on his skin and every other cliché that was the province of great poets and bad writers. He wanted to savour those things. He wanted to make the most of every single second that was to come.

Unless they just whack you with a shovel as soon as the coffin lid is lifted.

'No, they won't do that,' Paul said aloud. 'They can't risk killing me. Not now. Not yet.'

'What did you say?'

The question echoed around the inside of the coffin.

Paul started. He'd almost forgotten the voice.

That means there's only one of them digging.

'You spoke,' the voice continued. 'What did you say?'

'I need to get out of here,' Paul said. 'The oxygen must be nearly gone by now.'

'There's enough left.'

'How can you be sure?'

'You'll be out in five or ten minutes.'

'And if I'm not you'll have wasted your time.'

There was a touch of desperation in Paul's tone now. The pain in his chest was growing more intense. It felt as if someone was sitting on his ribs, pushing down harder with each passing second. He tried to take a deep breath but it was as if his lungs wouldn't expand.

'Oh no, not now,' he whispered. 'Please.'

Above him, the sound grew louder. The impact was more distinct.

'Hurry,' he called, as if the entreaty would speed his rescuer. 'Get me out.'

He closed his eyes, keeping the lids clamped shut.

'Tell him to hurry,' Paul called to the voice. 'Tell him to get a move on or I'll be dead by the time he opens this fucking box.'

'Just calm down,' the voice chided.

'I'm the one in a fucking coffin six feet underground, not you. Don't tell me to calm down,' Paul roared. 'I'm only here because you put me here.'

'You're there because you murdered our daughter, in case you'd forgotten,' snarled the voice with equal vehemence.

Paul didn't answer. He was listening to the sounds from above him.

Surely it could only be a matter of minutes now.

But how many minutes?

The pain in his chest continued to grow in intensity. Paul was feeling faint. He banged his injured hand against the side of the coffin.

The pain shot through his hand and arm, jolting him from head to toe. It had the desired effect, though, momentarily clearing his head. Even the pain in his chest seemed to recede slightly.

Thank God.

The respite was fleeting and the pain flowed back through him with seemingly renewed ferocity.

This is it. You're going to die. It's going to end now. After all these hours of clinging on to life and to hope, it's all going to come to an end right here and now. Moments before your release.

Paul tried to shift on to his side as much as the confines of the box would allow. It was as if he was trying to shift the weight that he imagined was pressing down on his ribcage. He managed to twist part of his upper body but the effort was far more exacting than it had been earlier.

There was a thunderous crash from only inches above him and he slumped on to his back, his hands rising before him.

The shovel had struck the lid of the coffin.

76

This was it, his mind screamed. The time for freedom had come at last.

Beyond the coffin lay clean air and life.

And two vengeful parents.

That didn't matter to Paul. All he knew was that he was going to be out of the coffin in a matter of moments. Once the screws or nails were removed he would be free.

He heard another loud bang on the lid of the box and he lay still, waiting.

There was movement next to the coffin as well and Paul guessed that the person who'd dug him up was now standing in the hole that contained him. He could hear footsteps moving around and even across the box.

He wondered what he should do next. Considering his next move helped to take his thoughts away from the pain in his chest. He attempted to focus on the chain of events that would occur in the next few moments rather than dwell on the extreme discomfort he still felt.

He had, Paul told himself, had long enough to consider his course of action. It was now time to set it in motion.

There was more movement outside the box. He heard a scraping at the foot of the coffin. Something hard and metallic was being scratched across it. Was the person outside loosening the first of the screws that held the lid in place, he asked himself. When the same sound was repeated at the other side of the coffin just moments later, he was sure that was the case. There were two screws at the foot, two at the side and two at the top. Once those were removed he would be able to push the lid off. He would be able to spring upwards like some malevolent Jack-in-the-box and begin the fight against those who had imprisoned him and tried to kill him.

Whatever happened then, this particular part of the nightmare would be over.

Paul lay still and very slowly raised his hands so that they were touching the lid of the coffin, his fingers gliding over the satin there.

To his left he heard the sound of another screw being removed.

He kept his hands in place, tensing the muscles in his arms but not pushing against the wood and material just yet.

There was a loud thump on the lid and he pulled his hands away quickly.

It wasn't as powerful as the sound of the shovel hitting the box. This was a different kind of noise. Paul realised that whoever was out there had probably stepped on the coffin, using it as a stepping stone to reach the other side and, sure enough, within moments he heard the fourth screw being worked on. He also heard a grunt and a muttered curse as the screwdriver slipped. There was silence for a second then the work began again as the digger continued loosening the fourth screw.

Paul sucked in a lungful of the acrid air and held it, preparing himself. He felt as if his muscles were on fire but now they burned with the desire to escape and also with the strength that came with anger. For hours, held captive inside the coffin, he had swayed madly between one extreme of emotion and another. Fear, terror, frustration, sorrow and anger had all filled him at various points and now he was allowing the rage to take over. For with that rage came hope.

Paul's hands clenched into fists. He rested them gently against the lid once again then withdrew them slowly, repeating the procedure a number of times as if he was pumping his arm muscles in preparation for what was to come.

When he heard the fifth screw being loosened he could barely control himself. His entire body was shaking, filled as it was with adrenaline. His heart was thundering against his ribs and he could hear the blood rushing in his ears. He was breathing rapidly and the taste and smell of the vile air filling the coffin didn't seem to bother him any longer, any more than the light-headedness and the pain in his chest. He raised and lowered his arms again and again, the motions becoming faster but more controlled. He didn't want the one digging him up to know that he was prepared. There must be no warning. When he made his attack it must be with the benefit of surprise.

Paul heard more scrambling outside the coffin and his

head turned instinctively towards the head of the coffin and the area where he knew the sixth screw must be. He waited for the sound of the screwdriver but it didn't come.

His breathing slowed a little as he wondered what his captors were doing. Why the delay? They were so close to uncovering him now. What was taking them so long to remove the last screw?

Unless, he reasoned, they had some plan of their own they wanted to put into operation before the lid was removed.

He lay still, arms now at his sides, his eyes closed.

Waiting.

Somewhere above him he heard muffled speech.

He was certain of it. They must both be there now. Looking down upon the coffin and preparing to open it. Paul strained his ears to try and pick out the words.

One of the voices sounded further away than the other. But, whatever the case, Paul could now definitely pick them out as male and female and it sounded as if the man was the one standing over the coffin. Perhaps, he reasoned, that was why the woman's voice sounded further away; she must be standing at the graveside. The man was actually down in the hole with the box. And with the screwdriver, ready to remove the last screw. The last obstacle to Paul's freedom.

He allowed his head to loll to one side and tried to relax his body as best he could. This was all part of his plan. He wanted to make them think that he was unconscious when they opened the coffin. Lull *them* into a false sense of security until the time came to strike back.

Paul swallowed and managed to reduce his breathing to

shallow breaths. His chest was barely rising and falling as he swallowed and then exhaled the rancid air inside the coffin. But, again, his mind shrieked the question that was bothering him so much. Why were they taking so long to remove the last screw?

He heard the voices again. The man first.

Paul tried to pick out words once more and this time it seemed a little easier.

'This is it,' came the man's voice. 'Are you ready?'

'Open it,' the woman replied.

'Are you sure?' the man queried.

'We've got to,' the woman insisted. 'Do it now. Do it before he runs out of oxygen.'

Paul heard them for the first time with no distortion. Not through inferior speakers but separated from him by only the thickness of the coffin lid and the noises made him shudder. Especially the voice of the woman. He didn't know why but something deep inside him froze. His mind was telling him something that couldn't be possible. Something that every fibre of his being tried to deny and, yet, the feeling persisted.

'Open it,' the woman repeated. 'Before it's too late.'

Once more he was gripped by that same feeling. Shaken by a growing conviction deep within him. A conviction based on the sound of her voice.

Then, the sound he had prayed for. The sound of the sixth screw being removed.

77

The last screw was being removed with less haste than the previous five, Paul was certain of that.

Each turn seemed to take an eternity.

He told himself that he must keep calm. If his plan was to work he couldn't show that he was conscious. They had to think that he was unconscious. That was the only way this would work.

The screwdriver slipped again, gouging into the wood, and Paul heard more curses from beyond the lid of the box.

There couldn't be long now, he told himself.

The man returned to his task, the screw slowly but surely coming free.

And then there was silence.

It was done, Paul assumed. The lid had been freed. There was nothing more between him and fresh air except an inch of wood that he only needed to push hard to remove. But, for all that, he remained still, motionless, within his cocoon of wood and satin.

He heard more movement. He was aware of someone standing over him.

There was a scraping sound and the lid was moved slightly to one side, Paul could see that much through his half-closed eyes.

He had to fight to control his desire to yell out his delight and relief but he won that battle and he stayed silent and still as the coffin lid was slid further off.

Paul felt fresh air flooding across him and he had to resist the temptation to suck in huge mouthfuls of it for fear of giving himself away. They must not know he was conscious. They must think he was comatose at the very least. He had to make them think they were too late. That they'd played their murderous game for too long.

The coffin lid was eased a little further back and now he could see upwards through his slit-like eyes.

It was dark. The night sky was black and unforgiving. No light flooded the box, just more darkness, but it was blackness he could see through, unlike the horrific blackness that had enveloped him inside the coffin.

'He's passed out,' the man observed, pulling something from his jacket pocket.

He was aware of a figure bending over him and that that figure was trying to wrap something around his head. Paul recognised the smell of washing powder on the material just as he knew that what was being forced on to his head was a pillowcase.

'No, I want to see his face,' the woman called from the graveside, and now the feeling Paul had experienced earlier hit him so hard it was as if all the wind had been knocked from him. 'Don't cover his face.'

He jerked his eyes open.

He recognised her voice.

All thoughts of plans and all preparation were discarded.

Paul sat bolt upright and grabbed at the man, who took a step back, almost slipping on the wet earth. It was raining and obviously had been for some time. There were several small puddles around the graveside.

'Watch him,' the woman shouted and Paul looked up to see that she was standing not six feet above him but less than eighteen inches.

He hadn't been buried in a proper grave but, rather, placed in a hastily dug shallow hole.

The earth around it had not been packed tight but only tossed loosely on to the coffin lid. This had been no premature burial but merely a hasty act of concealment.

Paul tried to grab the man as he rose from the coffin.

He actually managed to rise to his haunches and beyond, his eyes darting back and forth between the man who stood in the grave with him and the woman who stood to his right.

He locked eyes with her briefly and saw the look of horror on her own face.

Then the man facing him grabbed the shovel and swung it.

The metal blade caught Paul on the side of the head and the impact sent him sprawling. For one terrible moment he thought he was going to black out again but he somehow managed to remain conscious despite the savage blow he'd sustained.

He landed face down on the wet earth but the sensation seemed to revive him and he rolled over on to his back in time to avoid a second swing of the shovel that missed him by inches and thudded into the earth at the side of the grave.

Paul kicked out and caught the man in the thigh rather than in the groin, as he had intended. However, the blow was enough to make him stagger and the man stumbled slightly as he tried to pull the shovel free to swing it again. But Paul too grabbed for the shaft and gripped it with one bloodied hand.

The other man was stronger and he tugged the shovel free from Paul's grip.

'Help me,' he shouted to the woman, but she was now standing transfixed, watching the struggle but seemingly helpless to intervene.

'Gina.'

It was Paul who called her name.

He could feel something warm running down the side of his face and realised that the impact of the shovel must have opened a cut just below the hairline, but that seemed unimportant now as he ducked to avoid another blow from what was fast becoming a deadly weapowe.

The woman was looking at him, dumbstruck.

'Help me,' Frank Hacket roared again. 'He'll get away.'

He caught Paul in the ribs with a powerful blow that knocked the wind from him and cracked a bone. Sharp pain lanced through his side but he fought on, advancing towards his attacker, launching himself at the man who couldn't reset himself quickly enough to repel the assault.

Paul slammed into him and knocked him off his feet as the woman screamed.

'You fucking bastard,' Paul shouted, pushing his hand

into the man's face, trying to shove his head into the soft dirt below.

Frank Hacket brought one knee up into Paul's groin with incredible force and the pain forced him to roll to one side.

He tried to rise but Hacket swung the shovel again and connected with a heavy blow across Paul's shoulder. The impact knocked him sideways and he slipped in the mud as he tried to get up. Hacket hit him again and, as Paul raised his hand to protect his head, the shovel shattered his left wrist.

White-hot pain enveloped his arm and he fell to his knees, unable to clench his fist, so great was the pain.

'You murdering bastard,' Hacket shouted, advancing on him.

'I never touched your daughter,' Paul screamed. 'I swear to God.'

'You said you killed her,' Hacket reminded him, his face contorted with rage. 'You told us everything.'

'I made it up to get out of that coffin,' Paul said, trying to back away.

Gina Hacket moved nearer to the two men, her eyes darting back and forth.

'Paul,' she murmured.

'I never touched your daughter, Gina,' Paul gasped. 'You know I wouldn't do something like that. You know me.'

'But all those things you said,' she muttered. 'How could anyone make up things like that unless they'd done them? How could anyone pretend to have feelings like the ones you talked about? You couldn't lie about everything.'

'He wasn't lying,' Frank snarled. 'That's why he's here now.'

'I lied about *everything*,' Paul told them. 'I used my imagination. Think about it. What information did I give you that you didn't already know? I asked you questions about what the police told you. I didn't give you information, I just embellished stuff that you told me. When you asked me something specific I couldn't tell you. You asked me the colour of her uniform and I couldn't tell you. If I'd killed her I'd have known that. Think about it. I knew that in your state you'd never realise. I knew that you'd believe me because you wanted to.'

'You killed my daughter,' Frank Hacket hissed at Paul. 'You fucked my wife and you killed my daughter.' He turned to look at Gina with hatred in his eyes. 'I should have buried you in that fucking hole with him, you slag.'

'You knew all the time?' Gina murmured.

'About you and him?' he rasped. 'Of *course* I knew. I'm not as stupid as you think I am. You'd be surprised at how many times I've followed you to that grotty little hotel where he takes you. I've waited outside there dozens of times knowing what you two were doing in that room.'

Gina took a step back, her feet sinking in the mud.

Paul was standing motionless, the rain coursing down his face.

Frank held the shovel before him, ready to strike again. It seemed just a question of which one of them he chose to hit first.

330

78

'Why like this?' Paul wanted to know. 'If you knew then why go to such lengths to get back at me? Why not just run me down in the street?'

'You deserved to suffer,' Frank told him. He glared at Gina. 'Both of you. I knew that you'd recognise his voice straight away unless I did something to the microphones and speakers inside the coffin. If you'd known you were talking to your boyfriend then you'd never have gone along with this. Why do you think he had a pillowcase covering his head when I brought him out? I couldn't let you see his face. But to have you talking to him as he died, that was real justice.' He smiled crookedly.

'Frank, I'm sorry,' Gina murmured.

'Don't insult my intelligence by apologising,' he snapped. 'How many times have I heard your apologies in the past? How many times will I hear them in the future? Keep your apologies, Gina. You don't mean them anyway.'

'Did he kill Laura?' Gina asked, looking at Paul and then at her husband.

'Of course I didn't,' Paul snapped. 'He wants you to believe that because he wants you to help him kill me.'

'Shut your mouth,' Frank rasped. 'Murderer.'

'Gina, you've got to believe me,' Paul pleaded. 'Why would I do that? I'm not a murderer and I'd never hurt a child. I told you what you wanted to hear because I wanted to get out of that coffin. I made it all up. Nothing was true. You should know that.'

'What about the other things you said?' Gina enquired. 'About hurting people? Hurting your girlfriend. Was that true?'

'You wanted a confession and you got one,' Paul told her flatly. 'I'd have said anything to get out. I'd have done anything to get out. Anyone would.'

'Liar,' snarled Frank. 'You told her what happened because that was what you did.'

'You know that's not true,' Paul countered. 'The only reason you wanted me dead was because I was seeing your wife. It was never anything to do with your daughter's death.'

'*Seeing my wife*,' Frank sneered. 'I like your choice of words. Very discreet. But, then, I suppose both of you learned to be discreet during your affair.'

'Frank, please,' Gina said quietly. 'You said you wanted it to finish here and it should.'

'She's right,' Paul said. 'Finish it now. Let me walk away and you'll never see me or hear of me again. I'll leave here. I'll go away.'

'And you think that will make things better?' Frank

chided. 'You think that will stop all the pain that you've both inflicted?'

Frank hefted the shovel before him menacingly, his eyes again darting back and forth.

The rain continued to lash down.

Paul wondered if he could turn and run. They didn't appear to be in a graveyard but on a piece of waste ground. The hole that he'd been lowered into was less than two feet deep, hastily dug and not even properly rectangular in shape. Rain was already collecting at the bottom of it.

'Gina, tell him I wouldn't hurt your daughter,' Paul said tentatively. 'You know that.'

'Don't speak to her,' Frank snapped. 'Who are you going to believe, Gina? How many lies has he already told you? What's he promised you when you're together? What's he told you he'll give you that he never will? He's a liar, you know that. You know you can't trust him. Why believe him when he says he didn't kill Laura?'

'On my mother's life,' Paul said. 'I don't even know what your daughter looks like.'

He took a step towards Gina, who looked first at Frank then met Paul's gaze. Rain was running down her cheeks and Paul suspected that some of it was mixed with tears.

'He killed her, Gina,' Frank insisted.

'I would never hurt anyone,' Paul told her, moving closer.

'He's a liar,' Frank went on. 'A stinking liar. How many more of his lies are you going to listen to?'

Gina looked imploringly at Paul, her eyes wide, her lips slightly parted. He took another step towards her.

Frank lifted the shovel a little higher.

'Why would I do it, Gina?' Paul asked quietly, some of his words lost beneath the increasingly heavy rain.

She looked blankly at him.

'He's lying,' Frank said. 'Like he always lies to you. Has he told you he'll leave his girlfriend and run away with you? I bet he has. I'll bet he's even told you he loves you, hasn't he?'

'No,' Gina murmured. 'He's never done that.'

'Because he doesn't love you and he never will,' Frank went on. 'Not the way I do. He wouldn't forgive you the way I have. He doesn't want you for anything else except those sweaty afternoons in that filthy hotel.'

Paul took a step nearer to her.

'He's crazy,' Paul said quietly. 'He'd have to be to bury me the way he did. What kind of man does something like that? He's insane. Don't listen to him, Gina.'

'I did it for you,' Frank insisted. 'For Laura.'

Gina sniffed back tears and kept her gaze fixed on Paul, who was now only a foot or so from her.

'What's he ever done for you?' shouted Frank. 'Nothing except lie. And now he's lying again.'

Paul looked at Gina and smiled gently.

She was sobbing quietly now.

'You know it's not true,' he told her soothingly.

'Then tell her the truth, tell her you love her,' snarled Frank. 'Go on, tell her.'

Paul put out a hand to touch her face.

It was then that Gina pulled the knife from her jacket pocket.

79

Paul saw the blade as it turned in the air, jerked free of Gina's jacket.

He took a step back, his smile fading rapidly.

'Tell me the truth,' Gina said breathlessly, her gaze fixed upon him.

'I've told you,' Paul protested.

'About Laura,' she went on.

'How many times do I have to repeat it?' Paul told her exasperatedly. 'I never killed your daughter, Gina. He told you that because he wanted me dead.' Paul jabbed a finger at Frank. 'He found out about us and he wanted revenge. It was never anything to do with your daughter.'

'So what about the others?' Gina said, turning her head to look at her husband. 'Why did they have to die? Did you know they were innocent as well?'

'They could have been the killer,' Frank explained.

'Others?' Paul blurted. 'You've done this to other people?'

'We would have done it to a hundred men if it meant punishing the one who murdered Laura,' Frank told him.

'But you picked on me because of my relationship with Gina,' Paul said.

'Relationship?' Frank grunted. 'How can you call it that? How can you dignify it by calling it a relationship? You met up for sex when you felt like it. When you could sneak away together. Don't try and call that a relationship.'

'Whatever you want to call it, that's why you put me in a fucking coffin and tortured me?' Paul protested.

'Do you blame me?' Frank bellowed, raising the shovel before him.

Paul readied himself for the attack he felt sure would come.

'So what you said about taking something from Laura, that was a lie, too?' Gina offered.

'It's all been lies, how many times?' Paul told her. 'I knew you'd never let me out of that coffin unless I confessed. I couldn't confess because I hadn't done anything so I had to invent something. Telling you I'd taken something from your little girl was my last chance. I knew if you didn't go for that then I was dead.'

Gina looked at Frank, tears now openly rolling down her cheeks.

'We're never going to find him, are we?' she said. 'The man who killed Laura will get away with it.'

'What more can we do?' Frank asked her.

'I'm so sorry about your daughter,' Paul offered.

'And are you sorry about what you did to our marriage?' Frank wanted to know.

'I never meant anyone to be hurt,' Paul confessed.

He looked at Gina and smiled thinly.

'Did you love me?' she asked, sniffing. 'Would you ever have loved me?'

'We both knew what we were involved in, Gina,' Paul told her almost apologetically. 'I would never have hurt you.'

'But you never loved me,' she cried.

Paul swallowed hard.

'Did you?' she sobbed.

He took a step closer, wanting to comfort her, struggling to find the words she wanted so badly to hear.

'I would never have hurt you,' he murmured, one hand outstretched towards her. I swear it.'

'What would you swear on?' Gina asked tearfully. 'You made me swear on Laura's soul.'

'I had to. It was the only way I could get through to you,' Paul protested.

Frank dropped the shovel in resignation. It landed with a wet thud at his feet.

'It's over,' Paul whispered. 'Everything finishes here and now. I'll walk away. Neither of you will see me again. I won't call the police. I won't press charges. Let's all get on with our lives. Let's all grab our second chance with both hands.' He even managed a smile.

Gina looked directly at him, her eyes overflowing with tears, a look of despair on her features.

'For eighteen months you wouldn't speak to me,' she sobbed.

'It wasn't that I wouldn't speak to you,' Paul countered. 'I didn't know what I could have said that would have helped. I thought it would be best for both of us if we didn't see each other.'

'I couldn't contact you,' she roared at him. 'I couldn't even speak to you on the phone. You wouldn't return my calls when I rang you at work and at the time I needed you most.'

Frank shot her an angry glance.

'When Laura was killed I wanted to speak to you,' Gina continued, the volume of her voice receding even if the fury didn't. 'I needed you but you didn't care.'

'I thought it was best to stay away,' Paul said apologetically. 'I didn't want to intrude. I knew what you must be going through.'

'You had no idea what we were going through,' Gina snarled. 'None at all. How could you?'

'I'm sorry,' Paul offered perfunctorily.

'Sorry?' she gasped. 'So did someone else take my place for a few months? Did you find someone else to fuck while you couldn't fuck me?'

'Don't be silly,' he cooed. 'Try and understand why I couldn't see you then. If I could have I would. I'm sorry if you thought I'd hurt you.'

Paul took a step towards her, his hands outstretched.

'I'm sorry,' he repeated and a faint smile flickered on his lips. 'Forgive me?'

Gina moved nearer to him, tears still coursing down her cheeks.

She was still crying when she rammed the knife into his throat.

80

The blade slammed into his larynx, sheared through it and penetrated as far as his spine.

Paul tried to make a sound but his windpipe had been severed and the only noise he could utter was a liquid gurgle as blood jetted from the wound. He pulled feebly at the hilt of the knife, trying to wrench it free, but the handle was slippery with his blood and he couldn't get a good enough grip on it.

His lips moved soundlessly as he tried to mouth words. Inside his head, however, the words formed and stood out briefly with searing radiance.

You're dying. Look at the blood.

There was curiously little pain apart from the edges of the wound. Paul was aware of a startling coldness around the blade, even the part of it lodged in his throat. The blood was pouring down his chest, soaking into his robe and spattering the wet mud at his feet.

Gina and Frank Hacket watched him silently, seeing him drop to his knees before them.

Gina had stopped crying and was now standing motionless, her hands at her sides as she watched Paul dying before her.

Not now. Not like this. I got out of that coffin and now I'm going to die like this. It isn't fair.

Paul felt dizzy and his entire body began to shake.

He saw Frank Hacket pick up the dropped shovel, heft it before him and take a step closer to him.

'What we do we do together,' Frank murmured and Paul wasn't even sure whom the words were directed at.

All he was aware of was Frank swinging the shovel at him as if it was a golf club.

The metal caught Paul full in the face and splintered his nose with ease. The sound of shattering bones was clearly audible and Paul was knocked backwards by the impact, his head filled with a dull ringing sound. He lay where he fell, eyes looking up at the rain-filled sky and at the two figures standing above him.

Consciousness was draining from him as surely as water from a cracked container. He gripped a handful of wet mud and felt it ooze through his clutching fingers. He felt so terribly cold apart from the warmth of his own blood that now covered his entire upper body and his face.

Frank Hacket raised the shovel over his head with both hands, glaring down at Paul, but there was a look of complete indifference in his eyes. He looked no more concerned than a man about to swat a troublesome fly.

Paul tried to lift one shaking hand to fend off the imminent blow but it was a feeble and pointless gesture.

Frank Hacket brought the shovel down with thunderous power and caught Paul across the forehead with a blow that almost split his skull in two.

There was a second of incredible pain and then nothing.

Gina and Frank stood looking down at his body for a moment.

'Is he dead?' Gina ventured.

'Yes,' Frank assured her. 'Or he will be pretty soon.'

Frank dropped to his knees and bundled Paul's motionless form back into the shallow grave. He pushed the lid back into place but didn't bother sealing it.

'Go back to the car and wait for me,' Frank said and Gina nodded but hesitated, watching as Frank began shovelling earth on to the box once again. 'Go. I'll take care of this.'

This time she turned and walked slowly away from the grave, her feet sinking into the increasingly liquid mud. The rain continued to pelt down and Gina shivered as she walked.

Behind her, Frank worked as quickly as he could, hurling shovels full of mud on to the coffin in a desperate effort to cover it. Dawn would be dragging itself over the horizon in less than thirty minutes and he had to be finished and away from this place. The rain, he noticed, was washing the blood from the soil and also from his clothes, cleansing the area round about. Another hour of such a downpour and there would be no reminder here about what had gone before. Even the hole itself would be virtually invisible to anyone coming this way.

Frank continued with his task, sweating despite the chill in the air. More than once he had to stop to wipe his face, sponging away sweat and rain with the sleeve of his shirt. There was blood on his trousers but that wasn't a problem. If the rain didn't wash it out sufficiently he'd burn them later. The shovel he would keep in the back of the car. No one was going to come looking for it anyway. Even their footprints would be washed away, he told himself.

By the time he and the weather had finished, there should be no evidence that anyone had been in this place. Where there was no evidence there were no questions and where there were no questions there were no enquiries.

Frank managed a smile as he shovelled the last of the wet soil into place, then he stood motionless for a moment, gazing down at the last resting place of Paul Crane.

Only then did his face crease into a frown. He hawked and spat on the wet earth. It was a final and dismissive epitaph on an unmarked grave.

Frank waited a moment longer then turned and headed off in the same direction his wife had taken. What was to come for them he had no idea. There would be time to consider that later. For now, all he wanted to do was get home and shower. He thought how wonderful it would be if the events of the last year or so could be washed away as easily as the dirt that had clogged his fingernails and his hands, but that would never be the case.

Some stains lasted for ever. Some pain was never eased.

The rain continued to fall.

'Better the world should perish than that I, or any other human being, should believe a lie.'

Bertrand Russell